Lily of the Valley

By Hazel Andrea Smith

JaCol Publishing Inc.

Copyright 2018 © by JaCol Publishing Inc.

Illustrations Copyright © 2018
by JaCol Publishing Inc.
FIRST PRINTING

Nov 2018
All rights reserved

JaCol Publishing Inc.
195 Murica Aisle
Irvine, CA 92614
818-510-2898

Editor-in-Chief: Randall Andrews

Managing Editor: Jessica Collins

www.jacolpublishing.com

ISBN: 978-1-946675-42-2

Cover Art: Kay Kelman

Acknowledgement

I am grateful to my grandparents, Mama, (Mother Mack) and Papa, (Cappie, easily my hero), and my auntie Dot Dot, for my happy childhood. Their gentle nurturing inspired my confidence. They doted on me and filled my youthful world with love, warmth, and happiness.

My husband, Dr. Vidal R. Smith Jr., my children, Hans-Christian and Cristal Morning and my darling grandsons, Joel and Brandon; thank you for your patience while I stole time away from you all to finish this book. I appreciate my husband's support and patience as he shared our bed with my laptop at wee hours in the morning when inspiration woke me.

Hans-Christian, thank you for being my sounding board as you listened to my ramblings. Thank you for the critiques and suggestions. You will be a writer one day.

Thank you Randall Andrews and R.L. Andrew for your coaching. You are marvelous critics and instructors. Also, to Kay Kelman, another islander for your wonderful cover art.

And last but not least, in fact, mostly, thanks to Jehovah for blessing me with creativity.

Table of Contents

LILY OF THE VALLEY

Chapter 1

August 1988

The emergency boomed with activity. Nurses scooted the dead out of the way, and doctors moved from trauma to trauma.

"Doctor, we have two coming in that are viable."

Doctor Edwards helped swing a gurney to triage and ordered, "Stitch kit, stat."

A young girl maybe seven years old held a doll and cried. "Please help my sister."

Doctor Edwards turned and asked, "Is that your sister?" Another little girl rolled on her side, more alert and less fractured.

"Yeah."

"She'll be fine. Let's take care of you, young lady."

"Okay."

Doctor Lily Edwards smiled. "She started stitching up a wound. "What you do you want to be when you grow up?" She tried to keep the little girl's mind preoccupied.

"A doctor like you?"

Doctor Edwards slipped to a time when she was about this girl's age, when she was just Lily.

When the worst of the quake victims had been treated, Lily ditched her scrubs, tossed her bloody gloves aside and took refuge in the doctors' lounge.

A low steady noise of soft music reminded her of so many years before. She remembered the children gyrated to the rhythm of ska music—all to the amusement of their elders. Their giggles sliding over the sound of music; thrill glowed on their faces.

This was the life Lily knew before the move, her comfort zone, where there was acceptance and admiration. She thrived on it, and the love her aunt and grandparents showered on her.

Lily was the center of attention, and she excelled in all the games they played in Bellevue. Dancing to Ska music, boys against girls in their dance offs. Winning to the cheers of the other girls, and the boos of the neighbor boys. Granny and Gramps feeding them ice cream for being good little children.

Every week, the radio played, and they danced. When the music ended, they told stories—sometimes ghostly, sometimes charming bits of life, but always to the delight of the children

Back then she went by Lillian Elaine McDermott, a name she would identify with for most her youth, one she never lost sight of.

She also never lost sight of wanting to be a doctor. Watching Granny hobble on bad knees convinced her she would one day fix them, and she would live happily ever after with the greatest parents she'd ever known.

"Earth to Dr. Edwards." A voice cut into Lily's thoughts.

"Excuse me?" Lily slipped back into the present.

"I said Earth to—"

Lily smiled. "I heard you the first time."

Doctor Burrell handed her a mug. "Your favorite."

She winked, held the rim of the mug to her lips and blew on some hot chocolate. "Thanks."

"What were you so deep in thought about?"

Lily shrugged. "Life before Maxine."

"You mean your mother."

Lily accepted. "Yes, my mother."

"What about it?"

"Just recalling some of the times with Granny and Gramps, and Aunt Liza."

"What do you recall?"

"Conversations about that week before my mother came and took me away." She looked at Dr. Burrell, "Alex, I always wanted to be a doctor."

"And you became one. Good thing your mother came and got you."

Lily shook her head. "I am a doctor in spite of her."

Dr. Burrell leaned back, an exhaustion from hours of tending to victims. "All things led to here, just remember that."

She patted his knee. "I know." She put her mug down. "I remember it must have been a week or two when I confessed wanting to be a doctor. We'd just had a dance off. I won of course," she grinned, "and one of the neighbor boys said he wanted to be a musician."

"Was that Bob Marley?"

"Ha ha, funny, but he did go on to be pretty good in reggae. However, with all the professions everyone aspired to be, everyone thought mine was a dream."

"Well, you made it."

Lily continued. "I stood up, puffed my chest out and said to the room. 'I want to be a doctor. I want to be a doctor to take care of Granny and Gramps.' I hated hearing Granny groan from arthritis. It kept me awake. At times I tiptoed to her room and asked her if I could rub her knees. I would have done anything for her."

"You've always spoken highly of her. I know you loved her dearly."

"They made life fun. After we danced on the weekends, we told 'duppy' stories."

"Do you remember any of them?"

Lily nodded. "Yeah, a few."

"Tell me one." Alex turned and gave Lily his full attention."

"Let's see…As I walked up the road, this big everlasting dog appeared out of nowhere…Gramps eyes would open with excitement as he told his story and I'd cling to him like a leech, even though I'd heard that story a dozen times…My head grew big so…he'd do all these hand gestures to make the story larger than life and everyone would huddle together, worried something frightening was about to happen…" Lily followed suit and tried to mimic what her Gramps would do, "Then he just disappeared, poof!"

"That's your story?"

Lily sighed. "There was more to it, it is a little long for a post shift story, besides there was always something we were supposed to do, and I always shouted it out."

"Which was?"

"I shouted, *'Throw salt over your left shoulder and say Jack Mandora I don't choose none.'* Or I would slip off his lap, put a sheet on and scare the other kids by helping Gramps with a ghost story. People claimed I was a chip off the old block, which at that time gave me so much pride in a father I didn't know. All I knew is he was coming back one day for me. "

"Are you ready to go?" Alex pointed to her mug.

"Almost. Can I get some of this off my chest first?"

"Of course. Keep going."

"I remember the night I heard them talking about Maxine coming. I'd just gotten done praying for Liza to not be an old maid—"

"Old maid? Liza?"

"Long story, but I was told she was going to be one if she didn't get married. Anyway, I'd prayed for that, prayed for Granny and Gramps, and for my father and mother to come for me. Little did I know I'd brought a whole lot of change with that prayer, because no sooner than I said 'Amen,' I hear voices in the other room, and they are talking about someone coming to get me. I hear Liza telling Granny, 'But she doesn't even know her. She doesn't deserve to have her. She was the one who abandoned the child. Can you imagine she left the poor little helpless thing on our doorstep, merely six months and skinny like a rat in the rain? We can't allow her to take Lily away!'" Lily took a sip of hot chocolate. "Wow, what a moment. I come running in there and ask, 'Take me away, who's going to take me away?' I jump in Granny's arms and she assures me it's nothing." Lily tilted her head at Alex, "First lie she ever told me, and it was a doozey."

"I suspect she was sheltering you, not lying."

"Promise me, Alex, you will never 'shelter' me."

Alex smiled. "Fair enough."

"So Granny tells me to go back to bed, that she will protect me, and that it was nothing." Lily finished off her drink, stood and faced Dr. Burrell. "And Alex, that was the last night I officially called Bellevue my home." Lily waved her hand, "And if that wasn't enough, I had the worst dream about flying dragons and mean witches."

Chapter 2

Bellevue/August 1962/7 years old

"Hello. Open up the door." Maxine Francis hammered the door.

"Mercy me, Maxine, what are you doing knocking down our door like a god damn bailiff at this ungodly hour on a Sunday morning?" Liza held the door ajar and glanced at the clock. "Darn, it's just 6 a.m."

Maxine didn't have time for this. "Well didn't you all get my telegram? I've come to fetch Lily. It's the only time I got, I work, you know, have to be at the post office every day, not idle like some people who have nothing to do but sit home all day minding other people's business."

"You better mind your tongue, missy; fancy you coming here at my house and be passing remarks."

Maxine might have contempt for the McDermotts, but picking a fight on their territory wasn't going to further her cause "Alright, alright, let's not start like that. I come to get my child. Where is she?"

"She still sleeping, it's early morning you know. Come in and have a seat. Would you like a cup of coffee or tea?"

Maxine came in. "Coffee, thanks."

"Sugar, milk?"

"Nah, black, no sugar, and wake up that little girl while you're at it."

"Nah, let her sleep out her lil' baby nap."

The McDermotts annoyed her. "That's the problem, you all here spoiling her. The principal tells me you all not sending her to school and she can't even read at seven. That's why I've come to get my child. No child of mine is going to grow up without an education."

"If you think we're going to let you take this child and ill treat her, you have another guess coming. You hear me, Maxine Francis. You, the one who abandoned her on our door step, and by the way, she can read. She's a smart little thing, that one."

"Well her father, your brother, is a worthless bastard. He was the one who abandoned us."

"Well I won't get into that with you; that's between you two. He's not even here, he's gone to live in England, so if you want to pick a fight, take a flight, ma'am."

Maxine's life flashed before her.

Her first baby, Margaret had barely turned two.

Maxine sighed as Lily's father's harsh words plagued her.

"Winston, I have news for you."

"What news? It had better be good." He stroked her hair and gazed into her eyes.

"I'm pregnant."

"Pregnant. But we've only been sleeping together a month now."

"So how long do you think it takes a girl to get pregnant? The first time, duh. Well, I am pregnant, what are you going to do about it?"

"What do you want me to do?"

"Marry me."

"I'm too young to get married. I'm only twenty. That's the end of the rest of my life."

"So what do you want me to do walk around with a belly and no ring on my finger? My mother will kill me."

"So what you want to do, have an abortion?"

"I just...I Dunno..." Tears flushed her cheeks. Instinctively she knew what had to be done.

But almost seven months had passed and she could not bring herself to get rid of the burden, but had tied her belly every morning to conceal it.

****

Granny heard all the fuss and walked with Lily into the kitchen. Both still in pajamas and not ready for morning arguments.

Granny sighed seeing Maxine standing there.

10

"Lillian McDermott, come here, little girl." Maxine reached out to Lily.

"Good morning, ma'am." Lily kept her distance.

"Come to me, girl. What? Do I have horns?"

"No ma'am." She wouldn't budge.

Maxine reached out and pulled her.

"When I call you, you come to me, you hear, girl."

"I don't know you, and frankly, I don't like you. Who are you and why are you even here?"

"I am your Auntie Maxine, and I am taking you away from these silly people who are going to make you grow up to be good for nothing."

"I don't have an Aunt Maxine, only Aunt Liza. Do you think I'm even going anywhere with you, I don't know you, you look like a witch and I hate you!"

"Don't let me have to give you a good spanking. You are rude and spoilt. I will set you straight very soon."

Lily backed against the wall, rounded the corner and left crying.

Granny intervened. "Can't you see you're scaring the child?"

"Scaring her? What is she, a retard?"

"Lily is not used to people bullying her, she's used to kindness; you must be gentle with her."

"I think you mean Maxine cuddling. No pun intended, because she will not be spoilt by me. You've all made a mess of this child, she's such a weakling. I need to take her under my wings before you all stunt her development."

"Just remember we don't have to let her go with you, but you promised that you would be kind to her, but now you're reneging on your promise."

"She is my child."

"I wouldn't have known that if you hadn't told me. Where were you all these years? Now you come from out of nowhere claiming her."

"Where is Winston? You all packed him up and sent him away. What? Wasn't he man enough to live up to his responsibility? Don't let me start, Mrs. McDermott. I am her mother," Maxine took a seat and eyed Granny, "If you were the one to push her out of your womb, try to stop me from taking my child. I'll report you to the authorities that you kidnapped my child."

"You and your mother never wanted this child; do you think I forget that you all dug a hole behind your latrine, waiting for her to die?"

"She was sick, premature and only weighing one and a half pound, of course we didn't expect her to live, at least when the doctor asked me what I wanted him to do with it I told him to keep it since it still breathed."

"It? Just listen to how you speak of the child. Do you love her, Maxine?"

"Love, what is love? Ask Winston if he loves her. Ask him if he ever loved me? Your son is irresponsible and spoilt and that's what you're trying to make Lily become—worthless, just like her father, your son."

"Miss Francis, I will not tolerate your disrespectful behavior anymore." Granny clenched her fist and walked out of the room to find Lily.

"Y'all just pack her things and let us leave!" She shouted at Granny's back.

The bus horn tooted in the distance. Kong's bus rolled up the hill. Maxine pulled Lily from Liza's grasp and ran with her with her suitcase. Lily wept.

Chapter 3

Plum Valley/Late summer 1962/7 years

Like that, Lily was whisked away. Unceremoniously, her Granny crying, her Aunt Liza shocked, she had turned to see them as the she rode away from the only home she'd known.

Puffy eyed and a throated lump, Lily's immobilized frame hunched over her knees while quiet tears streamed down her cheeks. Her whimpering attracted Maxine and her wrath.

"You've been crying all day; I'm not going to live this way, and you are going to be here a long time, so it's best you figure it out, Lillian McDermott." Auntie Maxine hovered over her beside the bed.

"I want to go home, please take me home." She held her head up and met Maxine face to face, searching for compassion.

"Home? This is your home, get used to it." Her tone sliced through Lily's heart.

"No, no, no this is not my home. I don't want to be here. I want Granny." A fresh stream of tears cascaded down her face as she stood in flight mode.

"Granny is old and ugly. Granny is going to die."

"Nooooo don't say that, you are a wicked witch." Lily covered her ears and shrieked.

"Watch your mouth, missy"

"Don't you ever say Granny is going to die, ever again?" she stomped her feet

"Yes she is. She is old, old people die." Auntie Maxine mocked her.

"Don't say that!" she stomped her foot again.

"You better stop your foolish crying before I give you something to cry about."

Another woman entered the room.

"This is your Aunt Patsy; she's a teacher at the nearby elementary school, the one you will be attending. Dry your face and say hi."

"No I won't. I want Aunt Liza." She turned away, willing Aunt Liza to appear.

"What's wrong with this little girl? Is she retarded?" Patsy walked closer and spun Lily around to face her.

"Leave me alone. Don't touch me."

"Whoa, this one's got lots of spunk."

"They've spoilt her rotten. We have a lot of work to do to tame her. She's a wild animal." They both laughed.

Lily glared.

"Did you see that? This child is so disrespectful." She raised her hand to hit her.

Lily cringed. "Please don't hit me."

"I will murder you!"

Lily slid off the bed and slipped past them and out of the room.

She made it out the back and in her defiance, roamed the bushes and vowed never to bend to Maxine and Patsy. She ate guavas and mangoes she found on the ground. She'd rather live in the wild than return. A butterfly perched on her shoulder. She smiled. "What would you do if you were me, miss butterfly?"

The butterfly fluttered away.

She chased the butterfly, but it eluded her. She pondered silly things like growing wings and finding her way back home to Bellevue. She wandered further into the bushes till she reached Domingo River. As she got closer, she noticed a girl. "Hi, what's your name?"

The girl turned but didn't say anything.

"I'm Lily."

The girl laughed—part pathetic, part humorous. "So you are the girl Aunt Maxine said would be coming to live with us?"

"You live there too?" Lily found hope that another girl would be with her.

"Yeah." She nodded for Lily to come closer. She looked up. "I'm Margaret. I'm ten. We also have another little one at the house, her name in Millie, she's real young though. You can't miss her, she's always chirping about something."

"I'm seven, gettin' close to eight though." Lily squinted, "Why are you here?"

"I'm here to wash these clothes."

"Wash clothes? Granny would never let me do that. Moreover, we have running water in our house. We don't have to go to the river to wash. We only go there to swim. There's a river at my house. We call it Swift River because it's very deep and swift. Many people drowned there. So Granny never let me go there by myself. But I can swim though. Can you?"

"Yeah, I can swim, but what are you doing down here?"

"Nothing."

"You know you're going to get into trouble though?"

"I don't care. I'm never going back to that place."

"So where are you going?

"Dunno."

"Don't be silly, you must go back with me."

"Nope."

"You can't stay here all by yourself."

"They hate me."

"No they don't, you just have to get used to them."

"Never!" Lily turned to the water. "Let's go for a swim."

"No, I'm not allowed."

"Come on, let's jump in. Let's see who can swim the fastest." She undressed to her underwear.

"You shouldn't, I'm going to tell."

"Scaredy cat, scaredy cat tanny nanny boo boo."

"I'm no scaredy cat, I can swim better than you."

"Prove it."

Margaret undressed and jumped into the river. Lily followed suit.

Margaret was at the furthest end and out of the river sitting on a rock laughing.

"I beat you."

"Only because you cheat, let's do it again. This time let's count to three, one, two, three!"

They were at it again neck and neck. They forgot time and cavorted for hours, oblivious to the passage of time till the shadows approached.

"Lily, we must go back home now. We are in trouble. We are going to get a beating."

"You, not me, cause I'm never going back."

"You're mad. Come on let's go."

"I said I'm…not…going…back, read my lips."

"Suit yourself." She walked away. When she made it to the top of the bank, she turned. "Come on girl, don't be an idiot. You can't stay here by yourself."

Lily didn't answer and she didn't budge.

It turned dark; Lily shivered but resolved to not go back.

Chapter 4

Plum Valley/late Summer/1962

"Lily!" Maxine's voice echoed. No answer. They reached Domingo. They peered into the water.

"Where the hell could this little demon be?"

"I don't know why you bother to take this child. She's just as wayward as Winston."

"Lily, where are you?" beads of fear gathered on Maxine's forehead. If something happened to Lily she would have to face Granny's wrath and the law.

"Lord Jesus!" Patsy stumbled over Lily's body.

"Is she alive?"

"I dunno, Lily." Patsy stooped, shook her and checked for a pulse. "Lily, wake up."

Lily stirred and rolled face up. Maxine and Patsy converged, staring down at her.

Lily let out a blood curdling scream. Her body shook violently, her arms flailing in the air.

"Witches get away from me!" She struggled with Maxine and Patsy as they lifted her up. "Help me, someone help me. The witches are going to kill me!"

"Lily, Lily, it's me, Aunt Maxine."

"Aunt Liza, you come to get me?" She calmed down. "Granny, is that you, where's Gramps, you all came to get me? Take me home before the witches get here. They're going to murder me."

"Stop your foolishness, child. Wake up; it's me." Maxine shook her.

Lily resumed screaming.

"Stop it, you hear me, Lily, stop it!" Maxine shook her again.

"Please don't murder me; please I'll do anything you say."

"Do I look like a murderer, stop it at once, you silly child. Stop it!" Maxine's impatience heightened. "We're here to take you home."

"Home to Granny?" Lily's eyes opened.

"No silly, out of the night air and the dew before you get pneumonia. I should give you a good thrashing for the trouble and the worries you caused us. What do you think you're doing going off like this without permission and staying out here in the night air."

"I don't want to go back to your house. I want to go to Granny. Please, can you please take me home?" She put her hands to a prayer, "Please."

"Come let's go."

"To granny?"

"Just be quiet and come with us." Maxine lifted her over her shoulder. Lily fell asleep.

They placed her in her bed. She shared room with Patsy. They locked the louvers and everyone retired.

****

In the still of the night, the child woke and sat upright in the bed. "I'm blind. I can't see. I must be blind." She called out to Patsy. "Aunt Patsy, I'm blind, I'm blind, somebody help me, I'm blind; I can't see anything!"

Patsy stirred. Lily heard her bump into a chair. A grumble followed by the light of a match. "It never ends with you does it, everything is drama, drama. What's wrong with you now?"

Maxine and Margaret ran into the room.

"What is it?" Maxine sounded annoyed.

"Sorry, I thought I was blind."

"You thought you were blind, what do you mean you thought you were blind, why on earth would you be blind? You went to bed with two perfectly normal eyes, why would you be blind?" Maxine huffed, "You know what, just go back to bed and let us all have a normal life."

"Maxine, sorry but I think this one is retarded, I know I said it before, but I'm certain now she is retarded."

They all laughed and went back to bed. The louvers made the rooms dark.

22

Patsy insisted, "Go to sleep, child."

"Granny always left a lamp burning low."

"Too bad."

An hour passed when Patsy was woken again. This time the child fretted over a sound outside. "What is it this time, Lily?"

Something out there is screeching 'buck wheat, buck wheat' over and over. What's making that sound?" "It's guinea chicks." Patsy swung from her bed, pushed her feet in her bed slippers and pulled the piss pot to do a wee. "Turn around, give me some privacy."

"Guinea chicks, never heard of that before. They sound scary." She turned her back to Patsy.

"They are birds." Patsy left the room with the piss pot.

When Patsy returned she noticed the sheet missing from Lily's bed, and Lily stuffing something between the wall and the bed. "What's that you're hiding there, Lily?"

"Nothing." She fidgeted.

"Let me see that."

"It's nothing, I'm hiding nothing." She dropped the bundle behind the bed. Patsy reached across and felt the sheet. She yanked it out and noticed the wetness. "Dam you, Lily, you pee pee the bed. Not only are you retarded, you're also nasty. Let me call Maxine. Maxine!"

"Please, Aunt Patsy, don't tell her. I beg you please, she will kill me."

Maxine entered the room.

"What is it Patsy?"

"Check the bed."

Maxine ran her hand over the bed. "What, she pee pee the bed?" Maxine raised her hand to hit Lily but stopped. "You know what; we'll just feed her to the guinea chicks. They love to peck children who wet their beds."

"Please don't do that, I beg you." Lily shuddered. "I want to go home, I want to go home." A new wave of weeping began.

"Pee pee bed, pee pee bed the guinea chicks are going to get you." Patsy jeered her as she cried.

"I will go to Domingo with you to wash them." Margaret volunteered.

Maxine shooed Margaret off. "Patsy, see she changes and have her put a new sheet on the bed." Maxine shook her head. You and Margaret can wash that before school."

After Maxine left, Patsy smiled. "You are lucky this time, Lily.

Chapter 5

Plum Valley/September 1962/First school term

Lily stood in line and as she watched each child spanked for not knowing the times table; she shuddered as she anticipated hers.

Her 'new' status exempted her.

"Lily, you can step aside. Class you have a new friend. Stand, little girl, and tell them your name and where you're from?"

"My name is Lillian Elaine McDermott, but you can call me Lily. I am from Bellevue.

A little boy rang out, "Bellevue? That's the name of the mad house in Kingston, where they keep mad people, right class?"

The teacher ignored his comment.

"Yeah!" the class chorused and laughter rang out.

"You mad?" He prodded her.

At that, the teacher gave a stern look. "Kevin, enough."

"No, I am not mad. Bellevue is a most beautiful place, where my real family lives; it's not a madhouse, you idiot." Lily stood her ground.

"Lily McDermott." The teacher cautioned her.

"So your entire family's mad then?" Kevin launched another attack—amusing the class.

"Kevin Baugh, stop it at once before I have to give you a spanking."

That did it. He relented, allowing Lily to continue.

"I am seven years old and I am going to be a doctor when I grow up so that I can get a new knee for my granny."

"She's going to get a new knee for her grannee." It seemed Kevin couldn't help himself.

At playtime, they all gathered around her.

"Lily from the madhouse, how do you do, madam?" Kevin did a bow; the girls curtsied and giggled. The playground ricocheted with laughter. Kevin initiated the bullying. Lily didn't flinch.

Another student came to her rescue. "Well, she's not mad, and I want her as my friend. Now she is in Plum Valley, she is now Lily of the Valley, got it?"

"Yeah." They chorused again. "Lily of the Valley, Lily of the Valley."

Lily didn't mind, in fact she found it cute. That's whom she became, Lily of the Valley. She turned to the girl who helped her. "Hi, what's your name?"

"I'm Sasha Murdock. Please to meet you."

"I'm—"

"I know, Lily McDermott, from Bellevue."

They laughed.

At the end of the day, the class said the evening prayer. Her teacher stood close and overheard her prayer.

"Sanctify those guinea chicks that pest us, kill 'em with fine salts and good teeths." Lily, who was deaf in one ear, made up what she didn't hear. She kept her disability secret for fear people would tease her. She discovered her deafness when a friend whispered in her ear and she didn't hear a word."

"You deaf eenh." Her friend had said. Lily had placed a finger over her other ear to check.

She nursed this revelation since, not even sharing it with Granny, although she had ear infection after ear infection, no one knew.

The teacher couldn't help giggling and called her aunt Patsy, from another class, to listen to her prayer after the other children had left. "Lily, say the evening prayer to your Aunt Patsy."

"Sanctify those guinea chicks that pest us, kill 'em with fine salts and good teeths." With her eyes still shut, she felt a sting across her back. Patsy leveled the belt on her back.

"What's that you say, child? Foolishness, say 'sanctify all our pleasures and bless us. Fill us with kind thoughts and good deeds!'"

Lily strained to hear and caught the prayer.

"Guinea chicks that pests us? Why would she say that?" her teacher's curiosity tested Lily to speak up.

"I haven't a clue." Patsy pleaded innocence.

On the way home, Patsy pinched her on the mute ear.

"No matter how much you pray, if you wet the bed again, the guinea chicks are gonna get you. She held her head back and laughed, quickening her steps with Lily in tow. Lily feared the approach of bed time.

Bedtime turned out to be six p.m. At Plum Valley, the motto was, 'early to bed, early to rise, makes a man healthy wealthy and wise.' With all the louver windows shut tight, the impenetrable darkness, the menacing enemy overwhelmed her by its blackness.

"Aunt Patsy, can you light a lamp? Back home they always just turn the lamp down so I won't be afraid."

"No, you're too god dam spoilt. There's nothing in the dark to be afraid of."

"I'm not afraid of the dark, I just can't see."

"What do you want to see? Moreover, you don't use your eyes when you're sleeping."

"Pretty please, can you, Aunt Patsy?"

"Just shut up and go to sleep."

Her thoughts were filled with ways of escaping the misery.

In the dark, with Aunt Patsy's snore threatening to saw the board walls of the house, Lily talked to her only confidante, her doll, Betsy, the only doll she ever had, given to her by Aunt Liza.

"Betsy, do you think Auntie Maxine might be my mother?"

She made Betsy answer, "dunno, Lily dearest."

"Would she beat me so much if she were my mother?"

"Dunno."

"Did you know that Auntie Maxine has two extra pinkies just like me?"

"Yep, she does?"

"Maybe if she were my mother, she would hug me and show me that she loves me."

Betsy didn't answer. "Wake up, Betsy, answer me, what kind of friend are you, you fall asleep leaving me in this monstrous dark all by myself."

The vacant place in her heart, in Aunt Maxine's presence, burned a dreadful longing. She had tried to find out from Granny and Aunt Liza, but they both shut down when she asked. She dared not ask Auntie Maxine such a presumptuous question.

She had a fitful sleep.

Tuesday morning, Lily woke as Patsy delivered several painful slaps to her thigh.

"You nasty girl, you wet the bed again! I am going to call the guinea-chicks and let them peck you, a big girl like you wetting your bed!"

"I'm sorry, I won't do it again. Please don't let them bite me!" trepidation built, trepidation so dense it dulled her senses. She didn't know which one to fear more: the beatings for wetting the bed, or the threats of having the guinea chicks pecking at her.

"Pee-pee bed Lily, guinea chick going get you!" Patsy's face scrunched at the smell of stale urine.

"Yeah, call the guinea chick," Maxine, who overheard the teasing, made sucking sounds with her mouth to call the birds.

"No, please don't call them I won't do it again!"

"Give me that ugly dolly!" Patsy wrenched the doll from Lily's hand.

"I want my dolly. Mommy, let her give me my dolly. Give it back!"

"What did you call me, child?"

"Nothing, Auntie Maxine."

"Who told you to call me that?"

"Nobody, Auntie Maxine," Lily cowered.

"Don't you ever make that mistake again, you hear me!" Maxine's eyes burned into Lily's.

Lily could not imagine what made her react that way.

Patsy had wickedly ripped Betsy to shreds…she was gone forever, just the remnants of despair and emptiness left behind. Her bewilderment left her dizzy. The tears flowed but Maxine did not beat her.

Life was just one big blur during those days before Friday. Nursing the pain in her chest, she barely existed. She survived on memories of Bellevue and counted the days to Friday. On Friday evenings she came alive!

Chapter 6

End of first week in Plum Valley-Weekend in Bellevue/September 1962

"Thank God it's Friday."

"Why Lily?" Lily's teacher frowned.

"Because today I get to see Granny, Gramps, and Aunt Liza." She counted her fingers.

"Awesome right? Those are your three favorite people."

"My three most favorite!" She skipped off to join Sasha. "Sasha, wait for me." They walked hand in hand to the nearby stream and tossed leaves in, floated in the current, tea cups bobbing and swirling. The two girl's squeals blended with the playground noises.

Kevin approached them. "Hello, Miss Madhouse, how do you do?" Kevin bent over sweeping his hand in front of him to take a bow. Lily tripped him. Kevin sprawled out on his belly. She'd make sure he never called her that again.

At the end of the day Lily's spirit soared.

"Sasha, last one through the gate is a dead donkey."

"Dead donkey, dead donkey, you're last." Sasha looked back as she cleared the gate, Lily right behind her. They both laughed and headed home.

Lily skidded through her front door.

"Hey slow down, what's the rush? Take your shoes off, Lily McDermott." Her Aunt Patsy had taken the day off sick.

"Sorry Aunt Patsy."

"And where are your manners?"

"Good evening, Aunt Patsy." Lily had one intention—pack her dulcimina grip—and wait for Aunt Maxine to take her to Bellevue for the weekend.

She waited.

"Why are you packed and seated on the verandah, Lily McDermott? Aunt Maxine sauntered in that evening.

"I'm going home for the weekend."

"In your dreams, I'm tired and not even ten thunder claps could get me to Bellevue tonight. Do you see the time? It's past bed time."

"But you promised."

"A promise is a comfort to a fool."

"But…" tears stung her eyes.

"But nothing, go inside and wash up for bed, you eat anything yet?"

"No, Aunt Maxine."

"Patsy, I can't believe it; you here all evening and didn't give the child something to eat."

"She didn't say she was hungry."

"So what about Margaret and Millie?" Auntie Maxine shook her head.

"Margaret took care of that."

"Oh well, come inside, Lily, let me fix you some supper."

"I don't want supper. I just want to go home."

"What?" She closed in on Lily, "Don't give me lip, one more tear drop and I'll give you something to cry for."

Lily's spirit fell. She heaved a heavy sigh, bit the insides of her cheeks and sniffled.

Lily hated yam and she hated beef. She hated Plum Valley. She went to bed without supper.

Lily woke at the crack of dawn, changed out of her wet pajamas, gathered her things, and sat on the bed.

"Lookie here what's this, you all dressed up so soon, going someplace? Phew! That pee pee smell! Go outside and get the wash pan and wash up, I hope the guinea chicks get you while you're at it."

"Can you come with me?"

"Geez, what's wrong with you child, I'll stand at the door and watch you." Patsy lit a cigarette.

Auntie Maxine called everyone for breakfast. Lily picked at her breakfast.

The household buzzed with Saturday chores.

"Lily, take out the piss pots, empty them and wash them."

"I hate doing that, Granny never made me do this." Lily folded her arms.

"I don't care what Granny does, she spoils you rotten. Margaret, you clean the floors. Millie! Stop playing in the dirt!" Aunt Maxine packed the laundry hamper and the breakfast plates for the trip to the river. "And when you're all done we're going down to Domingo."

Patsy went back to bed.

"Yay," Four year old Millie squealed.

"Aunt Maxine, when am I going to Bellevue?"

"Child, stop annoying me and do as you're told!"

Lily bit her lip as she fought back tears.

"You know what, let me put you on Kong's bus and ask them to drop you off at your Granny's before you drive me crazy with your Bellevue tirade. But only when you finish what you have to do."

Lily's heart did somersaults. She whistled as she worked.

Kong's bus honked its horn in the distance. She ran to Auntie Maxine.

"Auntie, the bus is coming."

She walked to the gate with Auntie Maxine. Auntie Maxine waved down the bus.

"Good day, Mr. Kong, take care of Lily here for me, drop her off in Bellevue at the McDermott's."

Anticipation and excitement accompanied her to Bellevue.

When she got off the bus, she ran to the waiting arms of Granny. "I missed you all so much"

"We missed you too, and look who is here waiting for you."

All her neighborhood friends greeted her.

Lily handed her Aunt Liza her suitcase and cheered to her friends, "Let's play Bluebird," Lily screamed with delight. Home in Bellevue, she could be a child.

"Bluebird, bluebird in and out the window…" It was one game after another.

"Say it again, Lily, one and 'farty'… no forty," one of her little friends corrected herself, "Say forty again, Lily. She says it so sweet you see. I just love how you talk, Lily, say it again. She talks nice eh."

They played all afternoon until twilight.

"Time to come inside, the rest of you go home!" Aunt Liza looked through the kitchen window.

The children all left, but resurfaced an hour later at Lily's home for Saturday night's top ten and for Gramp's story telling.

Plum Valley never happened. Back to being herself, Lily opened the floor.

"Come on, everybody let's shake our legs and twists our bodies." Her spirit resurged.

"Yes Lily, you little star, you're the life of the partaaay, come on everybody, let's dance the night away." Aunt Liza took Lily's hand and rocked with her.

Afterwards, Lily and Seven or eight of them gathered under the ackee tree in the front yard, forming a semi-circle around Gramps, Granny by his side for story time, Lily blurted, "I want to tell the story tonight, Gramps."

"Okay, Lily."

"Once upon a time, while Anancy slept in his own bed, some bad witches stole him away in the middle of the night. They took him to a place filled with creepy crawlies and snakes." She wriggled her fingers.

"Ohhhhhhh." The children shuddered.

"Anancy was afraid, so afraid he trembled all the time. The witches talked like this, grrrrrr, gabble gabble, blah, blah." She mimicked a throaty voice.

The children laughed.

"Go on, Lily" Amelia edged closer.

"And the snakes hissed like this, ssssssss."

Laughter again.

"I tell you the chip can't fall far from the block." Granny looked up at Gramps and smiled.

"The witches were ugly, very ugly, with long dirty, green teeth, with grunge growing on them and slime and froth came out of their mouths. They had long, dirty nails, and they fly on brooms, like this."

"Ohhhhhh." Aunt Liza spurred her on.

"They cast a spell on Anancy."

"What spell? Jay opened his eyes wide.

"They cast a spell so he couldn't find his way back home and to turn him into a duppy."

"What happened next?"

"Well he got lost in a maze filled with duppies. All the trees turned into duppies and they made funny sounds, wooooaaaannnn."

"ohhhhhhhh" her friends cringed; Gramps had a perpetual smile on his face.

"And they grabbed Anancy, Anancy screamed, eeeeeek. Let me go you bad, bad duppy!"

"Good Lord, poor Anancy." Granny beckoned for Lily to sit on her lap.

"He kicked and screamed, but one of the duppies bit him on his neck."

"What happened next?" Jay curiosity piqued.

"Anancy turned into a duppy. He had to find the secret potion to turn him back to Anancy."

"Oh no."Amelia hugged Aunt Liza.

"He got away from them, and I ran and ran till I got to a river. I jumped into the river to find the secret potion, I looked everywhere and I just couldn't find it."

"I Lily?" Aunt Liza noticed the change in point of view.

"Oh, I meant Anancy. So anyways, tune in again tomorrow night for the rest of the story."

"Aaaawww, that's not fair, Lily, tell us now." Jay prompted her.

"Nah, next time, I'm tired now."

Gramps took over. In no time, sleepy heads led to bedtime. Lily fell asleep on Granny's lap again.

Lily woke up in her bed, wet in the middle of the night. She felt the heat of shame in her cheeks and ears; she didn't want Granny and Aunt Liza to know about her new habit. She didn't know what to do. Granny checked on her. Lily pretended to sleep.

"Liza girl, come in here."

"What's the matter, Granny?"

"Lily wet the bed. She's not done that since she was a baby."

"That's strange."

"I wonder what that woman did to her."

"Her eyes are so sad and empty."

"Yeah, it's like something inside her died, you know, a fire, a light. Maybe we shouldn't send her back."

"I don't think we have the right to do that though."

"I'm very concerned. Maybe we could report her."

"But what proof do we have?"

Lily opened her eyes and screwed up her face. "I'm sorry Granny and Aunt Liza, I won't ever do it again, I promise." She held up her pinkie fingers to pledge with them. "And I don't ever want to go back to Plum Valley, I hate it there."

Her Aunt Liza cleaned her up and rocked her back to sleep. Lily slept in bliss and stayed dry.

Chapter 7

Bellevue–Sunday evening/September 1962

Sunday afternoon and melancholy tunes piped from the radio. They succeeded in performing the final rites on the last vestige of her happiness. The evening, oppressive and as morose as death, poised to drive the final nail in the coffin of mirth.

"Poor child, eat up your dinner." Granny placed her favorite part of the chicken on her plate.

"I'm not hungry, Granny." She didn't fight the tears. They purged her soul. Lily, already gangly and thin, lost her appetite at the thought of returning to Plum Valley.

"Eat up, look how skinny you are." Gramps shook his head.

"I'm not skinny, Gramps, I am petite."

"What did she say, Granny? Did she say she's petty?"

"No Gramps, petite. That's what Aunt Maxine says I am. I am petite," Her sobbing subsided.

"Petty, pettee or skinny, you need to eat up to get stamina. I can't bother with your pretty talk. Just one week you're gone and you return all speaky-spokey!" Everybody laughed.

"Auntie Maxine says I am in need of being taught to be a young lady" Lily replied.

"Young lady? You is a little child. Maxine is force ripening you, you know. It pains my heart to send you back there, cho…" Granny trailed off.

"Granny, Gramps don't say that. You only make things worse for the child," Liza scolded them and turned to Lily. "It is good for you to go to Maxine."

"No, it's not, she beats me to read." Lily sulked and pouted.

"Learning to read is good, right?" she smiled and helped her with another spoonful.

"But she shouldn't beat her to learn. That's abuse!" Gramps punched the table.

"Gramps take it easy, don't add fuel to fire." Aunt Liza cautioned Gramps. "Look how you pretty like Maxine."

The lump in Lily's throat crushed her appetite and made the delicious dinner difficult to swallow.

"May I have the wishbone, Aunt Liza?" She had a secret wish, an evil wish. Sometimes the wishbone broke in favor of her wish, and she waited to hear the news that would prevent them sending her to Plum Valley.

The wishbone didn't break in her favor. Another depressing and gut wrenching week lay ahead of her.

After dinner, Liza packed Lily's suitcase while Gramps and Granny sat in the sitting hall. Lily played with a new doll Aunt Liza got her. She sat on the floor in the sitting hall, next to Gramps and Granny.

"Gramps, I wonder why Maxine allows her to call her aunt." Granny rocked in her rocking chair, pensive.

"Dunno."

"I wonder if it's because she started having them so young. She had the first one when she was only seventeen, or maybe she doesn't love the children."

"Dunno, I guess she has her reason."

"The reason she came here hot-hot to take Lily is because Principal Smith told her that we keeping back Lily's progress, but as far as I see, she is doing the child more harm than good. I mean if she was happy, she wouldn't be bawling like this."

"Maybe she just misses us. That's normal you know."

"I guess. That girl Patsy lives with Maxine in Plum Valley, I wonder how Lily gets on with her."

"Patsy who?"

"Her sister."

"Oh you mean that lil' flighty one, who smokes like a pipe."

"She just barely nineteen. I hear they take her on at the Plum Valley School as a pre-trained teacher. Lily should be alright since she has her Auntie there, what d'you think?"

"Dunno, you never know."

"But then poor Lily said she mashed up her dolly and threw it on the roof. Liza had to go buy her another one."

Lily listened to their conversation. "Aunt Patsy is wicked to me; she shouts at me all the time and I hate her!"

Granny and Gramps looked at each other.

Aunt Liza interrupted. "Lily, come and get dressed, the Tiger bus will soon be here."

Like a sacrificial lamb she went to Liza, in tears.

"Cho man don't cry, remember you'll come back on Friday, don't cry, you're breaking my heart." Aunt Liza wiped her tears. "Heh, I hear the bus, quick get her dulcimina grip. Let me run up the gate to stop the bus. Aunt Liza hastened to the gate.

Lily's 'pity party' was cut short by the hooting of the bus in the distance.

"Come child, the bus reach top road now!" Granny urged.

"I feel sick, Granny!" The fire of her anguish burnt her soul and dug into the deepest crevice of her heart. She melted into a tearful mess.

"Come on, Lily, you must go or Maxine will be vexed with us." Granny nudged her.

"I don't care." Lily wished to miss the bus, she moved like a snail.

As the bus came down the gravel parochial road, the driver geared down to stop at her gate as Aunt Liza fanned it down. Granny was at the gate holding Lily's little brown dulcimina in one hand, while she waved at the bus. The old rickety red, white, and blue 'Tiger' bus screeched to a halt.

"Granny, I don't want to go, please don't make me go!" She ran into the house with Aunt Liza at her heels, slamming into Gramps, whose open arms welcomed her.

"Papa don't let them send me, let me stay here!"

He hugged her but insisted, "Go on, man, it's alright, you know; you're going to be alright, you have to go," he kissed her forehead.

The bus driver grew impatient and hooted the horn.

Granny gently pried her from Gramp's arms and brought her to the bus.

"Where's my doll, where's Jolly, I can't leave without my Jolly," Lily ran into the house, "I want my dolly!"

Gramps found the doll, tucked it in her arm, and urged Lily. "You have to go, child. The bus driver ain't waitin' another minute.

The driver flung the door open and sneered. As she cried, he jeered her, "Cry, cry baby moonshine darling take off your clothes an' go to bed, when you go to Sunday school, the teacher call you a big duppy fool." She ignored him and found a seat. The trees and houses scurried past.

With each passing tree, she moved farther away from Bellevue. She slumped on the hard bus seat, sobbing, clutching her dulcimina and Jolly.

When they arrived in Plum Valley, the bus delivered Lily like a package. The driver lodged complaints about her bawling, and she received a whipping for embarrassing Maxine.

Aunt Patsy made Lily feel very unwelcomed. "Don't put your old dirty dulcimina on the bed!"

"Sorry," Lily removed the suitcase. As she did, the strong smell of eucalyptus oil from the dulcimina drifted through the air. A memory of home floated in its balm as it formed an impregnable barrier around her. It made her unreachable. It blocked the daggers of insults Patsy hurled at her.

"Yuk! What's that stinking smell? Don't let that dirty thing touch anything of mine!"

Lily removed the dulcimina and placed it at the foot of the bed where she slept, so she could inhale its potency.

She had a fitful sleep that night and awoke Monday morning to fight her life at Plum Valley.

Chapter 8

Plum Valley-March 1963/8 years

So went the daily ritual of surviving the verbal berating of Maxine, a woman barely to her late twenties, and her little sister, Patsy. She learned to speak only when spoken to, and became closer to Margaret and Millie.

Why she had to stay she didn't fully understand, but she survived a tear—filled year at Plum Valley. The visits to Granny and Gramps became fewer and fewer. Auntie Maxine insisted she spend more time on her lessons. In her desert of sadness, she's had mirages of escape, that's all they proved to be, mirages.

In a melancholy moment, Lily found herself in tears as Patsy entered the room.

"Why is it that every time I see this child she is crying; what are you, 'Sad Sack?'" Aunt Patsy tugged Lily's pony tail as she stepped past her at the doorway. Lily's lost eyes stared out as tears stung her lids, puffy from months of weeping.

"Lily! Stop day-dreaming and pay attention." Auntie Maxine pinched her.

"Ouch, that hurts!" She winced.

"You need to wake up. At your age, you still can't read."

"I can read."

"Well READ!" She pointed to the word on the page.

"'H-i-l' says hil, '-a' says a, 'r-i-o-s' says rios."

"Well, put it all together now."

"'H-i-l' says hil, 'a' says a, 'r-i-o-s' says rios."

"You did that already, now say the word."

"I'm afraid, if I say it wrong you're going to beat me, and if I don't say it you're going to beat me." Lily quivered.

Slaps from Auntie Maxine's belt rained on her back.

She grimaced. Her skin wailed.

"Hilarious, Auntie Maxine, Hilarious!"

"So what took you so long? I thought you said you could read."

"Bu…but I can read." She whimpered.

"Just shut up and continue."

Lily expected the torture at every reading session.

Auntie Maxine received a male visitor and cut the session short, much to Lily's delight, except she hated Auntie Maxine's visitor—the bus driver.

He is a presumptuous oaf, but a needed distraction, anything to get away from Aunt Maxine pestering and torturing me.

She mustered a smile to camouflage her misery, a skill she learned well at Plum Valley.

"Lily, come and sit on my lap and give me a kiss."
Sam, the 'Tiger' bus driver opened his arms. Lily refused.
She flinched at the very idea.

"Lily did you hear what Uncle Sam said?"

"He's not my uncle." She folded her arms and
recoiled.

"Well he is going to be your uncle, so get used to it.
Now show some respect and do as you're told."

"Respect!" Lily chuckled to herself. She didn't budge.

Sam guffawed. "She'll get used to me, no need to
rush."

Lily walked away with contempt.

"Come here, Lily, where are your manners?"

Lily walked back, fake smiled. "I'm sorry, excuse me."
Lily went to her room and played with her doll and hid in
the closet. "Jolly were you a good girl today?" she made her
dolly answer.

"Yes, Mommy, I missed you."

"I missed you too, let me cuddle you, you must be
cuddled, you're a little child."

"Thank you, Mommy, I love you, Mommy"

"I love you too, my child."

The door creaked open. Lily hid her doll and jumped
out of the closet. It was Millie.

"Hi Millie, want to play dolly house with me?"

"Yes, let's play."

"I'll be the mommy, and you'll be the Auntie. You must beat her, because she cries too much, right?"

"Millie, Millie, where are you?" Lily grabbed the doll from Millie and hid it under some clothes. It was Margaret.

"What are you two doing in here?"

"We're playing dolly house, Margaret, want to play with me and Lily?"

"Yeah, let's play." The three had hours of fun. They spoke in hushed voices.

Auntie Maxine left for the day with Sam. Aunt Patsy had already left with her man. They had the place to themselves. They didn't have to hide and play in the closet.

Lily bonded with her new sisters. The kinship grew and comforted her; the only sense of belonging offered her at Plum Valley. Margaret drew paper dolls and dolls' clothing. Lily lost herself in fond moments of joy.

During the holidays, when Auntie Maxine and Aunt Patsy left them home alone, Margaret took charge. Those days she didn't have to eat Auntie Maxine's daily insipid cornmeal porridge, sweetened with just sugar, sans spices and milk. She often gagged on the porridge and got a spanking for vomiting it. Instead, Margaret fixed them Kool-aid, and jam and bread, and on a good day, she got Jell-O. Even so, she missed Granny's cooking.

In their absence, Margaret played Frank Sinatra and Matt Munroe and sang all grown up and danced ballet. Lily grew to adore and admire Margaret, she emulated her. They sang and danced as they dusted and cleaned the house together.

On returning home, Aunt Patsy usually headed for her room with a cigarette in hand to light another. That evening was no different. She ignored the girls and went to her room crying. Lily presumed over her man. Auntie Maxine shattered those happy times when she walked through the door. The girls had lost track of time listening to their favorite music when the key turned in the door.

"It's Auntie Maxine!" Lily ran to the kitchen and grabbed a broom to sweep the swept floor and Margaret grabbed a dust cloth and dusted the dusted furniture.

"What kind of gallivanting is going on here? Why are you playing my records? If there is just one scratch on any of them, your little hinds will be laced. Did you do any lessons today, especially you, Miss Lily; you're so dunce. You need to be doing lessons in your sleep. Go get your book right now, Lily!" Fear froze Lily.

"Move! Why do I have to shout, are you deaf?"

"Yes, Auntie Maxine." Lily's nerves on the verge of snapping.

"Yes, you're deaf?"

"No...no Ant Auntie Maxine." Lily's tongue twisted.

"Sometimes I wonder about you. Something must be wrong with you." Auntie Maxine shook her head and curled her upper lip.

"Margaret, start dinner."

"Yes ma'am." Margaret headed for the kitchen.

"Where's Millie?"

"She's sleeping." Lily and Margaret chorused.

'Buck wheat, buck wheat.' Lily covered her ears as the guinea chicks cackled. "Those damn guinea chicks, why do they have to make that hideous noise? I wish they would just die, disappear. I hate them." Lily muttered.

"What did you just say, Lily McDermott? Did I just hear you swear? Damn?"

"It was me, ma'am, I just spoke." Margaret came to Lily's defense, Lily knew Margaret risked getting a spanking herself and spoke up.

"Yes, Auntie Maxine, but I'm sorry I won't ever do it again."

Auntie Maxine slapped her across the face. "That's for swearing." She then slapped Margaret across her mouth. "That's for lying. I'm not going to let you girls grow up to be loose women and liars. You hear me? So watch your mouth!"

Margaret protected her. She came to her rescue and helped her with her lessons so Auntie Maxine wouldn't beat her. She liked that most of all. Their bonding grew tight.

Chapter 9

Plum Valley-December 1963/8 going on 9 years

The household buzzed at four-thirty every morning. Even in the tropics, temperatures drop in December, and even then, Lily and the others bathed outdoor in the dark frigidity. It was five-thirty in the morning, twilight.

"Brrrrr, I'm freezing."

"Well hurry up and put some clothes on, girl, moreover it's getting late. The sun will soon be up. Come on, Millie, it's your turn."

Millie didn't complain.

"Miss Francis, don't you think it's a bit cold to be bathing the children outdoors, and my, so early." The neighbor, Mrs. Anderson strained to see across the fence.

"Mrs. Anderson, I'd rather you not breaking your neck to see what is happening in my back yard. Please mind your own business." Auntie Maxine's words frosted through the icy morning. Mrs. Anderson slinked away in the twilight like a phantom.

"Damned busy-body, mind your own damned business, what is it to you that we bathe, or when we bathe, or how or where!" She showed her middle finger.

Lily's nakedness succumbed to the cold; she breathed through chattering teeth as her breath congealed. Lily liked

Mrs. Anderson, and although forbidden to, often paid her visits. She gave her home-made confectionaries when she visited. She hid them, occasionally sharing them with Margaret and Millie in secret. Lily learned life at Plum Valley. She learned hunger and those goodies came in handy on hungry days, especially on porridge and yam days, when she hid and disposed of the porridge down the drain and the yam out the window, which at least the Guinea chicks were good for something.

As usual, Lily and Margaret arrived at school before everyone except the caretaker.

"Good Morning, girls."

"Good Morning, Mr. Tremble." the girls chorused.

"I really admire you girls, you're always so early. I bet you're going to be something big in this country. What do you want to be when you grow up?"

"Hmmm," Margaret leaned her head sideways thinking, her finger on her cheek. "I want to be a bank manager."

"Fine, fine, very nice, what about you uh..."

"Lily." Margaret reminded him.

"Yes, Lily, that's a fine name, the name of a flower. You are just as pretty and dainty. What do you want to become?"

"I want to be a doctor so I can take care of Granny and Gramps."

"Oh, that is wonderful. Would you take care of me too?"

"Oh yes, I will take care of everyone, but Granny and Gramps are special. Oh, and Aunt Liza, but she's not sick, she is young, but Granny says if she doesn't get married soon, she'll get old and be a maid, you know an old maid; maybe you should marry her, Mr. Tremble, because I sure don't want her to get old. She is very fine looking, even pretty. You will love her, Mr. Tremble."

Mr. Tremble's laughter echoed through the playground.

The school bell rang; time for devotion. The children gathered round the podium under the Lignum Vitae tree. The principal took the lead. In the midst of the devotion, a low murmur grew louder. The crowd stirred.

Lily felt faint, and the next thing she knew, something powerful smelling woke her.

"Where am I? What happened? Did I die?"

"No, honey, you didn't die, you just fainted." The school nurse beamed at her.

Mr. Tremble, Margaret, and Sasha stood beside the nurse. "Is she alright?" Margaret's brow wrinkled in concern.

"What did she have for breakfast?

"Cornmeal porridge, but she didn't eat it."

"Oh she is hungry then." The nurse charted a meal plan and wrote a note in her diary.

"Such a sweet little girl, she wants to be a doctor. I hope she makes it." Mr. Tremble took her hand in his.

"Lily you may stay here until you feel better."

Lily's focus grew clearer. She smiled. "Okay, thanks, Miss White." The nurse sent to the kitchen for a couple of biscuits with some cheese and a cup of tea. Lily ate with gusto, a welcomed change from porridge. She closed her eyes and slept until lunchtime. The cook served her lunch in the sick bay. Her teacher sent her work for the afternoon.

There are nice people in Plum Valley.

Lily warmed to the kind gestures. "Miss White, thanks for being so nice to me. I don't like it here, but it's not so bad after all."

"I'm glad you settling in nicely, Lily, it will take a while, but you will be fine." Miss White smiled.

On her way home from school, she stopped at Mrs. Anderson's. Margaret rushed home to start the dinner.

"Hello, Mrs. Anderson."

"Did you have a good day at school?"

"Yes and no."

"Huh."

"Well I fainted at devotion."

"What caused that?"

"I didn't have my breakfast."

"Naughty girl." Mrs. Anderson scowled at her.

"But I hate porridge."

"Oh you know what I have some almond drops here, would you like some?"

"Thanks, Mrs. Anderson, they are my favorites." Lily never said no to almond drops. She hid them in her knapsack. "Mrs. Anderson, would you like to see all my nice clothes that Aunt Liza makes for me. She's the best dressmaker ever. She makes all my pretty dresses. Come and see them."

"But won't your mother mind."

"She's not there. She won't be home till late, she works late on Tuesdays."

"Yeah, but I shouldn't."

"Pretty please, Mrs. Anderson, I really want you to see them, it would mean a lot to me. I never get to wear them here to show them off."

Mrs. Anderson acquiesced.

They made it to the house, and Lily took Mrs. Anderson's hand, "Right this way," and led her to her room. Lily pulled out her drawer and removed a frilly garb.

"See this pink one with the streamers? It's my favorite. And do you see this bolero? It's a Mexican bolero and it's woven with real gold thread."

"How do you know that?"

"That's what Aunt Liza said."

The key turned in the door.

"Oh my goodness, it's her, you have to hide." Lily tried to stuff Mrs. Anderson under her bed.

"No, Lily, I can't fit under the bed. I just have to try to leave through the back door." Mrs. Anderson hastened her steps.

"Yes, or she'll kill me, us…"

Maxine bumped into Mrs. Anderson as she slipped through the hallway leading to the back door.

Chapter 10

Plum Valley-December 1963/8 going on 9 years

"What the devil are you doing in my house, Adina Anderson?"Maxine barked and backed her in a corner.

"Miss Francis, I can explain." Mrs. Anderson pivoted.

You're trespassing! How do I know you're not here looking for something to steal?" Maxine tripped her.

Mrs. Anderson's body succumbed to the laws of gravity at a forty five degree angle but she regained her balance. She pivoted again and managed to dodge Maxine. She backed away. "Miss Francis, it's not what it looks like. I apologize profusely. I am out of my depths here, truly sorry." Mrs. Anderson held her palms up as a shield. She slipped out the backdoor, shame at her heals. She didn't look back.

"If you come as much as ten feet from my gate, I will be calling the police!" Her words trailed Mrs. Anderson with menace.

Maxine raised a fist. "I need to get a bloody dog."

"Now you, Miss Lily, what is that woman doing in my house and in your bedroom?"

"Nothing." Lily stared at her feet.

"Liar, if you stand there before me and lie I will slap you silly. Now tell me, what was she doing here?" Maxine's eyes burned into her.

"Nothing!"

"You're lying!" Auntie Maxine leaned in.

Lily quivered. Auntie Maxine noticed the opened drawers.

"She went into your drawers?" Auntie Maxine's eyes narrowed.

"No...I...I mean yes, ma'am." A puddle formed at Lily's feet. Lily felt a heat stinging her ears and ice water down her spine. If only the earth could swallow her.

Maxine's eyes fell to the floor, and then up again. She glared at Lily. "What the hell? You just stood there and piss up yourself, just like that?" Maxine rolled her eyes, then one smack across Lily's back.

Lily winced.

"On top of it, you have that woman here into our private business? Why on earth would you do something like that?"

"I don't know why." She hung her head. Talking about her folks in Bellevue kept them real. She didn't explain that to Maxine, she feared incurring more of her wrath.

"You do the stupidest things." She shook her head. "Only God knows what's going to become of you. You are not going to amount to anything." Auntie Maxine's nostrils flared.

"I'm sorry."

"Sorry, you're not sorry yet. If you ever bring that woman over here again, or if I ever see or hear that you have anything to do with her, I will give you a sound beating and tie you to a tree so the guinea chicks will peck you. Go and clean up yourself, you nasty little thing."

Lily shivered. "Yes, Auntie Maxine."

"I don't like busy-bodies, that woman is a busy-body." She throw her arms up and walked away.

Later that evening, Lily gave her the letter from school. She read it without emotion. Lily hoped for a show of sympathy.

"I won't bother to take you up with your book this evening. Just take a bath and have your supper."

Lily rejoiced as she bounded off.

Maxine changed her mind.

At school the next morning, Nurse White sent for Lily.

"Lily, what would you like for lunch today?"

"Dunno, Miss White."

"Okay, let's go to the kitchen and see what the cook is brewing."

She walked hand in hand with Nurse White to Cook's Parlor.

"What brings you both to my Parlor?" Ms. Cook, which Lily found humorous for a cook to be named, straightened her apron and dashed a toothless grin.

"Lily here is a picky eater, Ms. Cook, and I'd like to encourage her to eat."

"It shows, she's so skinny, skin and bones."

"Ms. Cook, that's not nice." Nurse White scowled. Lily looked from face to face as they talked about her in third person.

"Sorry, lovey, didn't mean to hurt ya feelings." She bent over to Lily's height and made eye contact, taking her hands in hers. "So what would ya like for lunch today?" Ms. Cook had a Cockney accent.

"Dunno." Lily shrugged.

"So how 'bout some good old bulgur rice and chicken?"

"I hate bulgur rice. It tastes nasty." She made a face.

"So how 'bout some yam and green boiled bananas?"

"No thank you." She shook her head.

"You're really a picky eater then, aren't ya? I know what I'm a gonna give you, my precious. Ms. Cook is gonna make you a nice bowl of white rice, you a white rice girl, huh?"

"Yes, thank you." Lily nodded. "And my Granny always gives me the chicken leg."

Nurse White and Ms. Cook looked at each other and smiled.

"You're gonna feel right at home then, Miss Lily." Ms. Cook rubbed Lily's head and flashed another toothless grin.

Suffice it to say, Lily gormandized lunch.

"Miss White, I really enjoyed my lunch, can I get that again tomorrow."

"We'll see, you could pay Ms. Cook a visit and tell her thanks though."Lily ran up the incline leading to the school canteen.

"Ms. Cook, Ms. Cook." Lily tip toed over the counter.

"Yes, Lily." Ms. Cook looked up from washing the dishes and wiped her hands.

"Thanks for the delicious lunch. May I get that again tomorrow?"

"Sure right ma precious, but you can't live on that every day. You must eat a variety of stuff to be healthy."

"That's what Nurse White said."

"Well, I'm sure one more day won't hurt."

"Thank you, Ms. Cook."

Lily left, made it out the building and down the hill to play with Sasha and the other children.

After school, Maxine briefed her on the school consultation. "So I had a talk with your teacher, the principal, and the nurse today about you."

Lily's apprehension grew.

"I didn't mean to do it, ma'am, I didn't know I was going to faint."

"Don't be silly girl, you can't make yourself faint. But what you could do is eat up your porridge in the mornings."

"But I don't like porridge."

"It's good for you. Miss White told me to give you what you like, but that is foolishness. You need to eat what's good for you and porridge is good for you."

"Yes, Auntie Maxine."

"Anyway on a different note, your teacher says you are well behaved and you are doing well with your lessons. See, all the work you're doing at home is paying off?"

"Yes, Auntie Maxine, thank you."

"And by the way, I saw Mr. Tremble. He offered to come down here and make a swing for you and Margaret and Millie. Says it's a reward for going to school early every morning. See, it's a good thing I wake you up early? And to think that busy-body next door is interfering."

"Thank you, Auntie Maxine, and that is very kind of Mr. Tremble, he is a good man."

Grateful for the way the day ended, Lily said a special prayer:

> *"Gentle Jesus meek and mild, pity my simple see, thank you for Cook and Miss White and Mr. Tremble. Amen."*

She hugged Jolly extra tight. Her dreams consoled her.

Chapter 11

Plum Valley/Rainy season begins, April 1964/9 years

The rain battered the roof and pelted the louver windows. The wind whistled ominous sounds through the trees. The eerie darkness petrified Lily and kept her awake. She crawled into Aunt Patsy's bed. She missed Bellevue. On those kinds of nights, she found the comfort of Gramps and Granny's bed or that of Aunt Liza's.

"Who's this?" Aunt Patsy drugged with sleep stirred.

"It's me Lily. I'm scared."

"Scared of what?"

"I'm scared of the dark and the rain. It sounds like duppies are tearing down the windows."

"Foolishness, go back to bed."

"Please let me stay here, I'm so very scared."

"There is nothing to be afraid of; get out of my bed. I need my beauty sleep."

"Please, Auntie." Lily clung to her like leech. Patsy pried her hands from around her and pushed her off the bed. Lily fell to the floor.

She got back in bed, covered her head with the sheet and lie on the side of her good ear to block the sounds. Tears competed with the rain. She remained vigilante until the Sandman took his toll.

She awoke the next morning to a less angry rain pitter-pattering on the roof. Calm washed over her. She drifted off until the loud chattering of the guinea chicks had their way. Her consciousness found her in a pool of wetness. She jumped out of bed and grabbed the potty to relieve herself. She caught the stream before it inundated the bed. She changed her clothes before the others rose.

Later that morning, the rain eased, and that meant going to school meant less drenched.

School prepared for Eisteddfod. Lily's teacher selected her for elocution competition. She had to study the poem, 'I Love to Walk with Mommy.'

"I don't like that poem."

"Why not Lily, it's a nice poem."

"I just don't like it."

"Why?"

"Nothing, Miss."

"Well okay then, study it and come prepared to practice tomorrow. Eisteddfod is six weeks from now."

"Okay, Miss."

The rain fell on and off all day. It was the rainy season, the season of muck and puddles. Again, the rain eased for the walk home time, almost, nearly to the house, it picked up, and they didn't mind. The children took off their shoes and walked bare feet in the streams running down the drains on the sides of the road.

Lily and Margaret joined the other children—bare feet slapping in the water and the rain pelting down on them, their laughter rang out with the showering of the rain, oblivious to the passage of time and the consequences.

Auntie Maxine sat on the verandah with the switch awaiting their late arrival. Lily spied Auntie Maxine and dashed into Mrs. Anderson's yard. Soaking wet, she hid under the cellar.

"Good evening, ma'am."

As Lily hid, she could catch the glimpse of Margaret getting the strap.

"Where is Lily?"

"I don't know, ma'am." Another blow fell.

"You know you must get home early to look after Millie, and you and Lily are on the road gallivanting. Go inside and change your clothes before you catch Pneumonia."

"Yes, ma'am." She scurried away to avoid another assault.

"I'm waiting right here for Miss Lily."

Lily shivered as the wetness soaked into her skin. She didn't know which was worse—the beating or the cold—she chose the latter. The evening sky turned mournful and

Lily contemplated sleeping at Mrs. Anderson's house. She walked up to the entrance to knock on the door when she spied Aunt Maxine on the verandah next door. She ducked and ran back under the cellar. Rats lived under Mrs. Anderson dirt floored cellar. They darted from pillar to post. They showed off their antics as if performing for her. She found them amusing. They took her mind off her predicament, but she knew she needed to get home out of the cold and dampness of the impending night.

Lily crept inside and hid under her bed.

"Lily!"

She'd fallen asleep in her wet state; the sound of someone calling her name jolted her awake. She curled up in a fetal position and kept still.

Muffled voices grew closer. She recognized Mr. Tremble's voice. He had joined Auntie Maxine in the sitting hall.

"We've looked everywhere for here, but, I'm sure she can't be too far."

"Have you looked under the bed? That's where children hide from beatings. When I was a little boy, I spent a lot of time hiding under the bed." He laughed.

"You must have been a naughty boy, Mr. Tremble."

"Let me check." Lily heard her footsteps getting closer. She shuddered. Auntie Maxine beamed the flashlight under the bed, blinding Lily.

"Mr. Tremble, you were so right."

Mr. Tremble joined Auntie Maxine in peering at her.

"Oh my, lying there in wet clothes, that's not good. Lily dear, you may get a fever."

"I am going to give her a hiding, that's the fever she will get."

"No please don't beat her, give her a chance. Foolishness is tied up in the heart of a child, so the Bible says. Give her a chance, Miss Francis. I beg for her."

"Get from under the bed, child. You're lucky Mr. Tremble begged for you. Suppose you get sick, eh, look at you. You better go change before you get a fever. It would serve you right."

Lily staggered out from under the bed and found dry clothing.

Later that night, she started coughing. She roasted. She stood by Aunt Patsy's bed. "Aunt Patsy, I feel sick."

Patsy huffed and pulled the cover over her head.

Chapter 12

Buff Bay, Portland/Hospital Day three/April 1964/9 years

Her fever grew worse, and after a few days of persistent fever, Auntie Maxine took her to the clinic.

"How long has she been having this fever?"

"About a week now."

"A week and you're just taking her to see the clinic?"

"Well I've been giving her garlic tea and other home remedies."

"We'll have to run some tests." The doctor shook his head.

A day later, the test results came back and Lily had pneumonia. The doctor recommended hospitalization. After a few days, she did not improve. The doctor ran more tests and discovered she also had meningitis. Her life hung in the balance.

"It doesn't look like she's going to make it. I think we better send for her Bellevue people."

"Lily, Lily can you hear me? It's me, Auntie Maxine."

Lily's eyes didn't open.

"I think you should tell her the truth."

"The truth, about what?"

"About whom she really is?"

"It's too late for that now, in any case, what's the point of that?"

"Honesty."

"Honesty is not always the best policy."

"Sometimes I wonder if we both grew up together, well, fairness then."

"When was the last time life was fair to me? Look at all the men that have saddled me with burdens and none of them hang around to put them in their saddle? Fair, fair indeed." Maxine chuckled.

"Lily, Lily can you hear me? Lily, move your thumb if you can hear us."

Lily moved her thumb.

"She's still with us. At least her beloved Gramps and Granny may be able to see her before..."Aunt Patsy tapered off.

****

Hope entered Lily's heart. She drifted off to sleep.

Bellevue decked with a plethora of flowers of all colors, more beautiful than she'd ever seen, stood in the distance. She walked through a mist smelling of eucalyptus. She stood in the mist for a while, savoring its balm. She floated on the mist. It took her to Bellevue. She walked over to a bed of white lilies and picked one for Granny, one for Gramps and one for Aunt Liza.

"Granny!" she waved. "Gramps! Aunt Liza." She waved again, her hair and her dress fluttered in a gentle breeze. They didn't respond. They chatted with each other about her, oblivious of her presence. She ran to them.

"That Maxine hasn't allowed Lily to spend any time with us recently." Granny looked perturbed.

"Yes, it's been a while." Gramps held Granny around her waist.

"I think we should go pay her a visit and see how she's getting on." Aunt Liza had a bunch of roses in her hand.

Lily listened without interrupting.

"I wonder if that little girl knows how precious she is to us."

"I'm sure she knows, Granny." Gramps squeezed Granny's hand and they all walked away.

"Granny, come back!" Lily called to them, but they kept walking. She tried to follow but lost them. She woke up whimpering, her face wet. The unrelenting fever burnt skin and brain, making her delirious.

Aunt Maxine leaned over to wipe her brow. Lily screamed.

"Witch, witch, go away. Leave me alone."

"Calm down, Lily, it's me, Auntie Maxine."

"Nooooo." She writhed and foamed.

"Nurse, nurse, come quickly please, I think she's dying."

****

The monitor beeped loudly.

"Can you please step outside, ma'am?" the nurse pulled the curtain and paged the doctor.

The doctor came. He invited them behind the curtain and spoke to them.

"The prognosis is not good. She's not responding well to the medication. We will have to relocate her to the Children's' Hospital in Kingston."

"Kingston, that's a far way off, she will die if she travels so far, what do you think, Maxine?"

"I think we should listen to the doctor."

"Don't worry; she will be transported by a helicopter. In the mean time we will give her something to calm her and keep her as comfortable as possible. Who will accompany her?"

"I will. Patsy, you stay and send a telegram to Bellevue."

"Bye, Lily." Lily squirmed and pulled away as Patsy touched her.

"Don't touch me, witch." She spoke with labored breath.

It took fifteen minutes to get to the hospital in Kingston. The hospital staff hooked her up with speed. Her blood pressure and heart rate fluctuated. Her breathing was shallow and labored. She drifted in and out of consciousness.

Maxine stared at her frail nine-plus-year-old body, a body that had grown gangly and thin, but grown nonetheless from the one and a quarter pound palm sized thing the doctor had asked what to do with. There in that hospital, she slid back to that fateful day nine plus years earlier:

"What should I do with it?" The obstetrician peered over his glasses and gave a sad smile.

"As long as there's life in the body keep it." Maxine had frowned and sighed.

"It may not live past a week." He rubbed his chin.

"Keep it nonetheless. I have kept this burden this past nine months. I don't think a week longer will make a difference." She exhaled. Too weak to cry, it couldn't even suckle at the breast.

She'd clean her mother's entire four-bedroom house, polishing the floor on her knees with a coconut brush that Christmas when labor pains began. Her mother, who had rushed her to the hospital, had no idea she was pregnant, because for the nine months of pregnancy, she had carefully tied her stomach to hide the growing fetus. As the story went, the baby was premature, the story she'd told everyone. When the belly ache turned out to be a baby her mother fumed as she announced the revelation to the rest of the family. She had gone ahead and had her older sons, Maxine's brothers, dig a hole behind the outdoor toilet to bury it, as the story went.

"It is not going to live. It is as small as a piece of codfish and pale. The doctor said it's not going to make it."

It seemed her life would end the way it began. It would die and the burden would be gone. Maybe that grave behind the latrine would be adequate, she was small enough.

Lily's frail chest continued to heave. The doctor placed her on a life support machine, with wires and hoses plugged into her lifeless body.

"What do you want us to do, Mrs. Francis?" The doctor cornered Lily's mother.

"If there's life in the body, keep it." Maxine's eyes glazed over. Maybe this time it will expire.

Chapter 13

Kingston/Children's Hospital Day seven/April 1964/9 years

She hovered over her own body. She hoped Aunt Maxine told Granny and Gramps and Aunt Liza to hurry to see her. The longing in her heart burned. Aunt Maxine sat in the chair next to her body. This is her second visit for the week. Aunt Maxine looked miserable and anxious as she studied the monitor. Aunt Maxine's face contorted in confusion, she didn't understand the readings. The oxygen tank hissed and fluids attached to her veins gurgled. The doctor brought a specialist with him.

"Good day, Mrs. Francis, this is Dr. Bell, she is the resident pediatrician."

Dr. Bell stretched out her hand. "Pleasure to meet you, Mrs. Francis. I can well imagine you're worried about her, but we're going to do everything within our power to help her."

Aunt Maxine shook the doctor's hand. "Thank you, doctor, what is the likelihood of her surviving?"

"It's hard to tell at this stage, we will just have to wait and see. She has a very bad case of meningitis. We have been able to control the pneumonia and she's still receiving some strong dosages of antibiotics, so we will just have to wait. We hope she won't need a blood transfusion."

"Oh boy." Aunt Maxine rubbed her chin.

"We're not too happy with the readings of her vital signs right now, they are somewhat below normal pediatric range, but we're hoping that things will pick up and take a turn for the better."

"Oh boy." She bit her lip and shook her head.

"Plus the fever hasn't broken. That is critical, as we don't want her to sustain any brain damage."

"Good Lord. Brain damage, no I hope not, I really couldn't deal with that." Aunt Maxine swallowed hard.

Fancy she should say that, because Aunt Patsy always called her a retard. It's impossible to be more retarded

Lily pitied her condition as she floated over the scene. She felt no pain.

As the doctors spoke to Aunt Maxine, the beeping from the monitor slowed as her vital signs began to fail. The situation rose to a critical level.

"We're losing her!" Dr. Bell rushed into action as she attached a CPR machine to her chest. Two nurses ran to assist the doctors.

"Oh my God, what's happening?" Aunt Maxine eyes froze open. She threw her hands across her abdomen squeezing hard into her womb. Her knees wobbled.

A Nurse held her up and escorted her from Lily's bedside as another pulled the curtains. The doctor began CPR.

Lily drifted off to a place of peace.

Tall trees provided shade as families sat and picnic baskets spread out with food of all varieties, colorful and appetizing. Lily helped herself at a fruit stand and no one noticed or turned to greet her or shun her. She bounced off to a stream lined with rows and rows of colorful flowers. She tried picking them, but they would not leave their stems. They had delightful aromas, the scent of jasmines and lavender wafted up and comforted her. Rainbows arched over cloudless skies, and birds sang tunes she'd never heard. She saw children playing with lions and tigers.

She floated to a group of children playing games. She tried to join, but no one paid her any mind. She lowered her head and turned away. A soft voice spoke from behind her. She turned around to see a stranger in the mist.

"Hello, Lily, welcome to Paradise." The stranger's dimpled smile eased Lily.

"How do you know my name?" Lily's eyes narrowed.

"I've always known you." The stranger stretched a hand out but withdrew when Lily tried to take it.

"You know me, how comes?" Lily stepped back and chewed her lip.

The stranger gave her an adoring gaze.

"It's so beautiful here, but no one wants to play with me." She frowned.

"They will play with you when the time is right." The stranger consoled her.

"When the time is right? What do you mean?" she cocked her head to one side.

"Just that, when the time is right." The stranger smiled.

"I don't understand."

"This is just a promise; in time you will be able to really enjoy this place. For now just be the best Lily you can be." The stranger gave a reassuring smile.

"Can Granny, Gramps, and Aunt Liza come here too?"

"It's for everyone."

"Everyone, even witches?"

"Everyone, who is not evil, but if they change they can live here, because in this place no one will hurt anyone."

"Hmmm."

"You need to return to your family. I hear them calling your name." With that, the stranger disappeared.

"Lily, Lily!" Dr. Bell urged her as she continued the CPR. "Lily, Lily, please respond." She bent over Lily's body and pumped. The monitor started beeping normal again.

"Thank God, she's back." Dr. Bell sighed with relief. Lily's vitals stabilized somewhat. Her out-of-body experience ended.

Dr. Bell left bedside and approached Aunt Maxine. "Mrs. Francis, so sorry about that episode, we're not leaving the hospital. We will be right down the hallway. We are keeping a close eye on her."

"Thank you, doctor." She had a vacant stare.

Aunt Maxine brightened as she saw Gramps, Aunt Liza, Aunt Patsy, and Granny approaching her. There was a tall gentleman holding on to Granny.

Chapter 14

Kingston/Children's Hospital Day seven/April 1964

Gramps, Aunt Liza, and Aunt Patsy hurried to Aunt Maxine. Granny wobbled to keep up, the arthritic pain shooting through her knees, while a tall gentleman bore her weight on his arm.

Maxine strained her neck to identify Granny's human crutch. As he got closer, her heart pounded against her rib cage. Breathless and choked up, she thought of running away. He had a familiar gait, heavier but still the same gait. Could it be Winston? Winston lived thousands of miles away in England. She dismissed the notion. "Winston McDermott!" she covered her mouth. Everyone and everything else dissolved out of focus. She melted as his face dimpled into a familiar smile. Her body shook. He stretched out his hand to greet her. She wiped her clammy hand into her dress but she refused an embrace.

"My first love." He whispered.

Her body stiffened. She remembered how he'd turned her down and abandoned her in her despair.

"Don't mess with me, Winston. Don't talk about love. Save your empty speech." She pushed him off.

"Aw come on, don't be like that, we haven't seen each other going ten years now. Is this the way you greet your baby's daddy," he spun her around, "Girl, you're still looking fine."

"Just get lost, Winston. I believe you're here to see Lily, let's get on with that, eh." She moved away from his reach. He grabbed after her. Maxine returned to Lily's bedside, he followed.

Dr. Bell stopped to inform Maxine of the MRI report. "She's a very lucky little girl. Diagnostic results do not show any brain damage." The doctor consoled her family. "We've put her on a stronger dosage of antibiotics. She is stable at the moment and we hope for the best."

****

"Thank you, Lord." Granny brushed a stray lock from Lily's forehead. "But she's still roasting with a fever, doctor."

"We're trying everything we can to reduce the fever; it's pretty stubborn. Hopefully it'll break within the next twenty-four hours. Otherwise, we may really have to worry about brain damage or other complications."

Granny joined hands with Gramps, Aunt Liza, Aunt Maxine, and Winston. She rested her free hand on Lily's forehead and prayed loud and long. After the prayer, they all filed out to the waiting area, except Granny. She watched over Lily like an angel.

Lily's eyes flashed open. "Granny." Her weak voice floated up to Granny.

Granny called out to the others. "She's back, she's back!" everyone filed back in the room and fussed over her.

Granny kept her focus on Lily. "Just rest, sweetheart."

. Lily closed her eyes.

Granny sat with her for several hours, when she noticed the fever breaking. "Lily, my baby, I missed you so much." She placed the back of her hand on Lily's forehead, the fever had indeed broken. "Thank heavens, it's gone."

"Lily, how are you feeling?" Aunt Liza joined Granny.

Lily didn't answer but smiled. Her eyes glistened.

"You had us all worried that we wouldn't hear anymore of your Brother Anancy stories." Gramps gave her cheek a soft pinch.

"Watcha talking 'bout, Gramps?" Lily made a playful pout.

Granny laughed and the others followed.

****

Lily weakly smiled, and she fixed on the stranger. She'd seen him somewhere before. The stranger who'd walked out of the mist.

"Hi baby, do you know who I am?" The man took her hand in his. Everyone left them alone.

"No." She shook her head, but calm washed over her. "Have you come to take me to paradise?"

"Paradise?" he cocked his head.

"Yes, paradise, you promised." Her chin trembled.

"I'm your father." His eyes moistened.

"My father?" she frowned.

"Yes, I'm Winston McDermott. Are you Lily McDermott?" His smile dimpled.

"Yes I am." She flushed.

"Then I am your daddy."

Lily's heart rose, a joy in all the pain leveled over her.

"Daddy, finally, you're here, where's my mommy, did you bring her with you?"

"Oh yes, she's here. Maxine, Maxine…"

"No, no, she's not my Mommy, she's Auntie Maxine. I mean is my Mommy here?"

"Bu…"

"No, she is not my mother."

"Yes she is."

"Nooooooo she's not my mother!"

"Lily baby, calm down, I know you're not feeling well, bu…"

Lily covered her ears and screamed. "She is not my mother!"

Everyone rushed back in.

"What's happening? Is she okay?"

"I don't understand, she keeps saying Maxine isn't her mother."

"She told me not to call her mommy. She is not my mother. I don't want her to be my mother!" Lily shook her head and writhed in the bed.

All eyes focused on Maxine. Maxine folded her arms and hung her head, her jaw clenched. Dr. Bell excused herself.

"If you need me, I'm down the hall." She walked away.

"Maxine?" Lily's father turned for an explanation, but she walked away.

****

Winston McDermott followed Maxine. "Maxine, why would you do something like that? You owe me an explanation."

They spoke in raised voices.

"Me, owe you an explanation?" Maxine demanded. "I owe you nothing, Winston McDermott. You left me with a baby to face the shame all by myself, that's why I left it on your doorstep. You were not man enough to deal with it. You ran away and left it for your parents to look after." Her nostrils dilated as she spat fire.

"I was too young to marry you, Maxine, I was just a boy."

"A boy indeed." She rolled her eyes. "A good for nothing boy. Do you know what it's like to walk around with an illegitimate child? No one wants to hire you, people don't respect you. I can't let people know my business. It's none of their business, only who needs to know, needs to know." She glowered.

"That's not a reason to disown your own child as yours."

Maxine narrowed the distance between them and shoved a finger into his face. "It is every reason to disown my children."

New Chapter 15

Journey from Bellevue to Kingston/1 week after release from hospital/April 1964

Just four feet-four inches tall, she peered out the window at the garden. The roses were wet with dewdrops, glistening in the morning light. She twitched with excitement at the thought of the day ahead. The curtains billowed in the breeze bringing in a rose scented morning as her silk ribbons flowed along with it.

She spotted the car. It was her daddy. She flung the door open, chiffon and lace bounded out the door.

"Daddy!" her arms outstretched, she jumped into his arms.

He scooped up her up. "My baby, how are you feeling now? You look a picture of health." He planted a kiss on her cheek as she returned his hug.

"I'm better now, Daddy." She scrambled down and ran to the car. She stepped back and stared at it. "Daddy your car is rather ugly, but I like the color. Why does it look like a toad?" she reached for the door, opened it, and stepped in. Her feet sank into the plush flooring and the huge seat swallowed her up. "Wow Daddy, I like this car. Can you keep it? What kind of car is this? I've never seen anything like this in my entire life?" She squealed with delight.

Winston chuckled. "It's a Peugeot"

"A what?" her brow knitted.

"Peugeot, it's a French car."

"I like it, can we keep it?"

"But I thought you just said its ugly? Anyway I won't be able to keep it because I have to go back to London. I borrowed it from a friend."

"Do you really have to go, Daddy? Can I come with you?"

"Not this trip, baby, but I promise I'm going to send for you."

"Really, Daddy? I can't wait." Her eyes sparkled.

As her father placed the car into gear and released the emergency brake, the car stood up like a camel. Lily giggled and tumbled as it threw her off balance.

They headed for Kingston, the capital city of Jamaica. It promised to be an exciting day with a rare visit of Her Majesty the queen, and a trip to the zoo. Lily's excitement had her bobbing up and down in the back seat.

"Lily, please put on your seat belt."

"Yes, Daddy."

"Lily, sit back and keep still."

"Yes, Daddy." She giggled as the car bounced over the bumpy road.

The trip to Kingston spanned the pothole riddled meandering roads of Portland through Junction in St. Mary, with its treacherous ravines and narrow roads. When they got to the Junction, Lily's eyes remained steadfast on the road as she clung to the side of the seat; her stomach jumped to her mouth as she gazed down into the precipices below the narrow road.

"Daddy, I'm scared."

"Don't be scared darling, Daddy is your hero, and he won't let anything happen to you. Just you make sure you keep that seat belt on and sit still." With the angry rivers below, she took that counsel seriously.

"Daddy, my stomach hurts. I want to throw up."

Her father stopped the car.

She threw up all over him. "Sorry, Daddy."

"Never mind, Baby, I'll get you some mints at the next stop."

They bonded. Lily fell asleep.

A witch cast a spell on her and dragons blew fiery breath at her. Out of breath she ran through a wooded area trying to find her way home to Bellevue. The witch had banished her to the woods and turned her into a toad, a turquoise toad. She tried to call out for help, but only croaking sounds escaped her lips.

"Help me, help me please." Her voice echoed. Shadowy figures moved around and made howling noises.

She fell into swamps with slimy swamp creatures and everywhere she stepped fiery balls fell in her path. She waded through the muck and fell into sinking sand.

"Someone, please help me."

Superman hovered in the sky, his cape fluttering in the wind behind him.

"Superman, please help me, I'm sinking!" She raised her head, screamed and waved her hands as she sank further into the mire. The more she wiggled the deeper she sank.

"Keep still Lily, if you move you'll sink further." He cautioned her.

"I'm scared superman, I'm so scared." She sank to her neck.

"Don't be afraid, Lily, I'm here to rescue you and break that dreadful spell." He used his cape to protect her from the fire balls. He scooped her up in his arms and flew off with her over the mountains and into the clouds.

"Oops that feels funny, Superman." She clung to him with all her strength.

"I'm going to teach you to fly."

"But I have no wings." She giggled.

"Don't worry, just follow me." He held both her hands, her legs dangling. He maneuvered in a circle with her until she glided. He let go one hand and then the next.

"Whee I'm flying, Daddy, I'm flying."

"Lily, did you say something?" Her father broke through her dream.

Lily's eyes snapped open. "Oh Daddy, I dreamt I was flying and that you're Superman."

"That's charming, Lily, I will be your Superman. I'm here to protect you."

She leaned over his seat and hugged him.

"That's exactly what Superman said." She hugged him again.

"Well there you go. That's what daddies do."

As the day unfolded, she grew closer to her father.

The queen looked spectacular in her royal attire as she waved and smiled. The thick crowd made it difficult for Lily to see the happenings, so her father walked with her on his shoulders.

"I want to be a princess, Daddy."

"You are a princess, you're my princess. Princess Lily."

When the procession ended, they had lunch and went off to the zoo. She saw the lions, tigers, and elephants, and even got a ride on an elephant.

On the way home, she had a heart to heart talk with her father. "Daddy, I don't like Aunt Maxine. I wish she would die."

"Not Auntie Maxine, Lily, Mommy." He corrected her. "It's not nice to wish your mother dead."

"But I don't want her to be my mommy. She's a witch. Every time I ask for the wishbone at Granny's." Lily pouted.

"What's your wish?"

"I wish that she would die, and then I don't have to go back to Plum Valley." Lily bit her nails and stomped.

"Lily, she's your mother, and that's not nice."

"No she's not." She stomped again.

"Yes she is."

"Is not." Her mood grew dark, but she had little time to dwell on how dark it was.

Her father turned a corner and a car came hurtling at them. Her father called out for Lily to hold on. She swerved, the car slid sideways and flipped onto its top then again and came to rest close to the edge of a precipice.

Lily's seatbelt tightened around her chest and gripped her like a visor. The excruciating pain in her leg numbed her mind. She couldn't move, and the last thing she remembered was her Daddy's still face and men shouting the car was about to blow up.

New Chapter 16
From Bellevue to Plum Valley/Six weeks after accident/May 1964

A loud scream escaped Lily's mouth. She'd been reliving the ordeal. It'd been six weeks since the trauma, but it remained fresh in her mind. She heard the loud thud from the collision and felt the jolt. She covered her ears and screamed. Her stomach churned as she felt the rolling motion of the car. She held her abdomen and braced herself. Her leg hurt and she choked on the smoke in the car. She smelled the gasoline. She felt the heat from the burning car. Terror built up as the flames grew. She screamed again.

Her hero had cheated death. He had a wound on his forehead and bled from his nostrils and mouth. She still smelled the raw blood. His right leg was broken. The steering wheel had pinned him. She blamed herself.

"Lily, are you okay? I just heard you screaming." Her father limped to Lily's room. He clutched his chest as he moved.

"I was having a nightmare again, Daddy."

"What about?"

"About the accident. The car was rolling over and over down a hill and into the river."

"Never mind, you'll soon get over it. I get nightmares about it too. But remember the doctor said it would happen." He lifted her out of bed and placed her on his lap.

"Yes, but it seems so real."

"I understand." He hugged her and put her down. They both walked out on the verandah.

"Daddy, it's all my fault." She hung her head as she sat with him on a love seat.

"No, Lily, don't think and say such a thing. Accidents happen. No one knows when they're going to happen."

"But if I wasn't naughty, that wouldn't have happened though."

"Naughty? Nah, I wouldn't say you were being naughty, you were just telling me how you feel."

"And I still feel bad."

"You will have to learn to love your mother."

"Never, she doesn't love me, she beats me all the time and she is always cross with me."

"Okay, I will have a talk with her."

"I heard a man at the crash site saying that it's a miracle if we survive. Daddy, do you believe in miracles?"

"Well, we survived, didn't we?"

"So that's a miracle? So God still loves me, even though I wish Aunt Maxine would die?"

"Yes, it's a miracle. And God loves little children."

"So do you think God loves me?"

"Yes of course God loves you, and I love you too." He poked her playfully.

"Daddy, try to catch me." She hopped off into the yard. She tested out her stiff leg. The doctor had removed the cast but the sensation lingered. "You can't catch me, you can't catch me." She dodged as she hopped around the yard like a rabbit.

Her father chased her, one hand on his side, the other on his hip. "You're getting too fast for me, Lily."

Lily giggled as she ran up to him, touched him, and ran off again. "Tanny nanny boo boo, you can't catch me." She sang.

"Okay, I give up." Her father held his chest, dragged his leg, and panted.

Granny called them for breakfast.

"This is my favorite—Johnny cakes and calaloo with codfish. Yum yum." Lily licked her lips.

Granny interceded on their behalf, her long prayer before the meal, thanking God for sparing her son's life and Lily's life for the umpteenth time.

Lily had one eye open all the time looking at her father, her heart full, and as soon as Granny finished, she added her bit. "And thank you for making my daddy stay longer with me."

Everyone chorused, "Amen."

Her father had had to postpone his return home to London, which Lily saw as a blessing in disguise. She wished he'd stayed with her on different terms.

Her robust appetite had something to do with her present state of contentment. What else could she hope for?

Granny burst her bubble. "Winston, will you be taking Lily to Plum Valley today? She's been out of school for a while, and that Maxine will soon come and scrape her up if we don't take her back soon."

Lily's countenance changed. She gagged. "My tummy is hurting me. I'm going to be sick." She ran to the bathroom and vomited. She wobbled as her knees weakened beneath her. Aunt Liza held on to her.

"It's alright, Lily. Calm down, baby, calm down." She knelt to make eye contact with Lily. "This is not going to be forever, your daddy is going to send for you."

"When?" Her brow knitted.

"Soon." Aunt Liza promised.

"Okay." Lily felt relieved.

After breakfast, Lily packed and her father drove her to Plum Valley.

The usual struggle to free herself from home was lessened by her daddy's presence. Not having to take the bus with Sam made the morning's event more palatable.

The car hit a pothole and her memories threw her back. "Daddy, what's that?" She stretched to the edge of the seat and held onto her father's shoulder.

"It's nothing baby, just a pothole."

She settled in his touch.

"We're almost there."

That was not a comforting thought. The ride, or the thought of Plum Valley, placed her between the devil and the chasm. Lily groaned. Every corner induced a return of the ordeal. "Daddy, you're going too fast. Can you slow down? I think we're going to crash."

"No baby, we're not going to crash." Her father turned the radio on. Sunday morning melodies from a Mormon choir filled the car with mournful tunes.

She drifted into a dreamless sleep. She woke in her father's arms. "Where am I?"

"You're home in Plum valley."

"Noooo." She resisted. "I'm not staying here; please don't leave me, Daddy. Take me back with you, please."

"I promise I will send for you to come live with me in England."

"I want to go with you now. Don't leave me here." She clung to him like a leech.

Maxine pulled her from his hand, but she ran back to her father.

"Please, Daddy, save me."

"In the little time you spend with her you spoil her already. Now, she is a fully spoilt fish."

"The child needs love, Maxine. Love her. Be nice to her, I beg you."

"Winston, I don't spoil people." Maxine scowled.

"Frankly Maxine, you're hopeless." Her father shook his head.

Lily peered up at them with a silent wish in her heart. *I wish she would die.*

"Call it what you want, this child needs toughening up, or she won't make it in life. At the rate at which you're all going, nothing good is going to come of her. Come to me, child." She pulled her from Lily's father and walked with her into the house, shutting the door in her daddy's face.

"Maxine!" Her father's voice echoed through the door.

Lily bawled and ran to the window. "Daddy, I love you, Daddy." She kissed her palm and threw it in the air.

He returned the kiss and waved. "Bye baby, see you soon."

The unkempt garden, with its prickles and weeds, formed the backdrop of her existence at Plum Valley. She stood by the window, peering out into the wilderness and waved till the car disappeared.

The dream ended, but she treasured the moments and held on to the promise.

Chapter 17

Plum Valley/Eisteddfod evening/May 1964

Lily returned to Plum Valley with flesh on her bones, toys her father had brought her, and a suitcase full of new clothes.

Back at school, she rehearsed her poem with Miss Lecky.

"Okay Lily, you're doing great, just one thing though. I want you to hold your head up and find one person in the audience to focus on and smile. Then you begin."

"Yes, Miss Lecky, I'll focus on you."

"The only trouble is, I'll be backstage, so you will have to find someone in the audience to focus on. How about Miss Francis, she's your aunt, right?"

"I'll find someone to focus on, Miss Lecky, I'll be fine." Lily hated that question; she hated the real answer as well. The world went silent on that question.

Lily practiced the poem and skipped all the way home. Margaret had stayed back with her to cover for her.

"Margaret, will you listen to me?" Lily thrived on praise.

"I'm listening, Lily."

"But you're not paying attention. You're not looking at me."

"That doesn't mean I'm not listening. If I look at you, I'll stub my toe and fall and you'd get to laugh."

"No I wouldn't, I'd hush you."

"No you wouldn't, you laughed when Kevin fell."

"Yeah, he deserved it, he's a bully. I swear I wouldn't laugh."

Lily recited again. Margaret pelted stones at a mango tree.

"You're not listening to me. Listen to me please."

"I am listening."

"But you're not saying if I'm good or not."

"Don't I have to listen before I comment?"

"Okay, let me say it again." She rehearsed for the umpteenth time until they arrived home. The glee disappeared.

"Where are you two coming from so late? This is the third time this week."

"We had extra lessons at school." Margaret lied.

"I had to practice for eisteddfod." Lily blurted the truth.

"Eisteddfod, is that what I'm sending you to school for? I'm going to have to let the headmaster know you must be home straight after school. The only time you're allowed to stay after school is when it's for a good cause."

"But it is for a good cause." Unlike Margaret, who knew Auntie Maxine's temperament, Lily didn't understand the woman's moods.

"What did you just say, child? Are you back chatting me, just go inside, both of you and have your dinner. After that, do your chores and wash up to do some lessons. I don't know what school is coming to these days? They're wasting time and tax payers' money with frivolities. I should report them to the Ministry of Education." She grumbled under her breath.

Lily sought ways to ask Auntie Maxine to listen to her rehearse and inveigle her to attend the Eisteddfod. "I'm going to say a nice poem. It's about mommies and walks and flowers and it's so very nice. May I say it for you?"

"Look here, child; what are you a circus or a clown? Don't play with me, just go have your dinner and finish your chores before you get a good slap."

"Please, please, please, it will make you happy."

"Happy? Did I tell you I'm not happy? The problem with you, Lily McDermott, you always want attention. I'm happy, okay."

"No you're not."

"What?"

"You never smile with me. Granny and Aunt Liza and Gramps are happy, they always smile with me. Can you be happy and smile with me. I can make you happy, because I love you."

"Love." The corner of her mouth lifted in a smirk. "What do you know about love? You and this lovey-dovey foolishness; you won't get that here. What you need is a strong hand to toughen you up. You're too soft. You can't survive in this world with your softy-softy attitude."

"But I love you." Lily walked towards her and hugged her.

Her mother, Auntie Maxine, pushed her off.

Lily's eyes welled up with tears.

"Okay, just this once."

Lily pulled all plugs, but before she got halfway, Auntie Maxine stopped her.

"That's enough, go and do what you have to do. I don't have the time and the stomach for this. All mushy and mumbo jumbo."

"But I wasn't finished though." Crestfallen, her chin dipped to her chest.

Auntie Maxine grounded her.

"I must go, Auntie Maxine. I have to do the recitation."

"Screw that, you're not going anywhere."

"Please, ma'am."

"If you wanted to go you would have come home earlier and done your chores, you are going nowhere until you've finished."

"Sorry, ma'am, but I had to go to rehearsal."

"You said that already. I can't see the point of that foolishness anyway. Don't the teachers have anything better to do with their time? They could use the time more wisely by giving you lot some extra lessons, foolishness."

"You said that already, ma'am."

"Watch your mouth, young lady."

"I'm sorry. Can I please go, Auntie Maxine, pretty please with cherries and strawberries and..."

"Read my lip, you...are...not...going...anywhere, that's final, now move."

"Bu...bu..." she fought back tears.

"But nothing, just stop provoking me to wrath." She warned and went to her room.

Lily fell into a crumpled lump, rolled into a fetal position and wept.

Unaware of the passage of time, she managed to pull herself together. She stood and brushed herself off.

"I will not let anyone steal my thunder." She muttered. She tiptoed into Auntie Maxine's room. Auntie Maxine slept like a log. Lily searched among her new dresses and took out her favorite.

She crept out of the house. As she neared the auditorium, she heard the choir belting its melodies. Goose bumps covered her.

"Lily, after the choir it will be time for the poetry competition." Sasha ran towards her. "Where were you? Miss Lecky has been looking for you."

"I had to do some chores."

"Oh. You look nice." Sasha sized her up. "Your dress is very pretty. Where did you get it?"

"My Aunt Liza made it. You should see my other pretty things she made." Lily gushed.

"I love it. You better find Miss Lecky before she crucifies you."

"Where is she?"

"Backstage."

Lily rushed backstage.

"Lily McDermott, you had me worried, thought you weren't coming. Is your auntie here?" Miss Lecky bustled about in frenzy.

"No, Miss."

"Never mind, you're the last out of five to perform. Go and practice."

The auditorium, jam packed with parents, teachers, and children heated up like a sauna. People fanned with anything they had in hand. The lone ceiling fan competed with body heat of five hundred people and tropical heat in an undersized auditorium.

Lily waited backstage, practicing. She glanced out her heart sank as she contemplated that she had no one there to cheer for her. She wished she had someone to share the moment, to cheer her, to be proud of her.

"Will Lily McDermott please prepare for the next reading." She brightened at her name over the microphone and found Miss. Lecky.

It was her turn. She walked onto the stage with confidence. She took the microphone, looked at it in awe, but it screamed at her. The screeching feedback from the microphone unnerved her. Her knees wobbled, her hand shook and stage fright took over. No sound came out of her moving lips.

Miss Lecky ran on to the stage and whispered, "Lily, take a deep breath."

Lily closed her eyes and inhaled.

Miss Lecky smiled and nodded.

Lily took another deep breath and commenced. Midway through, a ghost-like figure approached her. She continued in a trance. She focused on the figure as it got closer, could it be Aunt Liza? Jubilation.

Instead, Auntie Maxine walked up the aisle, switch in hand. Lily's ears burned as blood rushed to her face. She stopped in midsentence.

Everyone looked around and saw Maxine. Her auntie's position, whip in hand, gave the crowd pause, but as though the moment meant good versus evil, they began to cheer, calling out Lily's name. "Lily, Lily, Lily, Lily!"

One lone voice shouted Lily of the Valley. It launched a chorus, "Lily of the Valley, Valley, Valley, Lily of the Valley, Valley, Valley, Lily of the Valley!"

Lily knew right then, she had to continue, she had done the right thing. She regained her composure and finished to a standing ovation. She curtsied and the crowd exploded in adulation. Lily might be in trouble, but for that moment, her heart soared.

Her Auntie Maxine stood bewildered, shifting glances around the room. In an act Lily hadn't expected, she dropped the whip and applauded. Everyone applauded as the whip fell to the floor.

Maxine stayed till the end and watched Lily receive her first prize.

Lily found Auntie Maxine in the audience and smiled.

Maxine nodded and a grin plastered her face.

Chapter 18

Plum Valley/Two months after Eisteddfod/July 1964

"Auntie Maxine is getting so nice. She is so sweet. I love her." Lily imagined a change in Auntie Maxine since Eisteddfod.

"Heh."

"Don't you think she's getting nice, Margaret? She is very pretty too. Maybe we could call her honey, right?"

"Heh, heh, honey, heh, she'll turn into castor oil."

"Castor oil?"

"Yeah, castor oil."

"But that tastes bad."

"Yep."

"Hmm."

"Margaret, Lily."

"Yes, honey, coming, honey." Lily cooed in sweet tones.

Margaret's brows furrowed in expectation of a backlash on Lily. "Lily, stop sucking up."

"What did you call me, Lily?"

"I called you honey because you're so sweet."

"Sweet words will get you nowhere. Come, we're going to do some gardening today."

A heavy downpour left the soil saturated and the air fresh and cool. The front yard was an eye sore, the hedges overgrown and weeds everywhere. Maxine had bought a packet of seeds. She'd asked Mr. Tremble to get rid of the weeds and cut the hedges and make flower beds.

"April showers, May flowers." She gave Margaret and Lily a packet of seeds each.

"What does that mean, Auntie Maxine?" Lily took one packet and shook it.

"It's an old adage. It means that heavy rains in April prepare the earth for the growth of new plants and for the sprouting of flowers."

"So this is a good time to plant these seeds then." She read the instructions. "It says 'daisies,' and it says, 'daises need as much sunlight as possible.'"

"You're doing great, Lily, high five." Margaret slapped Lily's palm. "You can read."

"Hard work pays off, eh Lily? Let's put some hard work in planting these seeds, maybe we'll see some results."

"Yes, honey."

One corner of Maxine's mouth pulled up in a smirk and she stared at Lily.

They got to work. Afterwards, Auntie Maxine allowed them to play outside.

Margaret and Lily ran around to the backyard by their new swing. They both dashed for the seat. They took turns until it became a 'me first competition.'

"It's my turn." Lily tussled with Margaret for the swing.

"No, it's my turn. I only just got on it." Margaret pushed herself off in the swing. Lily pushed her harder. Margaret fell out of the swing. She lay on the ground motionless.

"Margaret! Margaret! Wake up! Wake up!" Lily shook her. Lily screamed. "I killed her, I killed her. She's dead! She's dead!"

Auntie Maxine ran outside.

"What do you mean you killed her? What did you do?"

"I pushed the swing and she fell out."

"Oh my God! She is not moving! Margaret! Margaret! What am I going to do, Patsy is not home."

"I'm so sorry. I didn't do it for spite. Honest."

"Don't tell me that, tell the police."

"The police?"

"Yes Lily, the police. That's what happens when you kill someone."

"But I didn't kill her, she fell from the swing."

"Just move out of my way. I need to get help."

Auntie Maxine left her standing over Margaret. Lily waited until Auntie Maxine returned with Mr. Tremble.

Lily ran to Mr. Tremble, panic stricken. "Mr. Tremble, honest, I didn't mean to kill her, it was an accident."

"Calm down Lily, everything is going to be alright, calm down; I will ride my bike down to the clinic and get the doctor. This place is so backward." Mr. Tremble wasted no time.

In the rural parts of Jamaica, people relied on 'peenie wallie' fire flies, kerosene lamps, and torches. They had no telephones or other forms of modern amenities, including indoor toilets or running water.

The doctor arrived with an ambulance in tow.

They placed Margaret with care in the ambulance and sped off. Auntie Maxine accompanied her. Mr. Tremble volunteered to watch Lily.

"Mr. Tremble, is she dead?"

"She is unconscious, Lily."

"Unconscious?"

"Meaning she doesn't know what's going on and she can't respond to us when we talk to her."

"So she's dead then? Mr. Tremble, I'm scared, the police are going to come and put me in jail. Are they going to hang me?"

"What are you talking about, Lily?'

"Gramps said that when people kill other people they put them in jail and then hang them till they're dead. Mr. Tremble I don't want that to happen to me, and I don't want her to die. She is my best friend. I don't want to lose her.

Mr. Tremble got down on his knees before Lily, took her hands in his and held her gaze. "Lily, listen to me. Unconscious doesn't mean she is dead. She is not dead and nothing is going to happen to you. She is going to be fine, you'll see."

"Are you sure, Mr. Tremble?

"Well, only God knows for sure, but for now don't worry about it."

"See you're not sure; I am going to lose her and they're going to hang me." Lily's throat tightened and she wept.

"Lily, Lily, listen to me, love, don't cry."

"Go away, Mr. Tremble. Leave me alone before something happens to you too. Everywhere I go, I cause trouble. I want to go home; I want to go back to Bellevue. I never get in trouble there."

"Lily, Lily, calm down."

"No, no, don't tell me to calm down, I can't calm down, just leave me alone."

"Lily, Lily of the Valley, remember I'm your friend."

She didn't respond, she leaned back in a large chair as silent tears followed the beaten path and washed her cheeks until she fell asleep. She woke up and found herself in her bed. Mr. Tremble must have put her there.

Lily packed her dulcimina and left through the backdoor. She had no idea where to go, but she hoped to disappear before the police came. She thought of going to Mrs. Anderson's house, but she didn't want Mrs. Anderson to know she'd murdered Margaret, so she went the opposite direction. She hadn't gone too far when she noticed a stray cat tangled in a clump of wisp. He cried for help. She walked over to him and released him. He stayed close and she picked him up and stroked him.

"Oh, you poor kitty, what can I do to help you?" The cat purred. She opened her dulcimina and pulled out one of her ribbons and the bottle of eucalyptus oil. She dabbed some on the ribbon and tied the cat's leg. She placed him on her lap and sang lullabies.

Chapter 19

Plum Valley/Later that day/July 1964

Lily woke and found the cat gone. "Kitty, kitty, where are you? Sheeewheee, come kitty, kitty, sheeewheee, where are you?" Lily ran through the bushes looking.

"Lily, there you are! You had me worried sick, naughty girl. You shouldn't wander off like that." Mr. Tremble scooped her up like the lost kitten.

"Sorry Mr. Tremble, I…I didn't know what to do."

"Lily, you don't have to do anything, you didn't do anything. It was an accident."

"Is…is she alright?"

"Haven't heard any news yet."

"Auntie Maxine not back yet?"

"No not yet. But I think I best get you home before she gets back, so we don't get in trouble, eh Lily?"

"I have to find my kitty first. Come kitty kitty sheewheee, sheeewheee." She wiggled free of Mr. Tremble's hand.

"Your kitty? Didn't know you have a kitty."

"Yeah, my kitty. I found him. I need to keep him well, Mr. Tremble. I'm going to be a doctor when I grow up, you know."

"Oh, I don't forget that, Lily." Mr. Tremble chortled.

"Come Kitty, kitty." She ran in search of the cat, Mr. Tremble in tow.

Lily found the cat. She stooped and called him to her. "Sheewhee, come kitty. Come, Cotton. The cat turned and walked towards Lily and purred. Lily lifted him and caressed him. "I'm going to call you, Cotton, because you wear a white coat. Do you like your name?"

The cat purred.

Lily confided in Mr. Tremble. "He likes his name, see he's smiling."

Mr. Tremble smiled. They walked back home. Lily carried Cotton in her arms.

Not long after they got home, Auntie Maxine arrived. As she stepped out from the taxi, Lily ran to greet her with Cotton in her hand.

"Hi Aunt Maxine, how is Margaret?"

"Why do you have that puss in your hand? Put it down this minute! Get rid of that thing! It may have leptospirosis or…or rabies put it down now!"

Lily's heart sank. 'bu… bu…"

"But nothing, do as I say at once!" Auntie Maxine stomped. She grabbed the cat from Lily and threw him in the bushes.

Lily stood gob smacked, eyes tearing up and stone-faced.

"How is Margaret?" Mr. Tremble looked around in confusion.

"She has been admitted, concussion." Doctor says she may experience some kind of brain damage."

"Brain damage, what do you mean?" Lily squinted.

"She may become a vegetable."

"A vegetable, how could she become a vegetable, that's stupid, people don't become vegetables; we eat vegetables, that doctor is dumb. I bet I'm going to be a better doctor than that."

"No, Lily, it doesn't mean real vegetables we eat; it means she will be unable to function like she used to. She…" Maxine broke down.

Mr. Tremble comforted her. "There, there, that's not going to happen, you'll see, she's going to be just fine. She's a strong girl."

Guilt consumed Lily. "It's all my fault." Lily hung her head.

"She's alive. Thank God." Mr. Tremble tried to improve everybody's mood. "I hope she will pull through alright without any brain damage."

Lily clasped her hands and looked heavenward.

"Mr. Tremble, thank you for staying with Lily for me."

"My pleasure, she's really a sweet little girl." He didn't squeal on her.

Lily, grateful for his confidence winked. He smiled. He waved as he left.

"Lily, water the garden before you go in."

"Yes, ma'am." Lily missed Margaret. "When is Margaret coming home?"

"Dunno. But you can go visit her tomorrow."

"Can I?"

"Yes you may, I will have to take her some stuff tomorrow. You may come with me."

A taxi honked, and out popped Sam with an overnight bag. He approached Auntie Maxine and gave her a hug. She moved away and looked in Lily's direction. "Sam, you know I don't like when you do that in public."

"Aw, come on, Maxine, I'm just showing a little affection." He kissed her in spite of her resistance.

"Sam Nugent, behave." She blushed and they both walked towards the house. Sam placed his arm around Auntie Maxine's waist. He leered at Lily, behind Maxine's back.

Lily snickered at the display of affection to Auntie Maxine and her response. She turned to water the flowers. She loathed Sam.

After watering the garden, Lily crept away to find Cotton.

"Cotton, Cotton, where are you? Sheewheee," Cotton hadn't gone far, she found him in the backyard. Lily gave him some cheese and followed him around until he ended up in Mrs. Anderson's yard. Cotton headed for the cellar. He pounced on an unsuspecting rat and devoured him. Lily stood motionless. She couldn't believe her cat's aggression.

"Cotton, you are so mean, what did that little rat do to you? You disappoint me. If you ever do that again I'm going to spank you." Cotton continued on.

She climbed up the verandah steps to Mrs. Anderson to show her pet. She knocked on the door, no one answered. She pushed the door and stepped inside. "Mrs. Anderson, Mrs. Anderson. Hello, Mrs. Anderson." Still no answer, she proceeded to the bedroom. Mrs. Anderson's lifeless body hung from a rope on one of the roof beams. Lily's knees buckled under her. She felt faint.

As she came to and saw the lifeless body again, she let out a piercing scream, grabbed up Cotton and ran out of the house. She heard Auntie Maxine and Sam calling her.

"Lily, Lily, where are you?"

They met her at Mrs. Anderson's gate. "How many times am I to tell you not to go to her yard and give me that damn puss?" Auntie Maxine grabbed the cat and flung him in the bushes once again."

"This child needs a father figure in her life. You know what, I'll be moving in full time. I can see that she needs to be under strict discipline."

"And why are you acting as though you've seen a ghost, you're shaking like a leaf. What is it? What's wrong with you, child?"

Lily pointed to the Anderson house and ran home. She made it to her room and sank into her bed, curled up in the fetal position and wept.

Chapter20

Plum Valley-Next day

Lily jumped out of her sleep to the sound of the cackling guinea chicks. She trembled as the previous day's events weighed on her thoughts.

Margaret may die and Mrs. Anderson is dead and the police are going to lock me up for killing Margaret and for finding Mrs. Anderson dead.

She held her head in her hands and moaned.

She got out of bed and sat on the steps of the verandah immobilized with fear and grief. She'd had a fitful night, filled with nightmares of the lifeless body hanging from the ceiling, but afraid to seek comfort. She just lay there all night trembling. Every time she closed her eyes, she saw the gruesome image.

She'd heard the ambulance and the police arrive, but had covered her functional ear to block it out. She passed the night in sheer terror. For all she knew, Margaret could die too and she would go to prison.

A pall hung over the village as the news of Mrs. Anderson's demise permeated their lives. A crowd gathered at her gate in confusion and disbelief as wild stories spread. Auntie Maxine and Aunt Patsy sat on their verandah as they observed the bundling and grief stricken crowd. The neighbors shook their heads and wrung their hands. They poured over the incident.

"What distressing news to come back home to. It's a good thing Lily was asleep last night when the ambulance and the police came to deal with Mrs. Anderson's situation."

Aunt Patsy, who'd just returned from her holiday, seemed disturbed by the recent happenings.

"For real, she saw too much already, a little child shouldn't have to see that kind of thing. But it's her fault. She's always wandering off somewhere. I told her over and over not to go over there and to mind her own business. I always knew that there was something wrong with that woman. Always hiding in the bushes and peeping over here." Maxine spoke about Lily as if she weren't there.

She listened to them theorize. She wondered if they'd mention her impending arrest for Margaret's possible death. She kept quiet and hung on every word, listening for any indication of what she'd have to face.

"That is weird."

"No wonder her husband left her."

"Poor woman she must have been lonely and heartbroken. No one should die like that. I guess the police will be probing to determine if there's foul play."

'Fowl' play, what's that, Auntie."

Do they mean puss instead of fowl. They always speak in riddles.

She'd taken Cotton to introduce him to Mrs. Anderson. Maybe they wanted to say she was responsible for Mrs. Anderson's death.

'Fowl play?' her imagination wreaked havoc.

"I Guess. Anyway it's no business of ours, I leave them to that."

Their conversation dug holes into Lily's heart, but still no mention of her fate.

"And then on top of all that, poor Margaret, they say that trouble comes in three. I wonder what's next. What really happened?" Aunt Patsy lamented. Lily's ear perked up.

"Lily pushed her out of the swing." She heard Auntie Maxine's accusation and stepped in for self defense.

"No I didn't." Lily found her lost voice. "How could you say that? I wouldn't do something like that. I hate you. I hate you. You want the police to lock me up. I'm going to tell my daddy that you are wicked and tell him to bring my mother to beat you. My mommy and my daddy would believe me."

"Speak when you're spoken to. Your daddy," Auntie Maxine smirked with contempt, "Your daddy is a wimp."

"Seriously though, Maxine, no offence, but do you know who her father is?"

"Excuse me, what do you mean?"

"But weren't you still along with Margaret's fa…"

"Shut up, Patsy. What I do with my life is none of your business. And how is this relevant anyway?"

Most of that went over Lily's head. "But I didn't do it though. Honest. And my daddy is a hero."

"Do you think she would deliberately push her out of the swing, Maxine?"

"Right now I can't even think straight."

She thought Aunt Patsy might take sides with her. "Aunt Patsy, please tell her I wouldn't do it and please don't let the police lock me up."

"Police?" Aunt Patsy scoffed. "Child you say the most insane things."

"Auntie Maxine says if Margaret dies the police will lock me up."

"Oh I see. Accidents happen, remember when we were kids, we were constantly bruising knees and getting head blows, and we didn't die. Here we are today."

"So she won't die Aunt Patsy?" Nobody answered her.

"Brain damaged and all."

"Speak for yourself."

They both laughed.

"So she won't die, Aunt Patsy?" Still no response; she remained lost and worried.

"I'm going to the hospital to see Margaret today."

"I'll come with you."

Lily wedged in, "Can I come?"

"I guess."

"Is she going to die?"

"What's wrong with you and your fixation with death?"

"I'm just worried that's all. I don't want to lose her like Mrs. Anderson, and I don't want the police to put me in jail."

Auntie Maxine looked at Aunt Patsy. "Just go inside and stop listening to grown up conversation, that's a part of your problem, always want to know everything. Curiosity kills the cat."

Lily got up and turned to enter the house.

"Look where you're going, child." She bumped into Sam as he entered the verandah with only his boxer shorts on.

"Sorry, Sam."

"Sorry, Uncle Sam." He corrected her.

She didn't auto correct.

Sam grabbed her by the arm and shook her. "Say Uncle Sam."

She refused. He slapped her across her back as she walked away. "You are a stubborn little girl. I will make you do as I say."

"Never! You're not my daddy."

"Come back here, Lily, apologize to Uncle Sam."

"He's not my uncle."

"Am I to go over that again? If you don't apologize you will not get to go to the hospital to see Margaret."

Lily thought about it.

If I don't go to see Margaret, I will have to stay with this horrid man, and I really want to see Margaret. I want to make sure she doesn't die.

"Sorry." She whispered.

"Sorry who?" Sam demanded.

"Sorry, Uncle Sam." She spoke under her breath.

"Speak up! I can't hear you." Sam shouted at her.

"I said sorry, already!" Lily matched his volume.

Auntie Maxine glared. "Lily!" she slapped her.

She winced as the blow landed. She ran to her room and curled up under the bed and cried.

She could hear him shouting, "Cry, cry baby moonshine darling." He teased her just as he had when he took her to Plum Valley on the tiger bus.

She crawled out from under the bed and took her doll from the dulcimina. "Jolly if I have to go away to prison, I want you to remember me as a good mother. Remember that I love you." She kissed her doll and crawled back under her bed and blocked out everything by lying on her good ear.

She listened to the silence and felt peace till the floor shook. Aunt Patsy entered the room. Aunt Patsy put on her going-out shoes.

Lily crawled from under the bed. "Are you going to the hospital to see Margaret?"

"Yeah, what about it?" Aunt Patsy walked towards the door.

"I'm coming." Lily searched her drawers for something suitable.

"Wait for me, please." She begged as she tumbled into her clothes and shoes and ran to the verandah.

"Don't you see you have your dress on the wrong side, go back inside and change."

"But you're going to leave me." She didn't trust them to wait.

"Go back inside and change the dress on the right side. Just hurry."

She rushed in, changed, and when she came back out, they'd left her. They'd even taken Millie but left her behind.

Chapter 21

Plum Valley/Later that day

"Go make me a sandwich, child." Sam walked up to Lily clad only in underpants and merino.

Oblivious of his presence, Lily stood cocking her head in confusion, her brows pulled together in a scowl, unable to grasp the fact that Aunt Maxine and Aunt Patsy went to see Margaret without her. She lowered her head and her eyes moistened.

"Lily McDermott, did you hear me?" Sam sneered and stomped his feet.

Lily met his eyes with an icy stare; without a word, challenge sparking in her eyes, she walked away.

He walked her down, spun her around, and glared. "Never walk away from me when I'm speaking to you. Who do you think you are, Miss Queen?" He straightened her up and came face to face with her.

"Let me go." Her nostrils dilated, and she pulled away.

His hand trapped her wrist like a handcuff.

She struggled to release herself from his grip and dropped like a rag doll dangling from his hand. He pulled her up, shook her and slapped her across her face.

She winced and her free hand covered her cheek. She didn't make a sound, but rage screamed in silent defiance.

Her eyes remained dry. She refused to give him the pleasure of seeing tears. She suppressed an urge to kick him. Instead she spoke through a clenched jaw, "Why did you hit me? I never did anything to you."

"I never did anything to you," he jeered, "you're not a woman, I am the man of this house and when I speak you're going to do as I say, or you'll be getting more of this."

"Let me go, Sam, or whatever your name is. You're not my daddy." Her posture tightened and she refused to be bullied.

"Uncle Sam, say Uncle Sam." He raised his hand again to hit her.

She used her free hand to block the strike.

He jostled her and let her go. She fell to the floor and he lifted his leg to kick her, grinned, and spat on her instead. "You like that? Maybe I'll just spit on you every time I see you. That's what I think of your disrespect."

Lily gathered herself as Sam walked away. Her disdain grew as she laid memory to her cheek with a soft touch as she rubbed it. She flinched as she eased herself from the floor; she had hurt her leg. She walked to the back door and contemplated running away.

Biting the inside of her cheek, Lily sat on the back-door steps and pondered her next move. She missed her daddy. If only time had wings, she'd be gone to be with him. She looked heavenward with sparkling eyes. Soon she would be flying on the BOAC to England to be with her daddy. That thought filled her with hope. Granny always said 'time is the master.' But what did that mean? If time was the master, then where did that leave her, at the mercy of time and Sam and Maxine and Patsy?

Everything came crashing down: her predicament, Ms. Anderson, Margaret. She allowed her tears to fall. The hanging figure plagued her memory every waking moment. She shook her head as she tried to erase the memory, but it stood in front of her like a stubborn mule. It hung over her like 'Damocles sword.' Her thoughts trapped her. She had nowhere safe to run to and no one. She sought the fortress of her room—under the bed.

An intruder peered at her with eyes that twinkled. She flinched. She made out the intruder. Cotton had found his way in the house. "Cotton, there you are, you're my true friend." She stroked him. He purred. "Are you hungry? Of course you are. Let me get you some milk." She tiptoed to the kitchen.

As she looked up from the fridge door, she saw Sam leering.

"Girl, you still haven't fixed my sandwich, get to it." He walked towards.

"Never, fix it yourself!" Lily's eyes narrowed and she attempted to match his steps backwards.

He grabbed her by her hair and spun her around. "You either fix it or face another slap." He tugged at her hair then let her go. "Now do as you're told." He pushed her to the kitchen counter.

While she made the sandwich, she gave in to tears.

Sam watched with amusement.

She left the sandwich on the table and walked away.

"Excuse me, what am I, am I a dog? Give it to me in my hand."

She looked him up and down, and without a word, slapped the sandwich in his hand.

He roared and pinched her butt as she turned to walk away.

She despised him. Lily flushed and gritted her teeth, willing herself to remain calm. She waited until he left the kitchen to pour milk into a saucer for Cotton. She placed the saucer on the floor in front of the bed and coaxed Cotton to come out from his hiding. It didn't take much. He slurped the milk and purred when he finished. Lily sat beside him and scratched the side of his neck and petted him. He crouched down on his front legs and raised his rear in the air. She giggled

"Cotton, you're so funny. We have so much to talk about." She stroked and kissed him.

Cotton drew closer and rubbed his face against her. She placed him in her lap.

"My sister Margaret is still in the hospital and it's all my fault. If she dies I'm going to jail. Do you think she's going to die?" she scratched his neck as she spoke. Cotton looked at her with wistful eyes.

The sound of keys opening the front door and voices broke up Lily's pity party. Lily didn't know what to do with Cotton.

"I don't like the way Margaret is looking." Aunt Patsy's voice permeated the hall as they entered the house.

"Me neither." Maxine's voice boomed concern.

Sam greeted them. "How's she doing?"

"Not too good."Maxine responded.

"Oh no, don't worry though, I'm sure she'll pull through." Sam sounded genuine. Lily balked at the sound of his voice.

"Where's Lily?" Maxine enquired.

"Oh that one, she's here. She has absolutely no respect."

"I know. We have to train her. Her spunk is getting in the way of her decency." Maxine added.

"And she's lazy. We do have a lot of work to do." Sam spoke with authority.

We?

Derision for him festered in Lily's heart. How did he become we? He was not her daddy; she would never bend to him.

"I hate Sam, I wish he would die." She cursed him under her breath.

She returned to Cotton. She needed to hide him.

Millie waddled into the room and shouted with glee over the cat and let out a "Kitty Cat!" and pointed.

Patsy walked in behind her "What the hell is going on in here? Maxine come and deal with this one. Move puss!" She shooed Cotton and took off her slippers to hit him. "This is one animal I hate. They are sneaking and disgusting."

"What is it?" Maxine spoke from the sitting hall.

Cotton took the cue and jumped up on the dresser and squeezed through the louvers.

Lily knew the torture she faced as Maxine entered the room.

Chapter 22

Plum Valley/Same evening

"Lily McDermott, come to me this minute." Maxine shrieked.

Lily saw a huge anaconda with a venomous tongue wagging at her as the belt snaked from Maxine's hand, it dangled at her side. Lily wiped beads of sweat and shifted from one leg to the other.

"I'm coming, ma'am." Lily moved towards her, but not fast enough. Maxine dragged her by the ear.

"Ouch!" She screeched and winced.

"How many times am I to tell you not to bring that puss in here, eh? You're a very disobedient little girl. I hate disobedient children!" She measured her words with ferocity.

"Sorry, ma'am. I didn't mean to." Lily cowered.

The snake bit into her skin as Maxine continued to spew venom.

"How many times am I to teach you manners? Why were you disrespectful to Uncle Sam? Apologize to your Uncle Sam, apologize now."

"But he's not…I wasn't…" Lily faltered.

"Shut up your lying mouth and apologize now."

"But really, I didn't."

"Are you calling the big man a liar? And don't talk back!" she shook Lily and pelted her with the belt. Lily wailed and twisted in agony as the snake wrapped around her legs.

"Apologize!"

"Sorry! Sorry!"Lily surrendered.

"Sorry who." Another taste of venom stung her bare legs.

"Sorry Uncle Sam, sorry!" She spoke through sobs, mucous and tears mingled on her face.

The beating finished as abruptly as it began.

"Now go with your Aunt Patsy to Domingo to wash the dishes and your sister's clothes." She handed Lily a bag of dirty clothes.

"Yes, Mom...Auntie Maxine." She took the bag as if she had just been handed a trophy and moved briskly to avoid another assault.

Patsy emerged from the kitchen with a basin of dirty dishes. She placed the pan on Lily's head. She returned for another on her head. Lily balanced the pan and used the other hand to carry the bag of dirty clothing, all the while whimpering.

They set out for the river. With every step she took, Lily shed tears.

"Girl, shut the hell up, why are you still bawling. You're getting on my nerves with that sound you're making. What, do you want more?"

"No, Aunt Patsy." Lily wiped the tears away, but they continued to flow as grief enveloped her.

"Or maybe I should call the guinea chicks." She laughed and made the cackling sound of the birds.

Lily feared they'd finally come for her She slowed her pace and lingered behind Aunt Patsy in hopes that her Cotton could keep them at bay.

"Come, kitty kitty." She whispered. Cotton appeared and it quelled her anguish. A soft smile curled the sides of her mouth.

"Walk up, Lily, it's getting late. I don't want it to get dark before we get home." She turned and shook her head, "shoo cat, shoo." She stooped and picked up a stone.

Cotton made scarce, but Lily could hear him stalking from the brush.

"Lily McDermott, walk up!"

"I'm coming, Aunt Patsy." Lily quickened her pace, but kept vigilance for Cotton.

By the river, they removed their load and prepared to wash. Lily waded in the shallow, raising small stones and cupping her hands she caught a crayfish.

"Lily, stop the idling and start the washing."

"Yes, Auntie." She caught one more crayfish and tossed it in the brush by where she knew Cotton waited.

They washed in silence and rushed against the hastening twilight. At the end of the wash, Patsy counted the cutlery.

"Lily, you lost three spoons, see, we should have ten. You better bottom the river and find them!" Patsy shouted.

"But I didn't wash the spoons, you washed them, I washed the knives!" Lily answered.

"Lie, you washed them!"

Lily's eyes glazed over as she stared into Domingo's green glassy countenance. The evening sun peeped through the trees and flickers of light danced on Domingo's face. It was calm and inviting, yet Lily knew its depth, the avid swimmer she was, she had gone there countless times. What if she lost herself in its belly, deep into the pits of forgetfulness, where Aunt Patsy and Auntie Maxine and the whip would never reach her again? As one lone leaf fell on its surface, ripples formed, and she tumbled back to her anguish. Lily jumped into the waiting arms of Domingo. She lingered in the deep as her young tortured mind strangled her. The world above held little joy for her. Down there in the deep she experienced peace and quiet, solitude, escape. Lily heard a popular Negro spiritual Granny taught her going over and over in her head as she held her breath. She held on to the freedom the watery deep gave her. She hovered around in the depths and left herself to the mercy of Domingo's current.

She heard Aunt Patsy's faint call from above, but remained unresponsive. She stayed there for what seemed like eternity. When she contemplated the world above, her heart sank to the bottom of Domingo with her, the heaviness made it difficult to float back up to the surface. She could hide in the darkness forever and become one with the river and its inhabitants. Her lungs on the verge of losing oxygen threatened to burst in her chest, but she refused to get out. She remembered a story Granny read for her about Jonah. He stayed in the belly of a whale for three days and three nights, maybe she could stay in Domingo's belly forever and be rid of the evil that followed her. The pressure continued to build and her chest and her nostrils began to fill with water.

Chapter 23

Plum Valley/Late evening into night/July 1964

Her life flashed before her eyes. She got clarity as the pressure on her lungs overwhelmed her. It didn't have to be that way. Yes, life with Aunt Maxine and Aunt Patsy sucked, and yes, the devil dwelled in Sam, but hope shone on the horizon. It beckoned her as her life slipped away. She reached out in desperation flailing her hands around and forcing her body to climb Domingo's incline.

Her daddy, her hero, would come to get her and she still wanted to be a doctor to cure Granny's knee. She thought of how much she loved them and them her, and how much she needed to be with them again. She thought of Margaret, Millie, and Cotton. She knew she did not have to be in the same space and time as malevolence and foreboding forever. One day she would be delivered from the grip of vice. This temporary time bubble that dominated her fate would pass. With all the strength she had left in her body she pushed her way up against Domingo's force. She had given herself up to Domingo, now she had to fight back to retrieve her life. Domingo bore down on her and forced its way into her lungs. The grip of death encircled her as she sucked in more water.

A bright light appeared as a hand reached out and lifted her onto celestial wings and carried her off to safety.

On the riverside, she vomited water and slime as she gasped for air. Mr. Tremble knelt over her.

"Lily." he called her back to consciousness. "Lily, can you hear me, dear?"

She sputtered and coughed.

"What happened, man, were you trying to drown yourself? You gave your aunt Patsy and I a scare. You're so lucky I was just coming from bush and heard your Aunt Patsy screaming out for help."

Lethargic and incoherent her tongue tied. She felt a sharp pain on her leg, Aunt Patsy had slapped her.

"Lily, wake up, talk to me." Patsy shook her and pried her eyes open.

"No man, you don't have to slap her, she's just trying to come around." Mr. Tremble scolded Patsy.

"Mr. Tremble, I was just trying to revive her."

"Yeah, but you can't do that man, don't you see she's been through a lot, you have to be gentle with her." He hoisted her onto his shoulder and carried her to the house.

His feet slapped inside his wet water boots and his body rolled under her weight as he walked. His clothing wet and reeking of sweat of a bush man would have been more than most could stand, but she felt comfort in his arms. She held on to his shoulders and wondered how a man his age could carry her for so long. As her strength returned, she said, "Mr. Tremble, I think I can walk now. I'm afraid I might hurt your back."

"Don't be silly, you probably weigh a mere forty pounds, a meager little thing you are, and I am old but strong, man. Stay where you are." He neighed and bounced like a pony.

Lily giggled, felt her strength coming back.

"I'm going to have to make trips to get the other things at the river because of this silly child." Aunt Patsy complained. "I don't know what Maxine is going to say about all this, you there gallivanting and all on Mr. Tremble's back."

"Leave her be, Miss Patsy, and I will get the stuff for you." He continued to jiggle and neigh. Lily giggled all the way.

The twilight merged with the moonlight. The full moon hung in a cloudless sky as night creatures sang the night's opera.

As they approached the house, they saw Maxine and Sam standing at the back door, Maxine akimbo with a scarf on her head. She looked the part of a prophet about to warn. "Get down off that man's back immediately. Mr. Tremble, I cannot believe you would do something like that, and you Patsy allow this to happen. Get down, Lily, you there giggling like a Jenny ass. And why are you all just coming back, look its night time already?" she screeched waving her finger.

"Maxine I …" Aunt Patsy faltered.

Maxine interrupted, "What are you giggling about, you stupid child, get down at once. It doesn't look good." Her brows knitted together.

Lily got down and sobered up. Her fear and anguish returned as she re entered the old-time bubble.

"Sorry, ma'am." She hung her head and bit her nails.

Sam leaned against the door picking his teeth; he didn't say a word.

"It's not how it seems. Please, Miss Maxine, Lily here near drowned and I saved her life. She couldn't manage the walk home so I gave her a lift."

"Drown, what are you talking about? Lily is an avid swimmer. Lily can't drown."

"Well, you near lost her, ma'am. I heard the loud hollering, that's how I know something was happening, and thank God I was just going home from bush. I have a few bananas down there in the field and I went checking on them. If you want I could give you a few hands of my bananas." He rambled, oblivious to Maxine's ingratitude and anger.

"Well, in that case, thank you, Mr. Tremble; you're such a good man. It's a good thing you were there, because Patsy here can't swim to save her own life. Thank you." Her tone softened.

"You're most welcome, ma'am. I will bring the bananas for you tomorrow." With that he walked off.

"Okay then, Mr. Tremble. Walk good."

It had been a turbulent evening, everyone retired early as usual. Lily had a fitful sleep, dreaming of drowning, she awakened in the middle of the night, and found herself in a pool of wetness. The bed wetting had become infrequent and Maxine had spread a rubber over the bed so it didn't catch the mattress. Lily had learned how to hide her accidents. She got up changed nightgowns and the sheet, and stuffed them in a plastic bag.

She couldn't go back to sleep so she cracked the window and stared out into the moonlight. She listened to the night creatures. Dogs in the distance howled at the moon, a perfect scene from one of Gramps ghost stories. She remembered him fondly. She heard a scuttling noise in the room. Her ears perked up and she followed the moonbeams from the window to the origin. A curious mouse stared back. She grabbed him, and held him in one hand while she stroked him with the other.

"You're so lucky Cotton is not home, or he would have you for supper. What should I call you, mousy?" She whispered. "I know, I'll call you..." she paused and scratched her chin, "hmm, I'll call you Timmy."

Aunt Patsy woke up and screamed out into the night as if she'd seen a ghost. She stood on the bed and screamed again. "Argh! What are you doing with that rat child? Put it down, before you get disease. I tell Maxine all the time you're not a normal child. Why would you hold that hideous thing in your hand? And where is that good for nothing cat when you need it?"

Lily let the mouse go and giggled. "It's a mouse, Aunt Patsy."

"And you let him go into the room. How am I going to sleep in here tonight?" She stayed on the bed, her back against the wall, head to toe and trembling.

Lily giggled again.

"And stop that silly giggling, you're so annoying."

Maxine came into the room, drowsy and staggering. "What's all this holler-balloo about?" She yawned.

"There's a mouse in the house, Auntie Maxine." Lily stifled the laughter. She placed her hand over her mouth.

"A mouse? Oh my God! Maxine screamed and ran out of the room. Sam slept through the noise.

Chapter 24

Plum Valley/August 1965/10 plus years

Time moved on, Cotton grew, as did the three girls. Lily went to Granny and Gramps' place less and less. Seasons turned and life moved on.

Because of the rodent issue, Cotton moved in as an official member of the family.

One morning, Cotton heaped himself in a ball on Aunt Patsy's bed.

"Move puss, you presumptuous thing, don't you ever go on my bed." Patsy threw Cotton on the floor in a thud.

Cotton screeched and hissed.

"Know your place!"

Lily picked him up. "Oh, dear Cotton, did you hurt anywhere?" She held him up, checking for broken bones. "Good thing you have nine lives." She cuddled him. "Now let's go over the rules: rule number one, don't go on the beds, only mine." She whispered the last part of the rule. "Rule number two, don't tie up their feet, rule number three, don't go on the tables, rule number four, do not go to toilet in the house, and if you kill a mouse make sure you take him outside—and no stealing!" Lily looked him in the eye. "Understood?"

Cotton cocked his head and meowed. He rubbed his face against her cheek.

She ruffled his fur.

"Good boy." She scratched his chin and let him go. He followed her around.

It was three months since Margaret's release from the hospital.

"I like Cotton, Lily, can we share him?"

Lily hugged Margaret. "Sure Margaret." Lily's gratitude to Margaret for not dying, freeing her from a prison sentence, made her happy. On around her youth, like all kids do, Lily's wondered about in a quest for God.

The pastor had said good people went to heaven and wicked people went to hell. She never forgot Mrs. Anderson and assumed she'd made it to heaven. He said that in heaven people drink milk and honey. Lily hated milk and she hated honey. He said that in hell the devil stoked up fire and burnt the wicked forever while he poked them with his fork. She didn't want to burn forever and she didn't want to drink milk and honey. Maxine had told her that maybe a little God in her life might make her a good girl. She went to church.

A packed church forced her to sit in the middle of a long bench. The few fans circulated hot air, and the shoulder to shoulder seating arrangement mingled khus

khus perfume and sweat. Some ladies used fancy fans to ward off the heat. Others ignored it. Lily glanced up at the ceiling to will the fan to spin cooler air.

"Brothers and sisters, say amen!" the pastor used his handkerchief to wipe his labored brow and jumped in the air as if to take flight. He landed like a ballerina. His performance infused life into the multitude.

"Amen!" they railed with him.

"Let me hear amen again!" He stomped as he screamed. "Eeehhh, I feel the spirit!"

"Amen!" the multitude thundered.

"Praise the lord!" Some spoke in strange tongues and waved their hands in the air.

"Praise the lord, praise the lord." His open palms rose to the heavens.

"Praise the lord." The congregation opened their palms and raised them to the heavens in like manner.

"Do you feel the spirit moooving, mooooving in here today, brothers and sisters? Say amen." Perspiration dripped from his face and inundated his pastoral robe.

"Amen." The spirited congregation bellowed and the heat sweltered, drenched bodies gyrated.

"There's someone in here today that is broken hearted." He danced a jig. "Let me hear amen!"

"Amen!" They roared.

"There's someone in here that just lost a loved one, there's someone in here that is in financial despair." He did a jig again. "Praise the lord, church."

"Praise the lord." The bellowing magnified as the pastor whipped up the frenzy.

"The bank is about to take away your house and your land and all your belongings. I know you, I can see you. I can feeeel you." He twirled then faced the audience. "Let me hear you say praise the lord."

"Praise the lord." They groaned together.

"There's someone inside here who is sleeping with a married man. Adulteress! You need to give it up. Give it up, sister, give it up! Come to the lord, repent of your sins." He danced again. "Let me hear amen!" He pounded the rostrum.

"Amen!" the multitude went wild, spinning and dancing as the church band played and the choir rang out a lively chorus. Petrified, Lily watched the whirlwind, wide eyed.

A church sister left her seat and marched up to the altar weeping.

"Come to me sister, come to me, let me lay my hands on you."

As she got close to him, he spun her around three times then he hit her with his palm in her forehead. She fell to the ground. She got into spirit and foamed at the mouth and rolled.

Lily looked in dismay at the scene unfolding before her. Her mouth fell open and her eyes froze open.

Why is God letting him do that? Good thing Margaret didn't die, because as a murderer he would have done worse to me.

"Get out of her Satan, get out of her!" The pastor garbled in a strange tongue as he danced around the woman.

Lily gritted her teeth and gazed in amazement.

He chanted and danced as he poured oil on her. Two church brothers removed her through a door behind the pulpit.

The woman disappeared and Lily wondered if the woman died, and did she go to heaven or hell?

The pastor moved back to the pulpit, wiping his brows, his whole body trembled as he held his hand in the air and cried out in a strange tongue. He seemed to enter a trance as he lay still on the floor. Meanwhile the congregation sang mournful dirges and rocked to and fro. When he came to, he whipped up the congregation.

"Say Amen, church, say amen!"

"Amen!"

"If you are a Christian, stand up. If you have the Lord in your life, if you have accepted him, stand up." He ordered the crowd.

Parishioners stood one by one. A few people, including Lily, remained seated. The pastor pointed out a woman. "Are you a Christian?"

"Yes, pastor." She held her head high.

"Are you a member of this church?"

"No pastor, but I…"

"Sit down."

The woman hung her head and sat. A whole pew of persons on the other side of the aisle walked out of the church. Lily remained seated in shock.

The pastor continued his rant. "Repent! Repent you generation of vipers! This may be your last chance. The devil is waiting to receive all those wicked people, to burn them, to consume them, to roast them in everlasting fire." He stomped and ranted and pointed in the direction of the people leaving. "Repent ye, repent ye. Make your way right with the lord. Come to the altar now. Bare your souls and be saved. Leave your sins at the altar!" he wagged his index finger.

Lily chewed on her lips and made furtive glances as more parishioners made their way to the altar. Aunt Patsy once said that Lily had the devil in her. Her body twitched into the frenzy as a kaleidoscope of her escapades darted before her. Maybe she should go to the altar. She stood and then moved past a lady sitting beside her and then another, but fear gripped her in her tracks. She slinked back on the bench beside a woman, wrung her hands, and swallowed the lump in her throat.

The small crowd gathered at the altar. They moaned and bawled and trembled. The pastor danced around them sprinkling oil. They kneeled with their heads bowed on the altar like cattle for slaughter. The rest of the congregation stood with their hands swaying in the air. They raised choruses and beat their tambourines. Lily stood on tiptoes to see. She contemplated running out of the church but thought better of it, fearing that someone may catch her and take her to the altar to be sacrificed. She froze.

Everything around her blurred as the room took on a life of its own. It rocked and reeled and the fluid multitude flowed. It seemed a spirit rippled through the room. The infectious music engulfed and infused them. She covered her good ear to block the loud drumming and stomping. Terror filled, Lily eyed the exit as she willed herself to make a run for it, but she sat in the middle of a pew. The church sister beside her filled herself with spirit. The woman's body shook. Lily mustered courage and crouched, then crawled under a bench. She crawled until she got to the door.

The pastor continued to rile up the congregation. "This may be your last chance. If you don't come to the altar today, you may not get another chance." His raised voice thundered. "The end is near, or the end of your life could be near, you may be the next body lying in a casket right here in this room! Brimstone and fire will be falling from…" Lily didn't hear the rest—she'd fled.

She prayed that she would make it home before the world ended. She prayed some more when she got home. She felt a void.

Chapter 25

Plum Valley/End of summer holidays-August 1965/10 years

The quarrelling guinea chicks woke Lily. She had hated the noise they made until that morning, the morning after the threat of brimstone and fire and milk and honey. Happy to be alive and not burning in hell, she basked in the morning noises; stretched, yawned, and caressed Cotton as he slept cuddled beside her. He purred and stretched as if he too appreciated the reprieve. Lily had a restless night of red devils with horns chasing her and stoking fire with three pronged forks.

However, she'd had a dry night, no wet bed; in fact she'd been having dry nights, and the embarrassments and threats dried up as well. Lily counted her blessings. She yawned again and sat on the side of the bed with Cotton on her lap.

Aunt Patsy stirred. "Lily put the god dam puss down, don't you have anything else to do but be fondling that blasted cat. Put him down and go empty the chamber pot!"

A normal earth day had begun. Lily smiled at the chastisement in gratitude of life on earth.

With chores done, she sat on the verandah and read a book. Trying to impress Auntie Maxine, Lily practiced her reading. She wanted to create a morning of good feelings.

Sam and Maxine sat on the verandah. They didn't seem to notice her as they engaged in deep conversation. Sam had permanently moved in, walking around the house in boxer shorts and behaving like a man of the yard. He lit a cigarette and pulled hard on it as Auntie Maxine unfolded her plan.

"I'm sending Margaret to her father in Portie, so that she can go to high school. It's end of August, time for back to school preparations."

"Good for you, now you have room for one more." Sam kissed her square on her lips and ran his hand down her spine, holding the cigarette in the other.

"Don't even think it, Sam Nugent. Are you going to help me take care of my kids? And how many times do I tell you don't smoke around me?"

He put out the cigarette. "Anything for you, darling." He smirked. "I promise you to look after you and yours." He fondled her breast.

"Behave yourself, Sam Nugent, don't you see Lily sitting right there. Lily, get up. Why are you so presumptuous? You see big people talking and you come and put yourself right here. Have manners child. Go and take up your book!

"I have my book, ma'am." She held up the book and opened her eyes wide.

Didn't Auntie Maxine notice?

"Don't give me lip. Move."

I'm sorry, so sorry, excuse me." With ice water words poured down her back, she hung her head and stepped off the verandah into the garden patch. She bit her lip and her eyes stung. The flowering daises danced as a gentle breeze rustled their leaves.

"Margaret!" Auntie Maxine shouted.

"Yes ma'am." Margaret ran to her.

Have you packed your suitcase yet?"

"What time is Daddy coming to pick me up ma'am?"

"At eight tonight, make sure you're all packed young lady. You're going to high school now. You must work hard and make me proud. And don't let that wife of his push you around. I'm not sending you there to be her maid. As to her little pee pee bed children, don't play with them. I bet they're spoilt and ugly."

Margaret didn't respond.

Lily's heart sank at the idea of Margaret leaving. She and Millie would have to face them all without Margaret. For the last two and a half years, people often mistook them for twin. Margaret always stuck up and covered for her. Lily hurried around the back of the house and made it to her bedroom. She locked herself in the closet and sobbed.

"Lily, where are you?" Margaret called for her. She rattled the closet and Lily unlocked it.

"You've been bawling again, Lily, you should try not to cry so much, you know Mommy doesn't like it when you cry."

"Why do you get to call her Mommy and I don't? Aren't we sisters?"

"Yes we are."

"Then why? And why is she so cruel to me?"

"Dunno. That's just how she is."

"Well, I don't like it, and I don't like her."

"Is that why you are crying?"

"No." Lily bowed her head."

"Then why?"

Because I'm mad at you."

"Mad at me, what did I do?"

"You're going away."

"But it's not my fault though."

"No, it's not your fault. But you're my best friend and I'll be here with Millie, and no one to stop all the beatings when you're gone."

"Just don't cry so much and do your lessons right."

"But I miss home. I want to go home."

"After almost three years? This is your home now, Lily, you had to have gotten used to it by now?"

"Never! Guinea chicks, Aunt Patsy, Auntie Maxine, they hate me. Aunt Patsy is lazy and mean and smokes too much and she hates me. Auntie Maxine is wicked and she hates me, and, and the guinea chicks are scary and they hate me, I hate them all. I can't stay here all by myself." She wiped her tears with the hem of her dress.

Margaret offered her a handkerchief and offered her comfort. "Don't worry, Maybe you'll get to go to high school away from here too."

After Margaret left the room, Lily packed her dulcimina and slid it under her bed. The darkness of an eight o'clock departure suited her.

She and Margaret chased Cotton around in the yard one last time.

"Sheeweeweeweewee, come Cotton," Margaret cajoled Cotton, "sheeweeweeweewee," Cotton ran to her. "I like this cat; he's so soft and pretty. I'm going to miss him."

"Me too."Lily added.

"You too, where are you going?"

"No, I mean I'm going to miss you too."

Sam watched them. He stood on the verandah picking his teeth. He had few good teeth in his smile, the rest stained with nicotine hung like fangs.

"He's so gross," Margaret whispered.

"Yeah he's so gross, I hate him." Lily whispered back.

"Me too." Margaret glared.

"What you looking at? Sam snapped and stepped into the yard. Lily turned away and continued her conversation with Margaret.

Cotton jumped from Margaret's arms and skittered up a tree. Even Cotton seemed to understand bad news. He turned back, but appeared unable to backtrack.

"See that, you're stuck. Who's going to get you down?" Lily shook her head. "This tree is too tall for me to climb."

"Sheweeweee, come on down, Cotton." Margaret pleaded. Cotton didn't budge. "Uncle Sam, Uncle Sam, can you please get Cotton from the tree? He's stuck."

"Uncle Sam?" Lily murmured, "Don't call him that, he's not our uncle."

"I know, but just this once." Margaret snickered.

"What!" Sam snapped.

"Can you pretty please get Cotton out of the tree?" Lily backed Margaret.

"You little idiot, he's a damn puss, he'll jump down when he's damned ready." Sam scowled and walked away.

Both girls snickered and mimicked his sucking sounds when he picked his teeth.

Cotton did find his way down.

As the day wore on and Margaret's departure hung over them, they both became somber.

Chapter 26

Plum Valley to Port Antonio/late August 1965

The car horn tooted. Margaret's father arrived.

Lily's heart danced in her chest with excitement, her moment had come—her escape. Margaret's father alighted from the car and stepped on to the verandah. Her heart burned when she saw him. She felt drawn to him.

Margaret's belongings stood at the doorway.

"Good night, Daddy." Margaret greeted her father dryly, no lost love between them it seemed.

"Good night, child, where's your mother?" he peeped into the house.

Sam came out in boxer shorts with a cigarette in hand and a screw face. He nodded.

Margaret's father responded in like manner.

Auntie Maxine must have heard him asking after her, she stepped out and greeted him without emotion.

"Night. Put her bags in the car. Take good care of her now, Rupert. I don't want one strand of hair on head hurt or else." Auntie Maxine threatened him.

"Or else what? She's my daughter too, why would I allow something to happen to her?"

"Well, maybe not you, but I don't trust that slut you marry." Maxine sliced with malice.

"Maxine there really is no need to be bitchy, I mean if you don't trust my wife, then don't bother to send your child to live with us." His icy response crystallized.

"You hear that, you're such an irresponsible bastard! And I think you know exactly what I'm making reference to." Auntie Maxine's venom flew over the verandah. She lectured him on how she wanted things done. While she rattled on, Lily crept away.

Lily got her suitcase from under the bed and tip-toed out the backdoor. She came around the house and in the confusion of parents arguing, she opened the back door of the car and slid in. Lily knelt between the back of the passenger seat and back seat and lay as flat as possible, hopefully Margaret would jump in the front, and no one would see her in there.

The trunk opened and she heard a thud as someone threw Margaret's luggage in. The passenger door opened and Margaret got seated. Lily sighed, the toughest part was over, and no one realized she was in the back.

Margaret's father sat in his seat and ignited the engine. Lily wanted to see Plum Valley disappear into nothing, but she steeled herself to keep down.

The drive was long, but through it all, she didn't get discovered. Nightfall came, and the jostling of the car put her to sleep.

A sudden slam of the car door woke her.

She'd wait until they all went into the house and things quieted down before she moved.

All the lights in the house went out. She crept out of the car and crouched as she made her way to the front door.

Oh dear, silly me, I'm locked out.

She found a lounge chair in the corner of the verandah and made it her own.

The alien sounds of the town, whooshing of passing cars, car horns on the road facing the house, buzzing sound of machinery and glows from the street light, dogs barking, kept her awake.

When she grew tired of hearing them, she rolled over and covered her good ear.

With her eyes closed and her ear blocked, Lily imagined red eyed devils with horns and tails jumping around her. Lily covered her head and squeezed her eyes shut. She'd been naughty and might be punished for running away. She shuddered as she remembered the pastor and his sermon. Hell fire and brimstone awaited her because she had sinned.

You're a sinner; you're going to go to hell and burn, burn, burn! What you're doing is wrong; you need to go back home.

Plum Valley was not home. As soon as she could, she would find her way back to Granny and Gramps, and Aunt Liza. Just their memory comforted her.

Lily took Jolly from her suitcase and laid her close to her. She hugged Jolly and her dulcimina.

Just about to doze off she heard the front door opening.

Whoever it was didn't turn on the verandah light, and her position, tucked away in the corner wasn't discovered.

Lily stayed hidden and noticed it was Margaret's father.

Her father walked out to the car, and Lily took the time to slip off the verandah and below view. He returned with a briefcase. As he approached the verandah, Lily had a strong urge to sneeze. She clenched her teeth, squeezed her eyes shut and held on to her nose. She managed to smother it, but another one. Slipped out into a soft tither—the sneeze muffled.

Margaret's father turned and looked in her direction as if he heard or sensed her presence. She ducked and leaned against the verandah wall.

Her train of thought fragmented as Margaret's father walked to the end of the verandah, she could hear his steps just over the edge from her.

Her heart skipped. She held her breath. Her lungs filled up and threatened to burst in her chest. He could have been right over her if he leaned over the railing. She prayed he wouldn't turn the light on. She heard steps walk away and the door opened and closed.

Chapter 27

Port Antonio/Next day/Margaret's father's house

Lily survived the night outdoors. She had to face the unpredictable day without discovery.

Still twilight, she roamed the yard and found a hiding place to put her things in the back yard, amongst the tall grass. Lily heard the family stirring and wondered how Margaret would like her new world. The smell of bacon drifted and punished Lily. Oh, how she missed bacon. Hunger pangs chastised her. She salivated and imagined slices of bacon and sunny-side-up eggs. She licked her lips and drew closer to the house, wanting to enter and have some. She crept closer. She dodged as she jumped from grass root to grass root.

Someone stepped out the back door. Lily strained to see the person.

Margaret held the chamber pot in one hand and covered her nose with the other. Lily threw a pebble to get her attention. Margaret turned and Lily waved.

"Lily?" Margaret cocked her head and narrowed her eyes.

"Shh!" Lily puckered and placed her index finger over her mouth and beckoned her over.

Margaret looked around, placed the potty by the cistern and walked towards Lily. "Lily, what are you doing here, how did you get here?" The questions poured out in a whisper. Her eyes sparkled at the sight of Lily, but she gave a tight-lipped smile and knitted her brows.

"Shh!" Lily smiled, "Your daddy's car."

"What? How was that even possible?" Suppose you get caught, they will send you back and Mommy is going to kill you!"

"I'd rather die than go back there." Tears welled in her eyes and a lump filled her throat. "I'm not going back, Margaret. I'm staying here with you until I can get back to Bellevue and Granny."

"But how? Lily you can't stay here." Margaret held her voice down.

"Aren't you going to help me?" Lily panicked.

"How?" Margaret lifted Lily's chin, they connected in a soulful stare, and "I can't help you, Lily. You need to come inside and ask my daddy to take you back home."

"Never!" Lily's chin trembled as the tears cascaded down her cheeks.

"Shh. They'll hear you." Margaret cautioned.

"Never!" Lily backed up and realized she shouldn't have let Margaret know she was there.

Margaret motioned for her to come back. "But you must, there's no other way." A sad smile wafted across her face.

'I can't." Lily winced.

"Margaret, what are you doing out there so long?" Margaret's stepmother sounded irritated.

"I'm coming, Aunt Hilda." Margaret held her hands out. "Lily, I have to go." Beads of sweat formed on her forehead. A shaky smile snaked across her face.

Lily swallowed hard and flinched as she shrunk into the grassroots. She covered her face and sobbed.

The cruel sun came up and found her hiding place. She looked around for a more secluded spot. She hid behind the latrine. The stench made her dizzy.

A car engine revved. She peeped from behind the latrine. Everyone left. She had the house all to herself. She contemplated breaking in. Lily came out of hiding and moved towards the house. She tiptoed and peeped through the front window. She heard footsteps coming towards her. She ducked and ran back towards the bushes. She bumped into Margaret.

"Lily!" Margaret had a dish with breakfast for her. "I was just bringing you some food."

"I didn't know anyone was here." lily stood akimbo with curved and raised brows over wide eyes. "Thank you."

Her cheeks burned with desire at the sight of the bacon, eggs, and toast.

"They went shopping and they didn't invite me." Margaret crinkled her eyes. But, Lily saw it as a blessing in disguise.

Lily's belly showed gratitude, she belched and farted. They both laughed and rolled in the grassroots like old times.

"Okay Lily, so here's the plan." Margaret sounded mature. "We're going to the bus stop and put you on a bus."

"What? Do you even know which bus I should take?" Lily frowned.

"No, but we could ask." Margaret held both Lily's hands in hers.

"Okay. But I don't have money for fare." Lily pulled away from Margaret's grasp.

"Let's go inside and find some money."

Margaret gave her a grand tour of the house. They checked all the drawers and cupboards until they thought they had enough loose change for a bus. They went to Margaret's room, sat on the bed, and counted the coins they'd found.

"How much is that?" Lily asked.

"Not enough." Margaret shook her head.

"Why don't I just hide in your room, Margaret, until we have enough money, no one has to know I'm there?" Lily winked.

"That's not going to work." Margaret scowled.

"I'll be really quiet." Lily bit her lip.

A car drove in the driveway. They glanced at each other, their gaping jaws hung. They scampered around the room in confusion.

"Quick, hide under the bed." Margaret pushed Lily under the bed.

"Margaret where are you? Aunt Hilda's voice reached the bedroom.

"Lily, your suitcase, did you bring it in?"

"Yes."

"Where is it?"

"I left it in the hallway."

"If Aunt Hilda comes all the way through the house, she's going to see it. I have to go get it." Margaret's pitch screeched.

"Oh my goodness!" Lily trembled.

Margaret made a dash for it.

"What is your suitcase doing in the hall way. Remove it. We don't keep a pig sty here like you're used to. My ankles hurt, bring me my slippers from the shoe bag in my room. Quick girl!"

"Yes, Auntie."

A minute later, Lily heard the front door close, and the sound of a car engine fade into the distance.

Margaret came in with Lily's belongings and hid them under the bed.

Chapter 28

Plum Valley/next morning

In Plum Valley, news spread like wildfire: *Lily of the Valley missing*.

Maxine, Patsy and the residents of Plum Valley scoured the village. The night she went missing Maxine and Patsy searched the house and the yard and all Lily's secret places. Others in the neighborhood joined them. They lit bottle torches and searched Domingo and its environs, still no sign of Lily. Sam Nugent slept through it.

"I don't understand, we've searched everywhere and we still can't find her. I don't know what the hell next to do." Maxine sat on the edge of the verandah, her face moist and her body trembled.

"This is such a mystery." Patsy walked over to her, sat beside her and placed her arm around her shoulder. "Don't worry, we'll find her."

"I can't believe I miss her so much. I couldn't sleep last night." Maxine crumbled, hugged Patsy and wept.

"Me too. She's always going off, but it has never been this bad. I can't imagine where she could be." Patsy sniffled.

"You should report her missing to the police." Mr. Tremble who had mobilized the search party and first on the scene the morning after shook his head in consternation. "I just can't understand this."

Millie tugged on her mother's sleeve. "Mommy, where is Lily?"

Maxine dismissed her and turned to Mr. Tremble. "It's not yet twenty-four hours. Isn't that how long before we can report her missing?" Maxine looked askance.

"That's a stupid law." Patsy's shoulders sagged. "She could be dead by then, by now!"

"Don't say that, she's not going to die and she's not dead." Mr. Tremble consoled them.

"But do you even know how much trouble I could get into now?" Maxine wrung her hands and chewed the inside of her cheek.

"Why would you get into trouble, you didn't do anything." Patsy comforted her.

"They won't think so." Maxine blew her nose. "They may think that I killed her and disposed of her body somewhere. Can you imagine what's going to happen when her other side of the family gets wind of this?"

"They can't accuse you of that. You're a loving mother to Lily." Mr. Tremble complemented her.

Maxine shifted in her seat.

"They won't think so Mr. Tremble; you know how the law works. The closest persons are usually suspects." Patsy folded her arms across her chest.

Sam joined the party in his underpants. He pulled hard on his cigarette. "Good morning." He grunted, his greeting dry and cold, he then coughed up phlegm and spat. He remained silent.

Maxine conjured up all kind of images. "For all I know, she may be found in a pool of blood somewhere, or maybe someone kidnapped her, raped her and cut out her organs to sell her body parts. Isn't that what the liver man does?" Maxine repeated an urban legend. A lump formed in her throat and her stomach tightened and churned.

"Gosh Maxine don't get so morbid, nothing of the sort." Knowing Lily she'll soon turn up safe and sound." She hugged Maxine, injecting hope. "Let's keep positive, you know, look on the bright side.'

"There's no bright side to this. When I find her I'm going to kill her." Maxine sobbed.

"You can't kill her. You should be happy to see her." Mr. Tremble laughed.

"You know what I mean." Maxine sniffled and dried her tears.

A pall hung over them, in fact, over the entire village. It seemed even the guinea chicks missed Lily, they didn't cackle that morning. As for Cotton, he refused to eat. He just kept staring down the road. He meowed at every passing vehicle.

"Even the puss misses her, do you notice he didn't come in the house all night. I suspect he slept right here on the verandah all night." Patsy turned and looked at Cotton lying on the verandah.

"Animals are sensible creatures you know. Chances are if he could talk he would tell us where she is." Mr. Tremble picked up Cotton and placed him on his lap and stroked him. "Eh, Cotton, do you know where Lily is?" He rubbed Cotton's head. Cotton meowed as if he knew something. "If only you could talk."

"Mr. Tremble, you're being silly, the cat doesn't know anything." Maxine sighed.

"You would be surprised. Only he can't tell us." Mr. Tremble coaxed Cotton. "Tell us, Cotton, where is she?" Cotton looked up in Mr. Tremble's face and meowed.

People congregated on the verandah and in the yard. They turned up with rescue implements. The loud chatter offered sympathy.

"She was such a nice little girl, very pretty and smart." A woman commented.

"Yes, nice girl, isn't it the same girl who won that competition at the Eisteddfod?" another asked.

"Same one." Another remarked. The other woman shook her head.

"I wonder if that man, what's his name, has anything to do with it." One woman in the group muttered. Maxine overheard the comment and fumed.

"Sam Nugent. He is the Tiger bus driver, her mother's lover." Another woman whispered. "Anything is possible, but that's none of my business, I'd just love for them to get the girl back."

Maxine tore up inside and shook her head as she excused herself from the verandah and stepped inside the house. She never did like the people in Plum Valley, too many nosy people. Now Lily had put her in a predicament and she had to mingle with them.

"It must be very hard for her, let her go." Someone remarked.

"People, we have to get moving. Some of you go up the road and some go down the road. We need a good diver to search Domingo." Mr. Tremble orchestrated the group.

"I'll do it; I can dive up to one hundred feet in deep sea."

"Good." Mr. Tremble continued to issue instructions. "Anybody find any clues, shout or whistle."

"Aye!" the group grunted and they dispatched.

Maxine sighed as they filtered out.

Chapter 29

Port Antonio/Day 2

Margaret and Lily maintained secrecy all night and spoke in low whispers. Margaret ran water and food errands. The morning activities made it more difficult to keep covered as the younger siblings movements increased.

The loud squeals of animated children running down the hallway rang in Lily's ears. She wished to join them. Instead, she holed up in Margaret's room on edge.

The door handle turned. Lily's eyes bulged as she dashed behind the floor length curtain.

"Lily, where are you?" Margaret's eyes swept the room. Lily stepped out. "Oh, there you are."

"You gave me a scare. I thought it might be your stepmother looking for you." Relief washed Lily.

"Margaret, why are you talking to yourself?" Herman burst into the room. Lily ducked beside the chest of drawers in a dark corner of the room, her relief short-lived.

"Was I?" Margaret yawned, picked up a nail clipper.

"Yes you were. I heard you." Herman cocked his head.

"Maybe I was just thinking aloud." Margaret shrugged.

"Thinking aloud, what's that?" He sat on Margaret's bed. The chest of drawers stood on the opposite side of the room facing the bed. Margaret moved and his gaze followed her away from the chest of drawers. Lily crawled under the bed.

"Talking to myself I guess." They both laughed.

"Mommy says mad people talk to themselves. You're mad, Margaret." He laughed and jumped up on the bed. He bounced up and down, did a belly flop, and sat up in the bed picking his toes.

"Whatever, Herman. I'm busy, go and play with Gillian." Margaret dissuaded further conversation, with the hope he'd leave.

"Gillian is boring, you're more fun." He bounced on the bed. "Margaret, how comes you're my sister and mommy isn't your mommy?"

"I dunno. Will you please go and play with Gillian." Margaret's voice rang with annoyance.

"Herman, Herman, where are you?" Gillian barged into the room.

"What are you doing in Margaret's room? Mommy says we're not allowed. I'm going to tell." Lily thought Herman's cue to leave had arrived, but instead, Gillian jumped onto the bed. It became a trampoline for them both. The springs on the bed threatened to fasten into her hair. She laid flat on her back, using her hands to shield her face. She prayed they'd stop and leave the room. It seemed like eternity.

"Gillian! Herman!" Their mother called out. "What are you doing in here, didn't I tell you not to come in here?" she marched them out.

"But, why not?" Gillian pleaded.

"Because…"

"Because what?" Gillian fell to the floor.

"Get up, Gillian, don't be obstinate." She lifted her.

"Mommy, I think Margaret is mad, I heard her talking to herself." Herman hastened his step beside his mother.

"She…" Their mother's voice became inaudible. Margaret closed the door. Lily came out from under the bed, sweating.

"Phew, another close call!" Lily flashed sweat from her brow.

"I was so nervous. I swear they would blow your cover." Margaret sighed.

"Margaret I need to take a bath." Lily smelled her armpits.

"Yes, you stink." Margaret went close to her. "Phew!" they both laughed. They went quiet and listened for repercussions.

"But really though, I feel dirty." She sniffed again.

"Okay, this is what I'll do. I'll take your stuff outside to the bathroom and then when the coast is clear, I'll whistle and you run out to the bathroom. And you're going to need a whole case of deodorant!" they both giggled again.

Lily took a fresh set of clothing from her suitcase and placed them in a plastic bag. Margaret took the bag and added other toiletries.

"There are two small buildings in the backyard, the one to the left is the latrine, and the other is the shower." Margaret pulled Lily to the window as she pointed out the small board buildings to her.

Margaret opened the room door and peeped down the hall way. Lily looked over her shoulder. They pulled their heads in and slammed the door shut as they saw Margaret's father coming in the front door with a bag of grocery.

"We better wait until he goes to his room before we try again." Margaret sighed.

"But how will we know he's in his room." Lily swallowed hard.

"I'll check." she walked to the door and peeked out. "He's coming from the kitchen now and walking up the hallway. Now he's heading for his room." Margaret whispered over her shoulder to Lily, giving a blow by blow commentary.

"Now the coast is clear, I'll take your stuff to the bathroom." Margaret looked around and walked briskly out the door.

Lily waited for the sound of a shrill whistle. Lily looked up and down the hallway, and stepped out. She placed her back against the wall—her hands outspread as she tiptoed. She headed to the back door.

"Eeeeeeek, a little ghost girl!" Gillian coming out of her room bumped into Lily.

Lily ran outside and hid in a bush.

She heard the little girl screaming. "I just saw a ghost. It came out of Margaret's room!"

Chapter 30

Port Antonio/ Day 2 continued

Lily's heart pounded with the strength of a power drill. She could hear her pulse racing at her temples. Lily covered her mouth and held her breath. She released her breath in spasms. Her chest tightened as she gasped for air. She bit her lips and peeped over the bush. Margaret's father stepped onto the back porch and checked out the surroundings.

Please don't let them find me now or I'll die!'

Margaret's stepmother joined him. "I think there's something fishy, there's a ghost in the house."

"What, are you saying that Margaret is a ghost, or that she brought a ghost with her in the house?" He winked.

"I didn't say she is a ghost, come on, Rupert." She turned and gave him a stare. "I didn't say she brought a ghost in the house either, but it's just strange you know—sightings of ghosts. I just get this weird, eerie feeling each time I pass by Margaret's room. You know—strange sounds, I mean it really spooks me and I am an adult, can you imagine the kids?"

"That's what your children are saying. I think you're being superstitious and childish" Margaret's father stood a few feet from where Lily squatted.

"Our children, Rupert. And I'm not being superstitious and childish. I know something is happening in that room." Margaret's stepmother corrected.

"You know what I mean. Remember that children that age are very imaginative. Remember Gillian's imaginary friend 'Cher Cher' when she was younger?" He leaned into his wife.

"That's different. She screamed and said she saw a ghost, she wouldn't be afraid of an imaginary friend. Moreover, she's too old for that now."

Margaret's father shook his head. "First of all, there's no such thing as ghost or duppy or whatever you want to call it. As a doctor, I deal with life and death every day, and I have never seen a dead man get up and walk. When a person dies, he's dead, Hilda. I would have thought that, as an intelligent school teacher, you would be past that kind of gibberish." He guffawed, picked up a stone and threw it off the property. "I want to go bird shooting with the cronies this weekend. Wanna come?"

"Don't change the subject, Rupert. Are you saying that there's something wrong with our daughter. Are you saying she's schizophrenic?" His wife arched one eyebrow.

"Darling, I said nothing of the sort. I just said that there's no such thing as ghost." He gathered another stone.

"Rupert, something is wrong. I overheard your daughter talking to herself. Herman told me he heard her talking to herself." Her brow creased concern.

"Hmm, you sure about that?" he tossed the stone at a bird in the tree overhead. It pinged off a branch and rested next to Lily.

"Rupert, are you listening to me, you seem detached. If she's talking to herself, you ought to have her head checked." She nudged him.

"There's nothing wrong with my daughter. She's a bright precocious little thing. That's why she got a scholarship for the best school in the parish." He shrugged.

Lily's throat tickled. She resisted a cough, her sinuses about to burst. Lily swallowed hard and fought back the cough. It overwhelmed her.

"Did you hear that?" Hilda's ears perked.

"Hear what?" he asked.

"Someone just coughed. It sounds like it's coming around the corner." She pointed in Lily's direction.

Margaret came up behind Lily, from the side of the house, erupting in a rasping dry cough. Around the corner she bumped into her father. Lily squatting in a bush behind her, still holding in another cough

"Margaret, are you okay?" Her father held her shoulders. "I hear you've been talking to yourself, what's going on?"

"I dunno, Daddy." She circled them so they turned their backs to where Lily hid.

Lily's cough attack persisted. Margaret coughed to cover, but all eyes followed the direction of the other cough.

"Margaret, who is that? Are you hiding something?" Her father demanded.

"No, Daddy." Margaret's voice trembled.

"Don't lie to me, girl." They rounded the side of the house. Lily crawled away, but her cover lay bare. She shuddered.

"Hello, who's there? You there, stand up!" Margaret's stepmother shouted.

Lily dragged herself to her feet, stood frozen and hung her head. They stepped closer.

"Oh my God! It's not a ghost! It's a little girl, a real pretty little girl too. Who are you?" Hilda's brow furrowed.

"My God, it's Maxine's other girl, Lily. How did you get here, sweetheart?" Margaret's father's voice softened.

Lily continued to hang her head. She dug her toes into the dirt and swayed. Her tongue tied. The man pulled her into his spirit, the kinship she felt the day she stowed away with him strengthened.

"You know her? So much for me being superstitious and childish." His wife glared at Margaret's father and smirked. "I can't help thinking you know this child was in the house all along."

"Don't be silly, Hilda. How would I know? How did you get here, Lily?"

Lily looked up and blushed. She still hadn't found her tongue.

"Lily? Don't be afraid, I'm not going to bite you."

She hung her head again.

He pulled her chin up.

Margaret spoke up. "She hid in your car, Daddy, the night you came to get me."

"So you knew all along?" Her stepmother narrowed her eyes and looked at Margaret.

"After we got here." Margaret replied, twisting her hands.

"So why didn't you say something?" Her father asked.

"I was afraid to get her in trouble, and she didn't want to go back home." She continued to wring her hands.

"Why?" Her stepmother frowned.

"You don't want to know. Maxine can be really harsh." Her father bit his lips.

"Well, we can't just stand here and ogle, we need to do something about it. We need to take her home." Margaret's stepmother motioned towards the front.

"No, please, please don't take me back there. I don't want to go back. Take me to Granny. Please. " Lily found her tongue.

"She can speak." Margaret's stepmother sounded cruel. "Little girl, you need to go home. Do you even know how much trouble you're putting us in right now?" she folded her arms and stared at Lily. Your mother ought to give you a sound spanking when you get home."

Lily's eyes moistened and her shoulders drooped. She took a dislike to the woman.

"Moreover, we have more than enough to deal with." The woman complained.

"Hilda." Margaret's father cautioned her.

"But it's true though, she needs to go home. Our hands are full." She gestured.

"Take it easy, Hilda; she's only a small child, perhaps searching for love. If it weren't for the trouble we would be in sweetheart, you would be more than welcome to stay with us. But I know Maxine would make a big deal of it, especially to punish me." He got closer to her and placed his arms around her shoulder. Lily warmed to him, she felt safe with him.

"Come on in; let's get your things and go." He steered her towards the house. His warm tone contradicted his suggestion.

Lily shoved his hands from her shoulder and ran. Everyone chased her.

Chapter 31

Plum Valley/ Day 2

Lily trembled as she buried her face in her hands. She bent over in her lap with her jaw clenched for the entire journey. As the car slowed she held her head up.

The crowd, the police cars, the flashing lights and the windscreen wiper slapping the rain, stretched Lily's nerves taut. Beads of sweat gathered on her forehead. She sat forward and caught a glimpse of her face in the rearview mirror. Her puffy face, red eyes and wet cheeks stared back. Margaret had comforted her in vain. She pictured her funeral. She must have died and went to hell because no milk and honey awaited her at Auntie Maxine's.

Margaret's father's car rolled up in front of the house. Onlookers ignored the drizzle and peered in to see its passenger.

"It's Lily of the Valley, it's Lily of the Valley." A buzz drifted throughout the crowd.

Either a rock star or a serial killer, of which she'd choose neither, her reception lacked nothing short of fanfare. They stepped out from the car, Margaret's father, Margaret, and Lily, to loud cheers. Margaret's father held her hand. Her fear melted in his grasp.

"Lily, Lily, Lily of the Valley!" a path opened between human walls as they approached the verandah. "Lily, Lily, Lily of the Valley." they chorused.

"Thank God she's back." One woman shouted.

She felt hands on her cheeks and her head, hugs from perfect strangers. She blushed.

Auntie Maxine and Aunt Patsy towered on the verandah. Two police officers waited. They stood and walked towards the three.

The human arch way merged behind them, curious whispers leaked.

"I wonder why the police were talking to Mr. Nugent?" Someone said in a low tone.

"Maybe he was a prime suspect." Another volunteered. Other inaudible whispers pried. The crowd shuffled closer and went silent as Lily's group stepped onto the verandah.

Lily would have loved to have the police blame Sam for her disappearance. She wished she'd stayed away longer.

Hands rolled into fists, rigid cords in her neck about to pop, Auntie Maxine glared at Margaret's father as she hyperventilated.

"Rupert Edwards, you have some explaining to do." She snapped. Waves of emotion flowed between the two, Lily caught in the riptide, sank in the mire of despair.

"Maxine, don't be quick to jump to conclusions." Margaret's father defended himself.

"I'm not jumping to conclusions, Rupert. It is evident what is happening here. You kidnapped her." She moved towards him and grabbed Lily from him.

"Kidnap? Why would I do something so dastardly?" He waved her off.

The police focused on Margaret's father. "Sir, we would like to have a word with you." One of the officers walked up. "The rest of you go home." He waved away the crowd.

"We're going to take you down to the station for a statement." He turned to Maxine, "Make the little girl comfortable, we'll need a statement from both girls, but for now, they may be too traumatized for questioning. We'll inform you when we're ready for their statement."

"The older girl is my daughter, officer, she will return with me. So she'll have to accompany me to the station." Margaret's father spoke with indignation in his voice as he glared at Auntie Maxine.

She returned the frost.

"Okay, fine, so we may as well get a statement from her then." With that they asked Margaret's father to follow them. Margaret and her father left behind the squad car.

Lily watched with tears in her eyes as the car drove off. She waved until it disappeared.

Maxine turned her attention to Lily.

"I'm glad you're back and in one piece. What were you thinking?"

Lily's lips quivered and words failed her. Aunt Patsy brows pulled together, she stared at Lily.

"It's alright, never mind. I'm going to fix this problem once and for all." For the first time Lily could recall, Auntie Maxine hugged her. Lily stiffened and pursed her lips.

Chapter 32

Plum Valley / Next Morning

Auntie Maxine came home with the pastor.

"Lily, can you come out to the Verandah!"

Lily watched from the window, wondering why her Auntie Maxine came home with the pastor. She stepped out and into the fray.

"So this is the little angel, bless her soul." He nodded, holding a pious stance and wringing his hands, his raspy voice breathed over his words. He reached out his hand to her.

Lily recoiled.

"Hello, little girl."

"My name is Lily McDermott." Lily folded her arms and jutted out her chin.

"I'm sorry, Lily is it?"

"Yep! Lily McDermott." She put on a brave front, all the while shivering.

"Lily, have some manners, you can't talk to the pastor like that." Maxine wagged her finger.

"It's alright, my dear. I see she's a sassy one. Come to me, my dear. Don't be afraid, pastor won't eat you." Lily screwed up her face and looked him up and down. The man looked greasy and sloppy and carried a tattered bag. He reeked of oils and potions. He had a black plastic bag stuffed with who knows what. She dared not get close to him lest he push her down like he did to that woman at his church.

"I don't like him, he is a bad man. I see what he did to the lady at his church." She gave him an icy stare.

"She has a bad attitude, pastor." Auntie Maxine apologized and glared at Lily.

Lily remained stony faced and curled her lips.

"She has the devil in her if you ask me." Aunt Patsy could be heard as she stepped out on the verandah, smelling of cigarettes. "Lily needs prayers." Aunt Patsy made herself comfortable.

'You need more prayers than me, you smoke like a chimney and lazy like a lout.' Lily muttered under her breath.

"What did you say, I didn't hear that?" Aunt Patsy leaned towards Lily.

"I didn't say anything, Auntie." Lily smirked.

"Never mind, never mind. I'll deal with her." his gruff voice graveled in his throat. "Come, my dear, come to pastor, let me rub you down with some oils and pray for you. I won't hurt you." He reached into his bag and came out with two vials of oils. Lily walked backwards to the edge of the verandah.

He walked towards her.

"Don't touch me with your greasy hands." She jumped off the verandah and ran around the back of the yard. Auntie Maxine and Aunt Patsy chased her. They brought her back to the pastor.

"This one really needs help. She has a roaming spirit. I need to beat it out of her." he croaked.

Lily twisted and kicked and pulled as she tried to pry off their hands. The pastor held her and doused her with winter green and frankincense and myrrh. She bit into his arm. He yelped.

"Oh my God, this is a very powerful demon she has in her. We will have to tie her to the post." He reached into his bag and took out a sisal rope and tied Lily to the verandah post.

Lily wriggled and screamed, "Let me go! Let me go! Leave me alone!" She winced and kept snapping at him.

The pastor chanted gibberish and danced around her. "Ala-sa-ba-sta-lie!" He screamed, "Get out of her you devil! Get out of her now, by the authorities of the skies! Get out of her, you roaming spirit, never to roam again! Lily McDermott, you will never roam again!" He tied fever grass in a bundle and raised it in the air. Lily screamed and blacked out.

Chapter 33

Plum Valley/Mid-day to late evening

Lily revived. Still tethered to the verandah post, she kept her eyes closed for fear the pastor may try some new tactics to exorcise her demon. Her head spun with the mingled scent of wintergreen, frankincense, and myrrh. It permeated the air and near suffocated her. She played dead. She squinted and stood still, observing his actions and listening to his ranting. To her relief, the pastor only trashed the air with the bundle of fever grass. He spun three times and dipped as he spoke in tongues. He walked around the post three times and splashed a liquid from a vial. It reeked of ammonia. Lily coughed and sputtered.

The ritual subsided. The pastor called out for a cup of tea and something to eat.

Auntie Maxine placed a coffee table on the verandah and laid the food in front of him.

He ate the ackee and salt fish and green bananas, but left a morsel on the plate. "That is for the spirits." He grunted and spoke in tongues over the morsel, bowed and walked backwards as he left the table.

He ordered a cup of fever grass tea for Lily with milk and honey. He spoon fed her. It repulsed her, she gagged.

"You must drink this, darling; it is the food of angels."
He cajoled her.

"Drink it, Lily, drink it." Auntie Maxine sounded desperate. "Something has to work; something has to stop you from running away. Drink it baby, drink it." Auntie Maxine's voice softened but laced with urging.

Baby. Where did that come from?

She felt Auntie Maxine. She opened her eyes and made contact with her. Lily prayed that this evil man would stop his rituals and that Auntie Maxine would see through his facade.

"Drink it, lovey, drink it." He force fed her. Lily pretended to drink, but drooled and gagged to avoid swallowing. He thought she foamed. He chanted.

"Let her foam, let her foam, no more will she roam. This is your home, this is your home, from it no more will you roam."

Lily giggled.

He stopped and stared.

Lily giggled again. She saw through him and she knew he felt it. She made eye contact with the man. His shifty eyes looked away, unable to maintain his stare. Lily felt power over him. Fear left her. The ritual subsided, this time for good. He released her and gathered his paraphernalia.

"Madam." He turned to Auntie Maxine. "You now have your child back, she has been returned to you. She will never leave you or deceive you. She will be with you for as long as she lives. I bid thee farewell until we meet again. That will be ten thousand dollars, Madam." He stretched out his greasy palm.

Auntie Maxine's eyes bulged. "Ten Thousand dollars! That's preposterous. You didn't tell me there was a cost. I don't have that kind of money now, pastor." Auntie Maxine recoiled.

"Well, you know you can pay me in installments." He bargained.

"Pastor I don't have that kind of money."

"Well I guess you can pay me in kind.

"In kind?" Auntie Maxine's eyes crinkled, her cheeks raised as she grimaced.

"Oh yes, in kind." He smirked.

"What do you mean?"

"Well you know, you could send this little angel here with my dinner for a few weeks. And if I should go by the taste of that lunch you gave me, I'm sure the dinner will be delicious." He rubbed his belly and chortled. "I'll be lenient you know, it's the lord's work." He touched Lily's chin as he spoke. Lily recoiled and wretched.

"Okay, pastor." Auntie Maxine sighed.

"Alright then, so we have an agreement." He croaked. He picked up his belongings and turned to Lily. He blew her a kiss. Lily's stomach turned. He left. She felt relief to see the back of him but fretted about taking dinner for him.

After he left, Auntie Maxine fussed about her and even gave her a warm bath. She allowed her to sleep for the rest of the afternoon till the payment of the first installment.

Auntie Maxine woke her. "Lily, Lily, wake up. You must take the dinner for pastor."

"Er, uh," Lily stuttered, dazed and stunned. She rolled over and pretended not to hear.

"Come on, Lily, we promised the pastor dinner." She shook her again.

"We? You! I didn't promise that sick man anything." Lily muttered under her breath.

"What was that, Lily?" Auntie Maxine returned to her old self.

"Nothing, Auntie. I just said how grateful I am to pastor. I will go." Lily sat up in the bed, her heart heavy with sadness and foreboding. She covered her face with her hands, rounded shoulders, she leaned over and cried. She had lost the battle. She dragged herself out of bed and took up the mantle.

She didn't walk alone. She took out a pork chop and fed it to Cotton. He licked his lips and walked beside her.

The pastor lived on top of a steep incline. She got to the top, out of breath.

"Hello, hello, hello, pastor." she knocked at the gate.

"Who's there?" he shouted from the interior.

"It's me, Lily; I'm here with the dinner."

"Oh, it's you, my little angel." He sounded coy. Lily winced, her upper lip curled. "Open the gate and come on in, angel."

Lily and Cotton entered the yard.

"Come on inside my love, I'm in the bathroom. Just rest the food on the dining table for me."

Lily chewed on her lips as she tiptoed into the dining room. As she lifted her hand to rest the dish on the table, the pastor entered the room. In her fright she dropped it, the metal bowl made noises as the food splattered all over the floor. She stepped back and covered her mouth.

"I'm so sorry, pastor. So sorry."

"Oh that's alright, my love, at least you're here." He walked up to her and caressed her hair. She pulled away. He moved closer then reached for her budding breasts. Lily screamed and kicked him and ran. He grabbed at her, a smile on his face that was anything but saintly. He caught the lace on her sleeve and ordered, "Get over here, child!"

The dress tore and Lily dodge his outstretched grip. "Cotton, go, go go." She rushed out with her cat at her heels.

The Pastor fell and Lily had the time to open the gate with a clear head start. He got up and chased her down the hill. His potbelly jiggled as he ran, and age and sloth living kept him falling until she could hear his grunting from exhaustion.

"I knew you were no good." Lily wagged a finger at him, "and pretty soon, everyone will know too." Lily ran without looking back until she got home. Out of breath, she approached Aunt Patsy on the verandah.

"Lily! You look as if you've seen a ghost."

Lily bent over, held her abdomen and sobbed.

Aunt Patsy put her arms around her and called to Auntie Maxine."You better come and see to your child. Something is wrong; she's coming back from pastor in a fright and her clothes are torn!"

"What!" Auntie Maxine rushed out to the verandah.

"He…he…he tried to rape me." Lily shook.

"He tried to rape you?"Auntie Maxine covered her mouth.

"I told you I didn't trust the man." Aunt Patsy spoke up. "The man is a slime-ball, a fraud, everything is a hoax.

He could never be from God. He is a dam obeah man. I told you not to let him come here."

"No you didn't."

"I did. But that's beside the point now. You need to report the creep to the police! That's what you need to do."

Lily had never seen her Aunt Patsy so livid. Lily lie on the verandah floor curled up in a ball.

Aunt Patsy lifted her, took her to her room, placed her on her bed and covered her.

Relief poured over Lily. She heard them arguing in the hall.

"Alright, so you're right. I'm going to the police station right now!" Auntie Maxine's voice filled with anguish. Lily drifted off to sleep.

Chapter 34

Plum valley/September 1965/few weeks later

"Maxine, did he rape the girl?" Sam Nugent pulled on his cigarette and puffed smoke in circles.

"I wasn't there, I don't know. Can you put out the god dam cigarette?" Auntie Maxine gagged and waved the smoke away.

"That's the point; you can't take what a little ten and a half year old child says."He ignored her wish to put out the cigarette and pulled on it again, blowing it in Lily's direction.

"Why would she lie?" Auntie Maxine cocked her head and fanned the smoke.

"Maybe she doesn't like him?" He sucked as he cleaned his teeth with his tongue.

"What reason would she have for not liking a man of God?" Auntie Maxine walked over to a stone next to Lily and sat.

"You know your daughter; she's always playing the victim. Moreover, you must have proof, how are you going to prove it?" He made that sucking sound again and spat.

Playing victim, is that what he calls it when he gets me beaten for no reason?

They hadn't seen her sitting in the swing. She thought of Margaret and her father. She wished her own father would send for her like Margaret's father did for Margaret. Her father had not written to her since he left, already gone a couple of years. He began to fade from her memory. Without a hero, she felt defenseless against Sam Nugent, against the world.

"But Sam, how am I going to prove that? Auntie Maxine frowned.

"Does Lily even know what rape is? The poor man probably barely looked at her." He scoffed.

Lily dug her toes in the dirt as she listened to Sam explain away her dilemma. She despised him.

"It's amazing what kids nowadays know." Auntie Maxine rubbed her chin.

"Maybe we should ask her to explain exactly what happened." Sam suggested.

"Lily?" Auntie Maxine turned to the house.

"Yes, Auntie Maxine." Lily jumped to her feet from the swing.

"You mean you've been there all along. Come to me."

"You see why I don't trust her; she's so sneaky, little snake in the grass." Sam glared at Lily.

Lily's mouth twisted and her eyes narrowed as she walked towards them.

"Are you giving attitude, child? Fix your face!" Auntie Maxine raised her hand to slap her.

Lily cringed.

"Lily, I hear that you're accusing the pastor of raping you. Did he rape you?" Sam Nugent spat.

"I didn't say he raped me?" Lily scowled.

"You are changing your story now?" Sam Nugent sneered.

"No I'm not." Lily stood her ground.

"You're a little liar!" He pointed a finger at her.

Tears stung the back of her eyes. She walked off.

"What? Are you walking away? Have manners when big people are talking to you, you don't walk away unless you're dismissed. Come back here at once!" Sam Nugent croaked.

Lily continued walking.

"Lily, don't you hear Uncle Sam talking to you. Come back here before I take the switch to you." Auntie Maxine stepped quickly behind her.

Lily stopped, but refused to return.

"Let me get the blasted switch, it seems the only thing you listen to." Auntie Maxine frowned and broke a piece of the coffee branch. Lily walked back to them.

"You know better." Auntie Maxine's eyes bulged as she shook the twig.

"Now look at me. Did you say the man rape you. Do you know what it means to be raped?" Sam Nugent puffed on his cigarette and blew it on Lily.

Lily gagged, fanned and shook her head.

"Speak up! People like you put innocent people into trouble." Sam Nugent pointed his finger in Lily's face.

"But I didn't…" Lily's nostrils flared as she stepped back.

"Shut up and stop lying. I would drop the case Maxine. This child is dangerous, you have to watch her. She's trying to put the poor man into trouble. You can't trust anything she says." His lips curled. He dismissed her with a wave of the hand, turned to Auntie Maxine.

"Come, darling; remember you and I have a date. Let's go get ready." He pinched her rear and she blushed.

"Sam, behave yourself." They walked off hand in hand.

Auntie Maxine emerged at the backdoor.

"Lily, your uncle Sam and I are going into Portie. I want you to watch Millie for me."

"But, it's better if Aunt Patsy watches her." Lily pouted.

"Why? Auntie Maxine frowned, hands akimbo.

"Because she's a grown up." Lily folded her arms.

"Patsy, all she ever does is sleep. You just make sure that you keep an eye on Millie; you're the big one now. You take Margaret's place." Auntie Maxine walked away.

"Okay then Auntie, yes Auntie. I will take care of Millie." At least it made her feel big.

Lily and her eight year old sister Millie, played hide and seek and took turns on the swing. As the shadows grew longer, they sat on the verandah looking out for Auntie Maxine's return. Lily told Millie ghost stories and Anancy stories.

"Once upon a time there was a cunning little fellow. His name was Brother Anancy. He was the slyest fellow in the whole world, he could steal milk out of coffee and you wouldn't miss it."

Millie laughed. She sat at Lily's feet with her hands cradling her cheek as she stared up at Lily wide-eyed until Lily finished her story telling.

"Lily may I have some tea?"

"Sure."

Lily proceeded to the kitchen, made the tea and returned with it to the verandah. As Millie drank her tea, Lily continued her story-telling. Millie's eye lid began closing down. Lily allowed her to rest in her lap. Lily herself nodded off.

Lily stirred. A smell of burnt cloth emanated from the house, smoke poured from the windows. She came to her senses and remembered she hadn't turned off the oil stove, and it seemed the dish cloth she used to hold the pot fell into the fire. She woke Millie.

"Millie, Millie." She shook Millie. "Wake up! Fire! Fire!"

Millie woke up in a stupor. Lily held her hand and ran towards the gate.

"Wait here, I'm going to move the dish cloth and put the fire out." Lily ran back towards the house, but the fire had spread, she couldn't get into the hall let alone the kitchen. She remembered Aunt Patsy.

"Aunt Patsy! Fire! Wake up! Fire!" she heard Aunt Patsy screaming and saw what looked like a ball of fire running towards the sitting hall and then merged into the inferno. Lily's knees buckled under her. Someone pulled her away before the flames got to her. She came to coughing and found herself lying on the front lawn. She screamed out for Millie.

"Millie! Where's Millie! Millie!"

"Lily! Lily! Lily!" Millie looked back at Lily as someone walked away with her. She ran to Millie and squeezed her. Lily stood helpless her eyes bulging, hugging Millie.

Millie screamed, hid her face in Lily's chest, held her tight and trembled.

The neighbors formed a human hose passing buckets of water to put out the flames. Everything seemed to move in slow motion before Lily's eyes, she had flashback of the car accident; she remembered the pastor, the fiery place of torment, brimstone and fire. She remembered her father.

"Daddy!" She felt the heat searing her skin, she squeezed her eyes shut and screamed.

Chapter 35

Kingston/upscale residential area/May 1967

Lily would survive the fire, as did Millie, but Patsy had died. Lily had first thought the fire had been her fault, but through research, it had been Aunt Patsy's smoking, as she fell asleep while a lit cigarette burned between her fingers. They had no home though, and Auntie Maxine blamed Lily. She was good at laying blame on Lily, and Lily had become used to letting it roll off her back like duck feathers.

Two years passed, they moved in with Sam, and Lily lived with a knife tucked under her mattress. She made her bed and placed a knife under her mattress.

Auntie Maxine and Sam Nugent sat sipping tea in the sitting room. Lily lingered in the hallway.

"I can't believe it's been two years now since we lost Patsy in the fire." Aunt Maxine sighed.

"Thanks to that little gal, Patsy died a miserable death and on top of it, we lost everything."

"You know we can't blame her though. The people at the fire department said that the fire started in Patsy's room. They claimed she might have fallen asleep with a cigarette. That's why I hate this whole cigarette smoking thing." Auntie Maxine shook her head at Sam.

"Well, anyway you look at it; it's thanks to me for moving you all to Kingston. Just make sure you all don't burn it down too. I don't want to get in trouble with the landlord." He shrugged."

"I am forever grateful to you, my darling." She leaned over and kissed him.

Lily cringed and retreated. She couldn't see what Auntie Maxine saw in that man with his snugger mouth and bad breath. As to him putting a roof over her head, she believed Auntie Maxine could have done better, and moreover, Lily could have gone back to Bellevue to live with Granny and Gramps, especially since Aunt Liza had migrated to Canada. Maybe Aunt Liza will send for them.

"Lily, aren't you going to school this morning? Look at the time, you're going to high school now, you can't afford to be late. What are you doing so long in there?" Auntie Maxine shouted from the sitting room.

"I'm coming, ma'am." Lily hurried in.

"Say good morning to Uncle Sam." Auntie Maxine smiled as she looked over at him.

"Good morning," Lily muttered.

"Good morning, who?" Sam cleaned his teeth as he glared at her.

Lily sighed.

"Say, Uncle Sam, Lily, if it wasn't for your Uncle Sam here, I don't know how you would go to school. Your daddy has not farted on you since he came here making big promises, and I still can't find a job. So you better be grateful and have manners." She waved Lily away. "Get going, because you have to tidy the place and help Millie get ready for school before you go."

"Yes, ma'am." Lily hung her head and shuffled away, her heart bleeding from the dagger Auntie Maxine threw at her.

Did she have to talk about daddy like that in front of Sam Nugent?

Lily sang as she dusted. Granny always said that she had a good voice and that singing kept her spirit up.

"Oh what a beautiful morning…"Lily faltered.

"Shut up!" he turned the radio up.

I can still sing in my heart.

Lily finished her chores and went to Millie's room.

"Lily, Uncle Sam likes to play with me." Millie looked up at Lily and smiled.

"Play with you, what do you mean?" Lily's heart pounded in her chest.

"He likes to play the touching game." Millie blushed.

"Touching game, what are you talking about?"

"You know, he touches me, and then he makes me touch him."

"Touch where?" Lily scooted closer and rang in her ear. Her hands trembled.

Millie placed her hand on the body part Sam touched. Lily flung the brush at the wall and grunted. Millie's eyes bulged as she chewed on her lips.

"What's wrong, Lily, it's only a game." Millie looked up at Lily.

"A game? It's not a game, you need to tell on him. you need to tell Auntie Maxine." Lily fumed.

"No, no, no I cant tell," Millie shook her head. "I can't tell anyone, I only told you because you're my best friend. He says it's our little secret."

"What? It's not a secret, Millie. It's a very bad thing. You must tell." Lily paused.

"I can't, he says if I tell bad things will happen to me."

"What bad things?"

"Bad things, you know, like we won't have any food to eat, and we would have to live on the streets and gunmen will shoot us up and we will die."

"Lie, lie, lie. I'm going to tell Auntie Maxine." Lily pulled on Millie and turned to face her.

"No, no, no please, I don't want us to die." Millie's eyes opened wide.

"We won't die." Lily's lip curled.

"We won't?" Millie cocked her head.

"No, he might." Lily remembered the knife under her mattress. She gritted her teeth.

"But I will get into trouble, Auntie Maxine will beat me." Millie's chin trembled.

"Don't be silly, you won't get into trouble. He will."

"Are you sure?"

"I'm sure."

"Promise me you won't let him know I told you." Millie's eyes moistened.

"Don't worry, Millie, you're going to be just fine. You can trust me." Lily made eye contact. "It's okay. I Promise." She held up her pinkie and curled it around Millie's.

Auntie Maxine and Sam Nugent sat on the verandah.

"Maxine, you need to tell that little gal of yours to stop locking her door at nights. Anything could happen to her and we can't get in."

"Maybe she just needs some privacy."

"Privacy, what kind of privacy could she want at her age, what is it, twelve and a half?"

"Thirteen this year, almost a teenager."

"Even so, it's not safe. I don't want anybody locking no door in my house. I must be able to go wherever I want to go in my house, whenever I want to."

"But, I think she's entitled to her privacy, she's growing up."

"Well, the next time I find the door locked I'm going to kick it down!"

"Okay, Sam Nugent, you've made your point. I know it's your house."

Lily and Millie stepped onto the verandah. Pin drop silence.

"Bye, Uncle Sam," Lily waved.

"Just a wave? Come and give Uncle Sam a goodbye kiss."

Millie stopped in her tracks and hung her head.

"Come on, man, shy?" he walked over to her and kissed her on her lips. Millie cringed, Lily winced. Maxine chuckled.

Lily pulled Millie away and they stepped off the verandah. Sam leered at Lily.

"Sam, I have something to tell you." Maxine said.

"What?'

"I'm pregnant."

Lily's knees wobbled and her heart sank. She regained her balance as she fought back the tears.

Chapter 36

Kingston/Upscale residential area/ October 1969, Lily 14

"Why, why Lily, why didn't you come to me first?" Auntie Maxine's face muscles tensed.

"Because you wouldn't listen to me." Lily shook her head, not making eye contact.

"Why did you have to go and tell your teacher? We could have dealt with this as a family, now the whole world is going to judge us." Auntie Maxine's expression rigid as she waved her hands in the air.

"Sorry, Auntie Maxine, but that is the reason I have been sleeping with a knife under my mattress, and why I have been locking my door. He comes into my room at night and touches me." Lily bit her nails and frowned.

"You're a liar!" you're just making up stories because you don't like the man. And on top of it you're packing up poor little Millie with things she knows nothing about."Auntie Maxine's eyes burnt holes in hers.

"But it's true, Auntie Maxine, he did touch Millie, she told me so. She's afraid to tell you herself." Lily maintained eye contact.

"Well, I asked her, and she said it's not true. I asked her if you put her up to it and she said yes. Why are you so wicked, girl? You tried to get pastor in trouble, now you're trying to get your Uncle Sam in trouble. You're a cruel girl!" Auntie Maxine's face shook with the ire of a tempest.

"He's not my uncle!" Lily stood her ground.

"You're a cruel girl, you're going to burn in hell!" Auntie Maxine wagged her finger.

"I'd rather go to hell than be touched by th…that man one more time!" Lily's face splayed open her contempt.

"Then go to hell! You're an evil liar!"

"Well, if that's the case, I'll see you both there!" Lily shrugged. she's said her piece.

"What!" Auntie Maxine raised her hand to slap Lily.

Lily tilted her head, Auntie Maxine had no power over her. Would rage change her view?

Auntie Maxine lowered her hand. "Don't test me, little child." Auntie Maxine pointed her forefinger inches from Lily's face. "I don't believe a word you say."

"Believe me Auntie, or don't believe me, it's the truth, and in my heart, I think you know it is." Lily held her gaze.

"Do you have any idea how much trouble this is going to cause. Hmm, do you even understand what's going to happen? Can you imagine the shame this is going to cause. Look at the neighborhood we live in. This is not Plum Valley, this is Cherry Gardens, an upscale community. Do you even have any idea what that means? Do you understand what you're doing to us?" Auntie Maxine shook her head.

"Yes, I understand. We're going to get that creep, Sam Nugent, out of our lives and we're going to live happily ever after." Lily's eyes sparkled.

Maxine slapped her across her face and drew blood from Lily's lips. Lily didn't flinch, just covered her mouth as blood poured from the wound.

"Get out of my sight, you idiot!" The cords in Auntie Maxine's neck rigid.

"I will, but it doesn't change the truth, Auntie Maxine." Lily's face burned but her heart was at peace.

"Just get out of my sight before I strangle you! You've come into my life and have caused nothing short of pain, I should have…" Auntie Maxine shook her head and waved her away.

Sam Nugent walked in before Lily could leave the room. He grabbed her by her arm and pulled her to him.

"Who do you think you're playing with, gal?" He grunted, his eyes blazing.

Lily shrugged him off, but his grip tightened.

"That's what I was just talking to her about, Sam. I can't believe Lily would do something like this."Auntie Maxine shook her head.

"You can't believe it? I knew this would happen. You should have sent her back to her Granny in Bellevue." Sam Nugent squeezed Lily's hand and shook her.

She faced him and let out a grunt so blood would splatter from her lip onto his shirt.

"What the hell? Why you…send her back."

"I can't, I don't want her to be a dunce. She has made such fine progress. You see how she ended up in the best high school in Kingston." Auntie Maxine stared out.

"I don't give a shit about that. she's making a mess of my life now, spoiling my reputation. I don't plan to spend the rest of my days in workhouse." Sam Nugent's lips curled.

"Cho Sam, it won't come to that, I'll defend you. You know I trust you. I believe in you, Sam. I will stick by you. Remember I'm carrying your child." She tilted her head with a lopsided grin.

"How could I forget love. But does she even understand how I manage to pay the rent up here in Cherry Gardens?" he squeezed Lily's hand harder.

"I'll deal with Lily. She'll come to her senses and tell them that she made up the stories." She walked over to him, her eyelashes fluttering, she kissed him on his cheek.

"Of course she made up the stories." He shrugged.

"I know that, Sam, I'm beginning to find out the kind of person she is. She's conniving. She just likes to get other people in trouble, especially if she hates you."

"Yes, and she hates me." Still holding on to Lily, he shook her. "Listen to me, little gal, if you ever let me get into trouble, you will live to regret it! Regret it! You hear me? Regret it!"He pushed her off.

"You will live to regret it." Lily muttered arching her eyebrows.

Sam Nugent doubled his fist and lunged at her. Lily ducked. Sam lurched forward and sprawled onto the floor. Lily ran up the stairs, skipping steps two at a time. Sam Nugent chased her up the stairs. She stumbled. He grabbed her leg, Lily screamed. Sam Nugent slipped. Lily got to the top of the stairs, ran into the bathroom and slammed the door and bolted it. Sam pounded on the door.

"Open the door! Open the blasted door, bitch, before I kick it down!" He kicked and pounded the door.

Lily cowered in a corner on the bathroom, pale and trembling, her eyes fixed on the door, her thoughts fixed on what to do if the door broke open. "You go away or you will be sorry."

Sam continued swearing and pounding the door.

The doorbell rang.

Footsteps traveled away from the floor in front of her and she stood, ran over to the door and peeped through a crack. Lily cracked the door open and peeked out.

"Good day, madam, is this the home of Mr. Sam Nugent?"

"Who, er, er?" Auntie Maxine stuttered. "Who are you?"

Lily walked out to the landing and looked downstairs.

"We're from the Constant Spring Police department, ma'am. I'm Detective Norval Bertram and this here is Detective Damian Spence."

"Good day to you officers, so who are they?" Auntie Maxine enquired.

"Oh, oh they are from the child services department."

"So why are they here?" Auntie Maxine's voice trembled.

"Madam, please stay calm. We will ask the questions."

"I'm calm officer, how may I help you?"

"As I was saying, is this the resident of Mr. Sam Nugent?"

"Er, yes, er, it is. What is it officer?" Auntie Maxine stuttered.

"We wish to speak to Mr. Nugent ourselves, madam. Is he here?"

"Er, um, no, um, er yes. Let me call him." Auntie Maxine ran upstairs. Sam Nugent and auntie Maxine spoke in inaudible tones.

Lily heard boot steps rushing up the stairs. Sam ran towards the bedroom. The officers rushed past the bathroom door guns in hand, pointing in every direction, spinning in circles.

"Sam, Sam don't jump, you'll die!" Auntie Maxine screamed.

The officers ran towards the bedroom.

"Don't move; it's the police, don't try to unlock that window. we have a warrant for your arrest! Move away from that window! Now! We'll shoot. Step aside, man."

"Shoot officer, shoot, shoot an innocent man!" Sam Nugent shouted.

"Handcuff him, detective Spence. Mr. Sam Nugent, you are being charged with child molestation and drug dealing. You have a right to remain silent. Anything you say will be used against you in a court of law."

Lily crossed her arms and stood where Sam could see her.

As they filed past her, Sam Nugent's hatred bubbled up, but he had no idea how much more Lily despised him.

"Madam, please come down to the station for questioning. If it can be proven that the children are not safe here with you, they will be taken away from you and sent to a home."

"You can't take my children away from me. And you're arresting an innocent man. I'll see you in court!" Auntie Maxine's voice screeched.

"Madam, if you protest, we'll have to arrest you as well, so don't make this more difficult than it needs to be. Please come with us to the station."

Lily caught Sam's attention and smiled.

"You will have your say, Madam. In the meanwhile be careful not to commit yourself. Please come down to the station, bail may be discussed there."

The detectives led Sam Nugent through the door, Auntie Maxine followed. The Child Services officers made their way inside to take the children.

Chapter 37

Kingston-Upscale neighborhood/January 1970

"Lily, you have to change your statement, or we are going to suffer."

"Suffer?"

"Yes, suffer. We don't have any money to pay this rent."

"Then we can move, can't we? We don't have to live in this big house."

"What about food, bus fare, school fee? You forget about these things."

"Remember I got a scholarship, we don't have to pay school fee."

"You're selfish, all you can think of is yourself. What about Millie? She's going to a private school, how am I going to afford her school fee? Now I have to move her to public school. How are we even going to eat? You couldn't go to school today, because you have no lunch money or bus fare. I am pregnant, who is going to hire me now?"

"Auntie Maxine, don't fret so much, we'll survive without him."

"You can say anything, you're a young breeze, you don't know a hurricane."

"I can run errands."

"For whom?"

"The neighbors."

"Hey gal, where's your shame? You can't let people know we are having hard luck. They'll know if you go begging them for work. Moreover, they'll report me to child services. You and Millie spent just two weeks in the Children's home and you couldn't stand it. Do you know how many strings I had to pull and how many lies I had to tell to get you out of there? Unless, you want to go back to the Childrens' home."

"No, no, I don't want us to go back there."

"Well, we better lie low for now, and you better change your story. For now we just have to suck salt through wooden spoon. Right now you have the power in your hands. I beg you, Lily, change your story."

"I can't, I just can't"

"What do you mean you can't? There's no such thing as can't."

"I can't live like that."

"Like what?"

"With him, I hate him."

"Oh so that's why you lied, you hate him, that's what I was telling the officers."

"I didn't lie!"

"You're a scheming little liar! And now everybody has to suffer for your selfishness. You know what? This conversation is over, you know what you need to do." She turned and walked away.

Millie ran to Auntie Maxine.

"There are some people at the door."

"Who?" Auntie Maxine bellowed from the staircase.

"I dunno."

"Let me see who it is." Auntie Maxine padded down the stairs, walked to the door and used the peephole. "Those dam people from Child Services. What the hell do they want? It's like once they get in your skin, you can't shake them off. Cho!"

"Hello." A voice at the door.

"Quick! Quick! Hide! They're going to want to know why you're not at school." She waved the girls away and opened the door.

"Please, come in ladies."Auntie Maxine welcomed them.

"Good day, Miss Francis. Do you remember us? I'm Dorothy Green and this is Miss Karen Hall."

"Please have a seat, ladies. May I offer you some lemonade or anything like that?" Auntie Maxine's voice sang like a hostess.

"So, where are the girls?"

"It's a school day, at school of course." Auntie Maxine giggled.

"Oh yes, that's right, dumb question. So how are they getting on? Has Mr. Nugent tried to contact you or the girls. We are concerned he might try to approach them while they're away from home. Is there anyway you could pick them up from school, or have them picked up?"

"I will look into it."

"You have to more than look into it, Miss Francis. Some of these predators can be very aggressive and vicious."

"Well, that's true, I will do something about it."

"Please do, asap."

"Yes, madam."

"We're really here to assess the girls' conveniences. So may we have a look around. When we were here last time we felt rushed."

"Oh, er, um, sure." Auntie Maxine stammered.

"Miss Francis, I thought you said the girls were at school?" Lily's and Millie's chins touched their chests as they poured out of the powder room.

"Oh, er, um I er um made a mistake." Auntie Maxine stuttered.

"So why arent they in school?" The woman cocked her head.

"Ah, I, um, er, basically, um, er, I wasn't feeling so good, seeing that I'm pregnant and all, so I woke late and didn't get to send them off on time. And you know how these schools are, they are a stickler for time." Auntie Maxine flushed.

"They're also sticklers for attendance. I'm sorry, madam, but that is going to be a strike against you keeping them." The woman scowled.

"I'm really sorry about that, it won't happen again." Auntie Maxine glanced away.

"So Lily, how are you feeling these days? Good?" The woman's eyes crinkled at the corners.

"Yes, thank you. I'm good." Lily smiled and nodded.

"How about you, Millie? You're both such pretty girls, just like your mom." She looked at Auntie Maxine.

Auntie Maxine blushed.

"I'm fine, thank you." Millie hung her head and dug her toes in the ground.

The probing continued until they nodded in satisfaction. The girls and Auntie Maxine gathered at the door, smiled and waved the Child Services' officers goodbye. They looked like a happy, stable family.

Relieved, Lily flopped on the sofa with a novel, Maxine went upstairs to her bedroom and Millie sat on the rug and played with her doll.

The door crashed open, wood splintering, and a masked man demanded, "Hey gal, get up! Where's your mother?" he held a fire arm burst and grabbed Lily off of the sofa.

Lily and Millie screamed. Millie hid behind the sofa.

"Auntie Maxine!" Lily bawled out.

Auntie Maxine ran down the stairs.

"What is it?" Auntie Maxine came round the corner and shouted, "Let her go! Who are you? What do you want?"

"I want you to clear the brethren's name. If this thing goes any further, you will all be dead!"

"Who sent you? Sam would never do this."

"I'm a friend of the cause."

"What cause?"

"You rich people uptown use your connections and keep down poor people. Now you're keeping down a trying black man. You're trying to keep down my brethren. You chew him up and spit him out because you feel you've arrived in high society. No sistren, this can't work. It's payback time."

"Let her go, I'm not afraid of you? Who sent you?"

"Never mind who sent me. This is just a warning. And if you go to the police, you're all dead meat." He waved the gun around the room.

Auntie Maxine stepped closer to the man.

"Woman, step back!"

Maxine reached out to pull Lily away from the gun man.

"Woman, don't come any closer, I'm warning you. These fingers are trigger happy today." He guffawed and pointed the gun at Auntie Maxine. She stepped back, her palms as a shield.

"She is going to tell the court it's a mistake." Auntie Maxine shifted from one leg to the next. She made eye contact with Lily and shook her head. "You will, right Lily?"

Lily gulped, she remained speechless. The masked gunman turned the gun on Lily, placed it against her temples. Lily's knees trembled, beads of sweat gathered on her forehead.

Chapter 38

Kingston/Upscale Neighborhood/January 1970, same day

The masked man spun Lily around. Lily's heart pounded against its cage and cold washed down her back.

"Answer gal, are you going to change your statement?" he dug the pistol in her temples. Lily mumbled a response out of a dry mouth.

"Speak up, I can't hear you!" he shook her.

Lily hyperventilated and wobbled. She stared at Millie.

The masked man followed Lily's stare and spun around. Millie picked up the telephone receiver, the man let go of Lily and lunged at Millie. Auntie Maxine grabbed the man from behind. The gun fell out of the man's hand. They both fell to the floor in a struggle. Lily eyed the gun, her heart thumping, she moved towards the gun as it slid across the floor. She fumbled and sprawled on the floor; she scrambled to pick it up and clutched it in her grip. Lily underestimated the weight of the pistol. She stood and pointed it. It pulled her forward and her hand shook. She steadied herself and used both hands to hold the gun. She raised it in the air.

"Don't move!" her lips trembled, her hand tightened around the pistol.

The man held Auntie Maxine at her neck and placed her as a shield, his eyes bulging, but he guffawed.

"Well, well, well, what have we here, David and Goliath?" holding Auntie Maxine, he moved closer to Lily. "This must be a joke."

"I said don't move. Don't come any closer!" Lily screeched, the weight of the gun pulling down her hands.

"Lily, please be careful with that thing!" Auntie Maxine stretched her hands to Lily, her brows raised and pulled together.

"Bring that thing to me, you little idiot, do you think it's a toy." The man stretched out a hand. "That thing will fling you across the room and damage you." He chortled. "Give it to me!" He edged closer.

Lily stepped back. She didn't want to miss her mark and kill Auntie Maxine. Lily shivered. She folded her fingers around the trigger, her fingers fumbled, the thunder that escaped pulled the gun upward and it fell to the ground, dragging her down with it. She froze and pissed. Her vision blurred.

The man retrieved the gun. "Everybody! Over here!" He pointed the gun.

They huddled on the sofa.

He ordered Auntie Maxine to stand in front of the girls. He moved closer to Auntie Maxine leering at her and fondled her breast.

Auntie Maxine pulled away.

"What, you have a problem with my touch?" His grin made Lily shudder.

Auntie Maxine pushed him away. "I'll have you know that I am pregnant."

"Oh, you're carrying Sammy's youth. Respect man, respect for the brethren. So that leaves me with you. Come here, girl." He pointed in Lily's direction. Lily's pulse raced in her ears. She retched.

"Oh no, if you put your stinking hand on my child I will kill you, boy!" Auntie Maxine clenched her fist at her sides, fire in her eyes.

"Shut up before I box you down!" he raised his hand in the air and gun-butted Auntie Maxine. She fell. He kicked her. "Get up! Sit on the sofa! You! Little girl! Get me a piece of string, rope, ribbon, anything." He beckoned to Millie.

Millie's body swayed as she walked to him. "Move it!"

The man tied their hands behind them. He took off his mask and grimaced. He pulled a joint of marijuana from his pocket, lit it and pulled hard. He spewed the smoke in the air and leaned back in the love seat, the gun beside him.

"Please, let us go, we're just harmless females, don't you have a mother, a sister, a daughter?" Auntie Maxine pleaded, blood pooling around the wound in her head. He pulled on his joint again, scratched his crotch and sneered. "Did I give you permission to speak?" he brandished the gun at Auntie Maxine. "I should cover your mouths. He left the room leaving the gun behind. Lily eyed the gun. She sat crumpled in the sofa, washing in cold sweat, her whole body shaking. Auntie Maxine moved to the edge of the sofa. The man returned with masking tape.

"Now I don't have to listen to you whine. I might not cover your mouth because you need to let me know your intentions. Are you going to change your story?" He pointed the gun at Lily. Lily's mouth moved, but no sound came. "What's wrong with you, gal, your mouth join church, you can't speak, answer me before I make you wet yourself again!" his laughter rang through the house. "You know what? I'm gonna fix myself something to eat, while you fix your mouth to speak." As quickly has he came back, he retreated to the kitchen again.

Auntie Maxine gestured to Lily to use her teeth to pull the string from her hand. Lily gnawed at the string, her teeth chattered. As it loosened, Auntie Maxine shook it off and grabbed the gun from the love seat. She sat with the gun behind her and waited.

He entered the room and looked across at the chair. Auntie Maxine pulled the gun from behind her and cocked.

"I am going to kill you, boy. They're going to have to scrape you off my floor. I know how to handle this!" Auntie Maxine kept a steely gaze. "Turn your back to me, hands in the air, boy!" he moved closer, "one more step and that pea sized brain of yours will be all over the floor. I said turn around and hands in the air!"

A commotion at the door, startled them, but Auntie Maxine kept the gun pointed, steely eyed and ready.

"Police! Open the door!"

Chapter 39

Kingston/ghetto /May 1972

Lily's visit with the counselor left her feeling in control of her possibilities, hopeful. With Sam Nugent and the masked man in prison, she felt safe, although they'd had to leave their home and into the ghettos, where the smell of danger lingered upon every footstep. The counselor made her see herself in five years. She imagined herself in medical school. With just two more years in high school the path seemed bright. She alighted from the bus and walked with her head in the air.

Lily walked down the alley leading home. Boys played football with juice boxes, while grown men sat on stones smoking and playing dominos. She clutched her school bag as her heart thumped.

"Good evening" she smiled.

Old men grunted responses; younger men ogled her; the young boys cussed.

"Hey gal, move out of the way." They chorused.

She increased her pace, held her head straight, ignoring them.

Graffiti on the zinc fences, sent messages to rival gangs. She called it 'Zinc Fence City.' Perimeter walls made from zinc provided privacy and kept the inhabitants safe.

The fences dotted with gunshot holes and rust, leaned from the soil that kept them standing barely clinging to nails that held them together. She opened the gate hinged to its fence by a piece of board. She entered the yard. The crude building painted light blue, greeted her.

Home sweet home.

Holes between the rows of board grinned and peeped. She opened the door to the one bedroom house.

"Evening Auntie Maxine." Lily placed her school bag on the floor. Auntie Maxine looked up from breast feeding the baby.

"Did you remember to buy the flour and the oil?"

"Yes ma'am, it's in my bag." She pulled the string on her hand-made bag.

"Take off your uniform and start the dinner. Make some boiled dumplings and cook up some onions with the oil."

"Yes ma'am." Lily pulled the curtain that divided her section of the room from Auntie Maxine's. She sat on the mattress they'd found in the Riverton dump, pulled off her shoes, the cardboard she'd used to fill the hole, fell out. She replaced it, put it aside and walked outside in bare feet.

Lily placed some coal into the iron grill, poured some kerosene oil and lit the coal. A flame rose and singed the hair on her skin. The smell of burning hair and flesh permeated the air. She yelped and ran to the all purpose water barrel. She dipped her entire arm, the relief only temporary, she winced.

"What's happening out there?" Auntie Maxine stood at the doorway. "Look here child; don't try to burn down this place too. Are you hurt?"

"Yes Auntie." Lily blew on the burn.

"You have to learn to use a coal stove, girl. After all, you're the one who brought us to this condition." Auntie Maxine scoffed. "Come inside let me put some cream on." She wheeled back into the room, baby Peter in hand.

Lily packed the dirty plates in a basin after dinner. She dipped the empty cheese pan into the barrel of water, washed the enamel plates and turned them down on the board runner alongside the house. She filled a wash pan with water for her bath.

"Hey girl, show me your tits!" Lily looked up and saw two boys staring down on her in the roofless zinc shower cubicle. She stooped, placed the washcloth over her breasts, ranted and screamed. The boys giggled.

"Auntie Maxine!"

"What's the matter?" Auntie Maxine rushed out in the yard.

"Boys, Auntie Maxine, boys, they're peeking at me!" Mortified, Lily covered her body, a downward gaze, her skin crawled, she wished she didn't exist and the earth swallowed her.

"You boys, Get away from there this minute. I'm going to report you to the Don!" Auntie Maxine shooed them off.

"Please ma'am don't tell on us. The don will have us tied up and beaten. We won't do it again." They begged.

Auntie Maxine chased them.

"Get away, you little perverts!" her voice trembling with rage and reaching a crescendo. The boys vanished. "Dam rude, it is clear what they're going to grow up to be." She escorted Lily into the house and slammed the door.

"Auntie Maxine, can we move back to the country?" Lily cocked her head.

"And which school would you attend?"

"I could go to the same high school that Margaret attended."

"Margaret isn't even there anymore; Rupert migrated and took her with him to Canada. Worthless Winston is a comfort to a fool." She sucked air through her teeth and changed the baby's diaper. "That's a backward move, don't even think about that. I'm not going back to that bush to live. Go help Millie with her homework."

Daddy, daddy had forgotten her, how could he? A lump formed in Lily's throat, her eyes moistened. She lie on her back and stared up into the ceiling at the naked zinc, held up by crisscrossed beams of wood, cold at nights and roasting in the daytime. She wondered if Winston lived in a big upstairs house with running water and electricity, one that didn't leak when it rained. She comforted herself with her five year plan.

She must have dozed off, but a loud banging on the door made her jump up.

"Who is it?" Auntie Maxine's voice shook.

"Open the door; it's me, Squiggle, the Don." The man insisted.

"Please come in, Don Squiggle." Aunt Maxine's voice animated. "Have a seat, er, um, sorry, no chair." She stuttered. "May I offer you a drink? Lily go outside and get me some water to make some lemonade for Don Squiggle."

Lily peeped around the dividing curtain. "Sorry Auntie, we don't have any lime." Lily bit her nails. She saw the Don, a surly, potbellied man, with scars on his face. His shirt front opened halfway down, he wore an oversized gold chain and a pendant that nestled in the thick hair on his chest. She shuddered.

"I'm alright man, don't worry about me. No problem. Come here, little lady." He shook his forefinger, beckoning Lily. Lily hesitated. "Come on, lovely lady, the Don is here to protect you, no need to be afraid. I run things around here. I call the shots." He folded his arm above his gut. His voice thundered.

Lily's heart flapped in her chest. She stepped out from behind the curtain wearing her nightgown. She held her head down.

"My, my, what a lovely lady. Hold up your head, don't be bashful." He curled his forefinger under his chin and gazed at Lily, all his fingers adorned with gold rings.

"I just come to let you know that I had those little rude boys beaten good and proper for their behavior." He winked.

"How did you know about that?" Auntie Maxine's eyes narrowed.

"Don't worry about that, I have my informers." He rubbed his palms together and smiled a toothless grin.

"Okay Lily, you may go back to bed now." Aunt Maxine held Lily by her shoulder hastening her behind the curtain.

"On a serious note though, you must understand that when she comes of age, she must be initiated." he cleared his throat.

"What do you mean?"

"I will have to be the first to sample her, to break her in." He pressed. "Yep, that's how it works in these parts.

Every young girl must be initiated, or the family cannot be guaranteed protection.

"What!" Auntie Maxine's voice filled with terror.

Lily's chest tightened.

Chapter 40
Kingston/ghetto/June 1973

Lily did the happy dance. Her daddy hadn't forgotten her, he had to sort out his life, and he'd moved to Canada, taken a wife and had a couple of kids. A letter from Aunt Liza had explained. He had relocated to Canada to join Aunt Liza. One big happy family, and soon she'd join them and then Gramps and Granny. Lily lay with her hands at the back of her head, dreamy; she stared up at the zinc ceiling but not seeing it, her eyes moist.

Two year-old Peter's banging on his toys pulled her out of her reverie. She peeped over the curtain and noticed that Auntie Maxine had left him alone. She cuddled him and played with him. Soon Millie joined them on the mattress. The ghetto barnyard came alive, hens clucked, chicks tweeted, roosters crowed, and mongrels yapped, the families stirred in the twilight. Lily heard Auntie Maxine approaching the house, a couple of male voices with her.

"Mind you drop it. Hold it good." Auntie Maxine spoke in an undertone.

"Yeah, yeah, I got it." A man grunted.

"Careful." Another snapped.

The key turned in the door.

Auntie Maxine gave orders.

"Lean it up over there and let me move the mattress."
Animated, she whistled.

The new beds stood elevated.

"Thank you gentlemen, how much do I owe you?" she
dug into her purse to tip the men.

"No problem ma'am, the don will take care of that."
one of the men bowed. They waved and left.

"Auntie Maxine, where did these come from? The
dump?" Lily cocked her head.

"Don't be silly child, can't you see that these beds are
brand new." She grinned, leaned back and admired them.

"But, we don't have money to buy them." Lily stood
and folded her arms and chewed on her lips.

"You don't worry about that, what you don't know is
bigger than you." She walked off towards the door.

"But, it's strange, this hour of the morning? The shops
aren't even open, you didn't..." Lily faltered.

"Steal them? No Lily, I didn't steal them, have you
ever heard of me being a thief?" Her hands akimbo, she
made eye contact. "Go and light the coal stove so we can
have some tea, Peter's hungry too, so make his milk for
me." She yawned.

Lily pursed her lips and walked off without
answering. Lily opened the door.

"Lawd Jesus Junior, don't murder me. Please!" a woman only in her panties and brassiere ran into the backyard, a cutlass wielding man running behind her. "Murder, murder!"

Lily retreated.

Slapping sounds made Lily cringe.

"Don't keep man with me, do you hear me?" another slap.

"I beg you please, Junior, don't kill me, I won't do it again!" the woman screamed.

Auntie Maxine ran to the window. "Hey man, leave her alone, mind you get yourself in trouble!"

Lily joined her at the window. The man paused and looked towards the window.

"Mind your own dammed business, woman!" he ordered her.

"It is my business, you're in my yard." Auntie Maxine asserted. He ignored her and continued his tirade.

"Give me one good reason why I shouldn't murder you here this morning, Eenh, give me one good reason. I give you everything to your comfort. When the don initiated you he set us up with everything we need and you're not satisfied. What more do you want?" Eenh? What more?" he slapped her again with the machete.

"Please, I am begging you. Remember our son." The woman used her hands as a shield and pleaded.

"You know that's the only thing that saves you." He slapped her again and dragged her behind him.

Lily shook her head, bit her lips, her eyes moistened, she moved her heavy legs to the coal stove. The smoke got in her eyes, tears streamed down her cheeks, her thoughts filled with what she'd just witnessed. 'Initiated, initiated, initiated.' A stuck record in her head, she wobbled, the echo reverberated. She held her head and ran to the corner of the house, stooped and cradled her face in her hand and sobbed, her body shook.

"Lily! What is taking you so long?" Auntie Maxine shouted. "Don't you hear the baby crying?"

Lily jumped up, wiped her tears in her hem. "I'm coming, Auntie Maxine." She sniffed.

"Hurry, don't let me come out there and pepper your skin with some licks. You could be old as Methuselah; you're not too old to get a beating."

"Coming, ma'am." She hastened her step as she served tea. They squatted on the floor as they ate, Lily sat at the doorway.

'Initiated, initiated, beaten, beaten.' Lily choked on the lump in her throat, the mint tea and the dry bread gagged her.

"What's wrong with you girl, are you breeding?" Auntie Maxine peered at her, "We don't need another hungry mouth to feed, so don't even bother with it, all those late evenings you've been coming home; who are you sleeping with?"

"Nobody, Auntie Maxine, I go to the library after school to do my homework." Lily sighed at her Auntie's accusations.

Jingling keys and footsteps approached the gate. Don Squiggly pushed the gate open. His gut prefaced him. A wide grin plastered his face and his gums flapped when he spoke. He opened his arms wide and invited Millie for a hug.

"Come to Uncle Squig, baby." He dragged his words and opened his large arms.

Millie hesitated.

"Come, baby, I mean well. I'm a good man." He cajoled her.

Millie didn't budge. He walked up to Lily. "You're growing into a fine young lady, my, my, my. How old are you now?"

Lily didn't answer, she stared him down. Auntie Maxine volunteered an answer. "She turns seventeen next year."

"Nice, nice." Don Squiggly nodded, looked her up and down, and walked around her. Lily wanted to disappear. She wanted to smack him with a broom across his pancake face. She gritted her teeth and walked away.

"So, Mommy, how are you enjoying the beds? I can't have you lovely ladies sleeping on the floor." He rubbed his hands together.

"I'm really grateful, don Squiggly, really grateful, thank you." Aunt Maxine's obsequious manner made Lily groan.

"No problem, Mommy, call me Squig. We're family."

Auntie Maxine giggled like a teenager.

"Anyway, I just came to make sure the goods were delivered and you're comfortable. Trala." He waved and left.

"What a nice man though, Eenh Lily? You all don't even have any manners, the man was trying to make much of you and you were so rude." She scolded the girls.

Lily rolled her eyes, her stomach heaved.

Chapter 41

Canada/late July 1973

Lily walked towards the airplane, luggage in hand, a glad bag in her chest and knots in her belly.

The air hostesses greeted her and showed her to her seat. She scanned the aisle, just like Kong's bus, except more expansive, with creature comforts. She took a deep breath, smiled, placed her hand luggage overhead, studied the three seats, and checked her seat number. She got the window seat. The airplane pulsated. Jonah in the body of the whale.

"Ladies and gentlemen, this is your Captain speaking, Captain Randall King with co-pilot Derrick Andrews at the helm welcoming you on board Air Canada, flight A249. Please sit back relax and enjoy your flight and our in-flight movies and wine and service. Thank you for making it Air Canada." The speaker clicked off.

The seat belt lights came on. Other lights flashed. Lily looked at the buttons overhead; she raised her eyebrows and crinkled her nose, but dared not touch anything, lest the airplane malfunctioned. She purse her lips and lifted her chin, glanced about, not focusing on anything in particular.

The speaker bell dinged. "Ladies and gentlemen, welcome aboard flight A249, this is your hostess speaking, please fasten your seatbelts, put out all cigarettes, put your seats upright and tables in place and prepare for takeoff."

The air hostess demonstrated the use of masks, life jackets, and pointed out escape routes. It confused Lily. Lily shuddered at the thought of an accident. She fretted. She fumbled trying to locate the life jacket and stared up at the mask.

I hope I don't have to use that thing.

Lily followed suit of her seat mate. She couldn't find the lock for the seatbelt. Her hand shook as she fastened it. The foreigner beside her struck up conversation.

"Your first time?" A blonde woman smiled and made eye contact.

"Oh yes, my first time." Lily grinned and nodded.

Not sure how to speak, should I twang?

In her own dialect, she offered "I'm going to see my daddy in Toronto."

"That's wonderful. I'm actually going to Quebec, but I have to make a brief stop in Toronto." The woman offered her hand. "My name is Fiona, yours?"

"My name is Lily, Lily McDermott." Lily shook her hand.

The woman turned her attention to a magazine and Lily followed the flow of activity outside the plane window. The engine roared. It taxied. Buildings and other aircraft and small airport service trucks passed her. The airplane began its ascent. Lily grabbed the chair handles and squeezed her eyes shut. The knots in her stomach tightened.

Her neighbor rested her palm over Lily's hand.

"It's okay. As soon as the airplane completes its ascent you'll feel better."

"My ears are blocked, I can hardly hear you."

"Do you have gum?"

"Gum?"

"Chewing gum?"

"Oh, chewing gum, no."

"Chewing is good to prevent blocking of your ears." She handed Lily a stick of hers.

"Thank you."

The airline settled.

Did it stop?

Through the buildings, cars and the road shrank, disappeared. Inside, she got a sense of inertia, the engine hummed.

"Ladies and gentlemen, we're passing over Cuba." The captain kept a steady narrative of the grounds covered. Lily thought of her examinations, geography, one of her favorite subjects. She awaited the results of her eight subjects. She'd applied for a scholarship to Oxford, and pending her results, her life was in limbo.

Maybe daddy will make me go to College in Canada.

He'd promised to file for her. "The sky's the limit."

"I beg your pardon?" her neighbor swung her head around.

"Oh no, I'm sorry, it's nothing. I guess I must have been thinking aloud." They both chuckled and returned to private preoccupations.

The air hostess offered her a light meal.

The aircraft dropped and vibrated.

"What's that?" Lily held on to the chair, her eyes widened, her stomach heaved.

"Cloud pockets." Her neighbor reassured her.

Lily gagged and covered her mouth. Her neighbor gave her a paper bag.

"Ladies and gentlemen, this is your captain speaking, we're presently experiencing turbulences, please remain seated and fasten your seatbelts. Thank you." Dead pan.

The aircraft dipped again and shook violently. Other passengers whimpered. Lily dug her nails into the chair and tensed, her eyes squeeze shut till they hurt. More jiggling and more dipping, the lights went out, passengers yelped, the light returned. The oxygen masks released and the airhostess demonstrated how to use them. Lily reached for the mask, but her hand shook, she missed it. The blonde lady retrieved it, fixed it over Lily's face and held her trembling hand. Lily said a prayer.

"Ladies and gentlemen, I'd like to apologize for the rather rough flight, but we're going through an unexpected storm. We're almost through it. Please remain calm and remain seated."

Lily muttered, "After every storm, there's calm." She remembered Auntie Maxine's words after the fire. She repeated the phrase and took deep breaths.

The aircraft settled down.

"Ladies and gentleman, this is your captain speaking, thank you for your patience, we've safely maneuvered the bad weather. Please relax and enjoy the rest of the journey. We're just one hour away from our destination. Thank you."

The humming soothed Lily's nerves.

The captain's voice woke her.

"Ladies and gentlemen, please prepare for landing.

When the plane landed, Lily thanked the blonde lady and separated at the immigration desk.

Although summer, the cold bit into Lily's body, unprepared for the change in temperature. She looked around for Daddy.

"Lily, Lily." a voice called out. She looked behind her. Aunt Liza carried a placard with her name on it.

"Aunt Liza!" Lily squealed with delight, her heart as light as feather. They hugged and kissed and squealed some more.

"Where's Daddy?" her words falling through grins.

"Oh, sorry, baby he wasn't able to pick you up."

"Why?" Lily frowned.

"Had to work, but you'll see him soon enough." Aunt Liza tickled her and she giggled. "How was your flight?"

"Scary." Lily rolled her eyes.

They laughed and chatted till they got home.

Chapter 42

Canada/August 1973

"Aunt Liza, I'm beginning to feel slighted by daddy, I've been here three weeks and he hasn't called, come to see me or anything. I don't understand. Sometimes I wonder if he's all that you and Granny say he is. You put him on a pedestal, so high I can't seem to reach him. What do you call him? Charming? He would do well to charm me back in his corner, because I'm hopping mad." Lily pouted.

"You'll see him today, Lily." Aunt Liza assured her.

"My, is that a coincidence or what?" Lily rolled her eyes.

"Is that sarcasm, Lily, watch your tone with me, just because you're all grown up doesn't give you rites of passage to be rude to your old people."

"Sorry Auntie, I'm not trying to be rude, I'm just disappointed." Tears stung the back of her eyes. "I thought I would have been staying with him, not that I have a problem staying with you, you know I love you and all." She hugged Aunt Liza.

"I love you too, baby. Do you still love to dance?" Aunt Liza changed the subject. "You used to shake a good leg when you were little, won all the top ten competitions. Do you remember?”

“I long for those days. They were the best days of my life. Auntie Maxine didn’t send me home anymore, she said I would learn bad habits, get dunce and not speak properly.”

“We never stopped loving you.”

“Nor I you.” Lily hugged her aunt again. Her eyes moistened.

“You can’t separate people from the love in their hearts even in absence of the desired object. Are you ready to go to the mall?” Aunt Liza squeezed her.

“I’ll just get my bag.”

The shopping malls intrigued Lily, she didn’t have to buy anything; window shopping satisfied her. She didn’t know when Aunt Liza became so cosmopolitan in her old age. She drove her own car, she owned her flat, but remained single.

Lily stayed with Aunt Liza, who chaperoned her, entertained her, and took her shopping.

After stopping at a café, they headed home.

“This is what I call ‘shop till you drop’ Auntie. I am so knackered right now; I can’t even try on my goodies.” She flopped across the bed. Memories floated back.

Aunt Liza, do you remember those cute little dresses you used to make me.

"Oh yes, how could I forget? You used to model in them at the local village fair and win prizes. You were ever so cute then."

"So what are you saying, I'm not cute anymore?"

"You're beautiful now. You've grown into a lovely young lady." Aunt Liza spun her around and gave her a playful slap on her rump. "Look at all your assets." They both laughed out loud.

"Thanks, Aunt Liza." Lily blushed.

"Anyway, let me leave you to get your beauty nap, because we're going out in a little while."

"Going out? I thought you said I was going to see Daddy." Lily squinted.

"Well, that's all a part of it."

"Okay, I'm in on that." Lily nodded.

Lily retired to her room, but she played over in her mind what she'd say to Daddy when they met again. Her racing thoughts stole her beauty sleep.

"Lily, let's get moving." Aunt Liza called out from downstairs.

"Coming, Auntie." She put on a little make up for the first time, glanced at her reflection. She liked what she saw.

They left the house, Lily twirling in her new clothes as they made it to the car.

"So where are we going?"

"Be patient." Auntie Liza winked.

They pulled into the driveway of a detached multi-level house, huge by Lily's standards. The well manicured lawn blended in with the general ambiance of Toronto, everywhere immaculate.

Aunt Liza rang the doorbell.

A woman opened the door. Two young children peeped around her. Lily presumed they were her own siblings.

"Hello." The woman narrowed her eyes.

"This is your stepdaughter, Lily." Aunt Liza presented Lily.

"Oh, I see, come in." she moved aside and didn't show enthusiasm as she waved her hand through.

"Lily, this is your stepmother, Alison."

"Nice meeting you Aliso…Auntie Alison." Lily stuck her hand out.

"Alison, I'm not your aunt. Come in." she ignored Lily's hand. Lily ignored the frost. She focused on seeing her father. She imagined how excited he would be to see her again.

Her stepmother escorted them to a family room, the largest Lily had ever seen, but the filthiest, tattered old green carpet, run down drapes and dust on every piece of furniture. It contrasted with the outside environs. Lily heard music blasting from the basement.

"What's going on? Is there a party or something here?" Lily smiled.

"Actually it's a party I arranged for you, you could call it your 'breaking out sweet sixteen' party."

"Oh! Aunt Liza, you're the coolest auntie ever!" Lily squealed, "But you know I turned sixteen earlier this year?"

"Well, I wasn't there to celebrate with you. Let's go downstairs and see what's going on. I won't be staying though, but I'll pick you up in the morning."

"Oh, that's okay; I'll be safe with my daddy." She exhaled.

Party in full swing, smoke filled the air and liquor flowed, ladies in their fanciest and men hip. Lily's head spun. Her mouth dropped open; she covered her mouth and froze.

"Where's Daddy?" Lily looked around.

"He's probably on his way home from work." Aunt Liza guided her to the stereo and introduced her to the Deejay.

"Ladies and gentlemen, let's welcome the lady of the moment, none other than Lily, Lily McDermott, from the paradise island of Jamaica, Miss Sweet Sixteen to her breaking out partay!" the Deejay revved up the party and played "Sixteen Candles."

Lily blushed. A young man approached her. She'd never danced with a young man before. Her heart skipped. She looked into his eyes and he hers. Their spirits met and danced. She'd never felt this way around anyone. She didn't understand the feeling, but it felt good. She loved it.

"I'm Andrew Richards. May I have this pleasure?" he bowed.

Lily bit her lip, covered her mouth with her hand and turned to Aunt Liza for approval.

Aunt Liza smiled and shoved her. "Go on, have fun, it's just a dance. Lily flushed and accepted.

He held her close, one hand around her waist; he rested his cheek on hers and moved with the grace of a swan. She felt safe, a warm glow pulsated through her entire body, her heart fluttered against her ribcage, and she swore he felt it.

"You're such a beautiful lady, when you walked into the room I thought I saw an angel. I know a number of young men here tonight wanted to have this dance with you. I jumped to it. I didn't want to take the chance of waiting. Please pardon me for rushing at you like this." He gazed in her eyes.

Lily made eye contact and smiled, their bodies synchronized. When the music stopped he led her to a table and got her a drink. They spoke and laughed together like old friends, kindred spirits.

Aunt Liza joined them at the table.

"Ah Lily, you'll be spending the night here at Winston's, I'm leaving now, but I'll pick you up tomorrow, or if you wish to stay longer, that's alright too. Just call me." She gestured a phone call.

"Okay Aunt Liza, love you." Lily hugged her.

"Love you too, darling. Have fun." She blew Lily a kiss. Lily watched her as she disappeared in the crowd.

"Would you like some fresh air, away from the noise and smoke?" Andrew pulled her back.

"I'd like that very much." she played with her hair.

The silver moonbeams mesmerized her; the crisp air stung her cheeks. She shivered. Andrew took off his sports jacket and covered her shoulders, placed his arm around her shoulders and leaned over to kiss her.

"What do you think you're doing, boy? Take your hands off her this minute!" Her father's rage burnt through the silver night with fury.

Andrew froze in his tracks and stood at attention.

Lily, dumbfounded, blinked and cocked her head. Cold sweat washed her. Mixed feeling overwhelmed her; she couldn't decide if she should lash out at her father for abandoning her, or that he ruined a precious moment in time. "Daddy…"

"Don't Daddy me; you're just like your mother, a little slut. You hardly know the man and you find yourself outside with him all by yourself. Get inside this minute! And you, boy, disappear. This party is over."

Lily glanced away and swallowed hard and shook her head.

Her father went to the basement and cleared out everyone.

Chapter 43

Canada/Next morning

Lily slept on the sofa, no one showed her to a room or a bed. The morbid atmosphere could fill a tomb. But the night's event played in her mind. Andrew. The thought of him picked up her spirit. How would his kiss have tasted? Dreamy, she closed her eyes and imagined it. She felt his strong arms around her waist, a new and strange sensation awakened in her body. She longed for his touch. Would she see him again? Her eyes moistened. Her father had humiliated him; he wouldn't want to see her again. That's that. Lily's heart broke into a trillion pieces. Her head tilted downward, she sighed.

She stretched, yawned and sat upright in the sofa. The carpet reeked of vomit and urine, toys strewn everywhere. She sneezed. The smell of dust tickled her nostrils. She sneezed again. The children's graffiti decorated the walls. Disgusted, she picked up the toys and placed them in a box in a corner. She sat on the sofa, her hand on her cheek. She heard movements upstairs. A child hurtled down the stairs, a second one—the two she'd seen the evening before. A third child, perhaps six years old, sucking her thumb dragged a dirty blanket behind her, followed by a fourth.

Like lost kittens, they huddled together and stared at Lily in silence. Lily remembered Cotton.

"Hi, my name is Lily. I'm your big sister." She stretched her hands out and smiled. The children recoiled. "Come on, I won't hurt you." She made eye contact with the eldest child. The child glanced away, held her head down and put her blanket to her mouth over her thumb.

"What's your name?" Lily pried.

The fourth child, maybe eight, stood at the stairs and smiled.

Lily beckoned him down. "Hi, I'm Lily, come on down."

The boy ran down the stairs to her.

"I'm Michael McDermott." He pointed to the three children, a wide toothy grin on his face. These are my sisters and brother, Arlene, Sheryl, and Tony. I have another brother, he's still sleeping, lazy bum." He laughed. "What are you doing at our house, are you going to live here?"

"I don't know yet. Maybe." Lily made eye contact and took her hands in his and made small talk, but the little ones just stared at her. The baby toddled off to the toy box; the four-year old followed him.

"You all must be hungry, let me fix you some breakfast." The kitchen made her gag; she fumbled her way through but managed to make scrambled eggs with toast.

Tony's nappies needed changing. She took him upstairs, changed him and headed downstairs.

"Shut up, woman!" Her father's angry tone whittled through the hallway upstairs. Lily stopped. A crash and a thud, Alison screamed.

"Winston, don't hit me!"

"Why did you let all those people into my house last night?"

"I didn't!"

"Woman, don't lie to me." Another thud, she screamed again.

"I'm not lying. Your sister, Liza, she planned her party, not me."

"In my house, without my permission? What kind of woman are you? You stand by and let another woman come into your house and have a party."

"She is your sister."

"And you're my wife, the woman of the house. You're a worthless good for nothing woman, all you do is stay here all day and sleep. I don't know why I married you."

"Why, why didn't you marry Maxine? Leave me. I beg you, leave me!"

"I'm going nowhere, and if you try to leave me I am going to find you and kill you!"

He walked out into the hallway and slammed the door.

"I didn't know you are here." his eyes bulged when he saw Lily.

Lily hung her head, too shocked to say a word, her lips pressed together; she stepped out of his way as he bristled past her, leaving a strong smell of alcohol.

"Lily, come downstairs, I need to talk to you." Her father's voice pressed of irritation.

"Coming, Daddy." She rushed down the stairs.

"Sit down on the sofa." He patted the space beside him.

"Thank you, Daddy." She forced a smile.

"About that boy last night, no girl child of mine is going to behave loosely. I'm very disappointed in you. I can't believe you grew up with my mother. She would have been shocked to see how you were locked down in that worthless boy's arms last night. Let me warn you. I don't want to see you with him or any other while you're here. Look around, can you see how many mouths I have to feed already? I don't need you to bring another one in this world for me to feed. You hear me?"

Lily dressed back without answering.

"You need to be more ambitious. Every generation must be better. You don't have to be like your mother. She's bad news, a disaster, with all those kids from different men. Is that what you want for yourself?"

"No, Daddy." Lily mumbled.

"Speak up, man, you had a mouth for kissing last night and now you can't find your blasted tongue. Speak up!"

Lily shuddered. She'd never seen him like that. "No, Daddy." She shook her head and swallowed.

"What do you want out of life?" he lit a cigarette.

"I didn't know you smoked." Lily crinkled her eyes.

He blew out a puff of smoke and ignored her comment.

"I asked you a question, what do you want out of life?"

His wife walked past them, her eye showing the signs of a hard hit. Winston pulled on the cigarette and looked askance.

"I want a lot out of life, Daddy, and it involves you." Lily sighed.

"Involves me? How so?"

"You promised to file for me to live with you and after all these years this is the first time I'm seeing you."

"I don't recall making any such promise, as you can see, I no longer live in England, I have a wife and I have five hungry mouths to feed."

"How could you forget something like that? Do you know that I spent all my life dreaming about being with you? You can't do this to me, Daddy. I would like the opportunity to live in a first world country just like them." She frowned and her eyes crinkled.

"Did you just hear what I said? I cannot afford it."

"Can't afford what?" Lily cocked her head.

"What did I just say? Take it out of your mind. You're better off where you are."

"But daddy…"

"Forget it!" he puffed on his cigarette, got up and walked off. Lily's eyes blurred, the tears lost their grip on her lids and fell over cheek. Granny had once said 'there's nothing worse than finding your hero washed up on the shore.'

Chapter 44

Kingston ghetto/End of August 1973

Lily sat on a tree stump in the backyard. She threw pebbles at the chickens.

"Why are you crying, Lily? What? Missing Daddy eh?" Auntie Maxine passed by Lily with a basin of dirty nappies. "I didn't expect you back here. Why did you come back?" she quipped.

Lily didn't respond; she picked up a stick and doodled in the dirt.

"Hey, you." Auntie Maxine tossed a pebble at her. "It's you I'm talking to, you're always playing deaf. What happened in Canada, did you piss Winston off?"

"No, I didn't."

"Then why are you back here? You got the chance to go to Canada and you didn't seize the opportunity to stay there. You have no ambition." Auntie Maxine scoffed.

"He didn't want me there."

"Why?"

"He said I'm better off where I am."

"Hogshit, he's just a selfish bastard."

"Whatever, Auntie. Maybe he's right; he's living a dog's life there."

"What do you mean? Come over here and help me wash these nappies and talk to me."

"Just that." Lily stood and joined her.

"Just what?" Auntie Maxine searched Lily's eyes.

"A dog's life." Lily made squeaky noises with the soapy nappies as she scrubbed.

"Talk to me, Lily." Auntie Maxine pressed.

"I don't want to talk about it." Lily sighed.

"Okay, ma'am, keep it to yourself." Auntie Maxine resumed her washing.

Lily blocked her father from her mind. Memories of the night she met Andrew lingered. She relived the moment. His sparkling eyes, ivory smile, and ruddy face vivid in her mind; his touch stirred her soul. She longed for him. Her body tingled and her tortured heart ached. Would she see him again? Her moist eyes gazed into space. Auntie Maxine snapped her fingers in her face.

"Lily, wake up, looks like your mind is thousands of miles away. I hear that the GCE A level results are out. Are you going to collect them?"

"Yes, I'll be going to check them in a little while, as soon as the school's office is open."

"So what's your plan?"

"I am going to study medicine."

"Lily, be realistic. How can poor little you study medicine?"

"What do you mean?"

"Do you have any idea how much that is going to cost?"

"I will find a way."

"What way, sell your body?"

"With all due respect, please don't insult me, Auntie Maxine. God will provide."

"Dream on." Auntie Maxine guffawed. "You better go look for a job and help me. I sacrificed to get you this far, you need to help me now."

"And I am very grateful, Auntie, but nothing will stop me from getting what I want. If it means I have to grow wings, I will."

"Well, grow wings then."

Auntie Maxine handed her a pan of nappies. "Finish these, I'm going to make some porridge, want some?" she looked back at Lily as she walked off.

"No thank you." Lily gagged.

"Suit yourself." Auntie Maxine waved her off.

She hung the last nappy on the line, ate a slice of dry bread and headed out.

Lily walked up the alley, drink boxes and Styrofoam lunch containers littered the ground. Men sat leisurely, pressing their palms on steps of dilapidated houses, kids running around in the yard. Dominos slapping tables, a police siren, mongrels barking, a rastaman beat a bongo drum, a joint in the corner of his mouth, a boom box blasted reggae music; a hopeful dirge rang out, 'Better Must Come' a cacophony of noise formed the backdrop of her thoughts. She had a queasy feeling.

Suppose I fail, suppose this is my destiny, the humdrum of Zinc Fence City, never! I shape my own destiny.

She held her head up and hastened her steps. At school, the secretary handed her two envelopes. She didn't open them, just headed home.

She leaned against the zinc fence, opened one letter then the other, disappointment in one hand and success in the other, mixed feelings, jubilation and despair. Her hands shook as she placed the contents of the envelopes back in place. She walked down the alley. Shackles on her heart, uncertainty placed her future in limbo. Her hands and her legs tingled, and her stomach churned. Maybe she should take Auntie Maxine's advice, go get a job. Her mind went blank to the surrounding sounds. She pushed her gate open.

"So, what's the verdict?" Auntie Maxine cocked her head.

Lily didn't answer. She walked past her, headed for the house. Despondent, she hid the envelopes under her mattress. There seemed to be no way out of that hell hole. If only her father had filed for her. She sat on the bed by the window, a vacant stare; she pressed her lips together and wrung her hands. So far she had managed to escape initiation, being away on holidays in Canada. She refused to allow any such violation. She'd rather go back to the country and live with Granny and Gramps, Auntie Maxine couldn't stop her anymore. She had reached the age of consent. She could make her own decisions. Her mind went a hundred miles a minute.

A loud knock on the gate startled her.

"Yow! Maxine, it's me, Squiggy."

Lily's heart jumped. She hid under the bed. The gate squeaked open.

"What's up, Mummy, long time no see. How's the fam?"

"We're okay, Don."

"I'm just in the neighborhood and decided to check on you, to see how the beds feel." He chortled.

"The beds feel great, Don, I really appreciate them and contrary to what other persons say, I feel quite at home and safe in the garrison. Thanks to you, Don, for making it such a safe place."

"Yeah man, no problem. That's how I intend to keep it. We have things under control around here. Where's that lovely lady?" he knocked on the door.

Lily's heart thumped hard against the floor, she swallowed hard and hyperventilated.

"Lily! Lily! Don Squiggly wants to see you." Auntie Maxine opened the door.

Chapter 45

Ghetto/September 1973

Without a father, her world had no sky, with a mother like Auntie Maxine, her earth molten and slippery kept falling away from beneath her. Lily held her breath; she heard the blood pulsing at her temples. She didn't want to see Don Squiggly. God did not bring her this far to be another of the Don's concubine. God forbid.

Hiding under the bed proved futile in a one room house.

"Lily come out from under the bed, and let me see the exam results."

Lily lay on the side of her functioning ear, everything muffled. She didn't budge.

"Lily, did you hear me?" Aunt Maxine peeped under the bed. "You're hiding like an ostrich, burying your head in the sand with its tail in the air." She guffawed. "Come on out, I'm sure it's not as bad as you're making it look. The Don is asking for you."

"You don't get it do you, Aunt Maxine, I don't want to see him. Go away! Leave me alone!"

"What! Who are you talking to like that? Come out now before I have to drag you out!" she stretched out her hand and pulled Lily. Lily resisted. "You're going to hurt the Don's feelings."

"Feelings? Why should I care about his feelings, what's he to me?" Lily spat.

"He doesn't mean anything bad, he's just being sociable." Auntie Maxine tugged at Lily again.

Lily sucked air through her teeth and turned her back to Auntie Maxine. Auntie Maxine jabbed her with a broomstick. Lily relented.

"Give me the results." Auntie Maxine insisted.

"Why do you care? You're only interested in me going to look a job." Lily responded.

"You're an ungrateful little bitch. If I didn't put my foot down you wouldn't reach this far." Auntie Maxine acted as though it were all her doing.

Lily took the letters from the mattress.

Auntie Maxine grabbed them from Lily. Her tone changed. "But Lily, you did well, man. You got all your 'A' levels with distinction." A broad grin pulled her face upwards. "So why are you behaving like it's the end of the world? Don Squiggly, Don Squiggly!" Auntie Maxine ran out of the room with the results.

"What's going on, Mummy?" Don Squiggly grunted.

"My girl got pure distinctions, look, see that? Now she can go get a job." She squeaked.

Lily stood behind the outdoor curtain and listened.

"Wow, I didn't know she was that good. Man this is the first time for the garrison. But didn't she say she wants to be a doctor? That's another first for the garrison. Let her do her medicine. Let her do it, Mummy, don't stop her. Hmm, 'Doctor Lily Mc Dermott.' Hmm, that sounds pretty eh."

"Sounds pretty yes, but, she has to go find a job. I've done enough. And I have the others to push through school. She has a responsibility to help me with the others now."

"No Mummy, don't stifle the girl's ambition. Let her do what she wants to do."

"Don, she would have to win the lottery to afford medical school. There's no way I can afford that. We shouldn't hang our hats higher than we can reach it. That's not for us poor people."

"Shame on you, Mummy, when you have the ability, nothing can stop you. "

Lily couldn't believe her ears.

"Lovely lady, may I have a word with you?" the Don's voice softened.

Lily smoothed her hair and her dress and stepped outside.

"Congratulations, lovely lady, you did yourself and this neighborhood proud. We've never seen anything like this in these here parts. I'm really proud of you." He opened his arms to embrace. Lily stepped back, but held out her hand.

They shook hands.

"Thank you." Her eyes narrowed.

"So now you can be the doctor you want to be." His toothless grin widened.

"Don Squiggly don't pack up her head with nonsense." Auntie Maxine scowled.

Lily felt shifting sands beneath her world. The other envelope she didn't share, the harbinger of bad news not yet revealed. Maybe she should acquiesce, go get a job at a government office. She didn't get the scholarship she'd applied for, her only hope dashed, she hung her head and her eyes moistened.

"But it's true, she can do it." Don Squiggly made eye contact with Lily, Lily looked away.

"How Don Squiggly, how?" Auntie Maxine asked.

"Let me think about It." he scratched his goatee.

Think about it, really? I don't want anything from this immoral criminal. What's he going to think about, initiation? Ravaging my body? Never!

Lily frowned. Her blood boiled as Auntie Maxine continued to allow him to play benefactor and father. She hated them. She'd rather fall prey to bears and tigers and wolves than to fall into the hand of an area Don. She retreated to the house.

Don Squiggly left.

Aunt Maxine chastised her for giving the Don the cold shoulder.

"Imagine the man was just trying to make much of you and all you could do is just show him bad face and then walked off. Is that how I grow you, without manners? He's a big man and he holds a very influential position in this community."

"Yes, Auntie, he is a big man and he must leave young girls alone to thrive." Lily snapped.

"I have not heard that man rude to you once. He always has glowing things to say about you." Aunt Maxine pushed Lily's head with her palm. Lily rolled her eyes, and gritted her teeth.

A truck drove up to the gate, and a loud knock startled them.

"Who's there?" Auntie Maxine inquired.

"The Don sent the sound system for the bashment." The driver announced.

"Bashment?" both Lily and Auntie Maxine chorused.

"Yes, ma'am, the dance." The man grinned.

The driver and his side men unloaded the contents of the truck.

Women with pans of mutton, and chicken and rice turned up, setting up coal stoves.

People entered the yard dressed up for a banquet. The music blasted. Lily hid in the room, she covered her ears and shut her eyes and sighed.

Maybe I should step outside and accept my fate, at times it can be cruel, but who knows maybe it will spare me some kindness.

She checked the mirror, wiped away tear stains, straightened her dress and stepped out.

A loud uproar greeted her.

Chapter 46

'Bashment'-At home in the ghetto/that night

Lily frowned at the skimpily dressed young girls who surrounded Don Squiggly, rubbing his cheeks; they kissed his pound of lips, massaged his shoulders, and giggled falling over him. He gloated. The music blared. A couple of young girls belly danced before him. He got up from a makeshift bamboo bench and started winding his large gut on one of the girls. The crowd egged them on, loud laughter and reveling ruled the twilight. Liquor poured and rum ran like a river. The smell of ganja and jerked chicken intermingled. The merrymaking thundered and rocked the yard in its lascivious festivity.

Lily sat in the shadows, folded her arms and remained detached, all the while rolling her eyes and pouting.

Auntie Maxine found her and sat down. She clasped Lily's hand in hers, but Lily pulled away.

"I can't believe you're allowing this to happen."

"This what?" Auntie Maxine acted clueless.

"The initiation party." Lily opened her hands. "You realize that, don't you?"

"Don't worry yourself, don't you need money to go to university. You don't have to sleep with him. We'll find a way to outsmart him. He's an idiot." Auntie Maxine smirked.

"We? You alone. I don't want anything from that criminal." If she could find a wishbone, she would wish Auntie Maxine dead, just the way she used to when she had to leave Bellevue.

An engine roared down the alley, Lily peeped through one of the gunshot holes in the zinc fence. A white limousine stopped at her gate. Two men dressed like bodyguards with long guns disembarked.

"Don Squiggly, the limo is here." someone announced.

"Good, but I'm not ready to leave yet, the party is just heating up and the girls aren't ready. We have to warm up first." He rubbed his palm together.

"But sir, you can't stay here too late, remember you have another movement to make." One of the bodyguards reminded him.

"No problem man, when I get to that bridge, I'll cross it. Right now, what's happening here is a special moment." He raised his hand to the Deejay and the music stopped.

Don Squiggly took center-stage. "Ladies and gentlemen welcome to tonight's celebration of our star and her home-coming party." He turned around to find Lily.

Lily melted into the darkness.

"Heh, where is she? Lily, please come forward."

Lily backed away into a corner and willed the earth to open. She wanted to run away, but her legs grounded her. A spotlight inundated her. She covered her eyes, the bright light blinded her.

"Come forward, don't be shy, tonight is your night." He walked towards her and led her to face the eager crowd. Lily stiffened as he placed his arms around her shoulder.

"Lily, Lily." the crowd shouted

"Lily of the Valley." Auntie Maxine gave away her Plum Valley nickname.

"Lily of the Valley, Lily of the Valley." the crowd caught on.

Lily froze. Auntie Maxine rushed over and nudged her.

"What's wrong with you, Lily? Move, walk with the Don." She pushed Lily forward.

"Leave me alone!" Lily snapped.

"Ungrateful, everyone here is being so supportive of you and you're behaving so snobbish. Don't embarrass me, child. Move before I take shame out of my eye on you." She raised her hand to hit Lily.

"Don't bother with that, Mummy, she's just shy." Don Squiggly stood between them.

"But she needs to show more appreciation, man." Auntie Maxine countered.

'It's alright, she'll soon get used to it." he tried to embrace Lily. Lily shrugged. He stepped back and scrutinized her.

"You see what I'm talking about, Squiggy? The girl has attitude." Auntie Maxine apologized.

"I love that; she has spunk. I love a girl with spunk." He chortled.

Lily sucked air through her teeth and pulled away.

"Let's drink a toast to her spunk."

The crowd's heightened anticipation peaked, they applauded and wolf-whistled. They raised their glasses.

"To her spunk!" they shouted. "Lily, Lily, Lily of the Valley, spunk, spunk, spunk!"

Lily looked up to the sky, shook her head, sighed and pouted. Her frost permeated the atmosphere.

"Why is she behaving like that?" one of the girls making a fuss of Don Squiggly pointed at Lily. "She thinks she's better than us."

"Leave her." Don Squiggly scolded the girl and continued.

"Ladies and gentlemen, this young lady has made our garrison proud. She has passed eight subjects in GCE with distinction and four A levels with distinction. This has never happened down here before. Let me hear a hurrah!"

"Hurray!" the crowd echoed.

Lily knew what would be coming next. She'd heard how the Don threw big parties for girls, then carried them away from their homes and ravaged them. She gathered her courage and moved towards the Deejay. She seized the moment. She took the microphone.

"I would like to take this opportunity to thank you all, but what I have done is no great feat. Anyone of you here tonight can achieve success. Young men, young women what I have done you can do. This is the kind of success story we want down here. If I can do it so can you."

The crowd applauded and some whistled.

"Poverty is not a crime. Let it motivate you. Don't allow yourselves to become slaves to a crime filled life, young women, don't allow anyone to use your bodies as a business. Education is freedom, its enlightenment, its independence. Don't depend on a Don to give you handouts, emancipate yourself. Let poverty inspire you."

Pin drop silence, everyone's mouth gaped and eyes bulged, looked from Lily to Don Squiggly and his cronies.

"I know you're also anticipating my initiation, as is the culture here, but that is not going to happen. I'm going to go to my little room with my womanhood intact.

Nobody is going to touch me. I may not have a gun, but I have ambition, ambition is my weapon."

"Lily, Lily, shut up; give the microphone back to the Deejay." Auntie Maxine ran up to her and tried to pull it from her hand.

Lily's nervous grip tightened. She looked in the direction of Don Squiggly.

He held up his palm to stop Auntie Maxine. "Leave her, let her express herself, I've never seen a young woman so brave. Let her talk."

"I implore you all to arm yourselves with ambition. Let it be your charge. We can win this war. Let's stand up for something." The deafening silence unnerved her, but she continued. She awaited a bullet to her chest. Her knees wobbled, and the microphone shook in her clammy palms. "So, I'm advising you to pack up and take your leave from my yard, as I had a rough day and wish to go to my bed in peace." The ominous silence laced the atmosphere.

One lone clap broke the silence.

"Bravo, bravo!" Don Squiggly cut through the silence. "Bravo!"

The applause trickled in, until it rose to a crescendo.

The Don signaled for his entourage and exited the yard without a word. He entered his limousine. A few young girls tried to leave with him.

"Did you hear what the young lady had to say? Get a life, get out of my car, get ambition." The car backed out of the alley. The crowd dissipated.

Lily cocked her head, pushed out her chest and strolled towards her house.

"You little idiot, the Don was going to give you money to do your medical course." Auntie Maxine walked up to Lily, glared at her, talked through clenched teeth, pushed past her and slammed the door in her face. Lily took refuge for the night on one of the bamboo benches.

Chapter 47

At home-ghetto/day after 'bashment' party

Lily awoke to the Zinc Fence city morning sounds and the clanging of pots and pans. Her hair and clothing damp from overnight dew. She sniffled and shivered, she wrapped her arms around herself for warmth. She recalled the night's event and the reason she'd slept on the bench. She'd rather sleep under a tree than to be violated. Her self esteem intact, she yawned, sat up, stretched, leaned back on the bench and smiled with satisfaction. She must contemplate her next move.

Auntie Maxine worked in silence by the fireside, not glancing at Lily. Lily assumed she still carried a grudge against her action the night before.

"Good morning, Auntie Maxine." She walked over to Auntie Maxine.

"What's good about it? You embarrassed the Don. The poor man left with his tail between his legs. You don't even know how to be diplomatic. That's not how wars are won. You have to take your time while you pull your hand out of lion's mouth, heh. Now I have to walk and hang my head. Just know that we don't have twenty-four hours protection in and out of the garrison anymore."

"So you'd rather allow your child to be sexually abused."

"But I told you that wasn't going to happen. All we would do is bargain with him to give us the money before he gets to touch you and then we disappear. We could try to migrate and you do your course abroad."

"Nothing is free, Auntie, not even air. Payback could cost us our lives. You know how the system works."

"Well, you've made your choice; you'll just have to pay the price. There's no hope of you being a doctor. You can kiss that goodbye."

"I will still be a doctor without selling my body." Lily's hands akimbo, her tone wooden.

"Sure." Auntie Maxine shook her head.

A loud knock on the gate startled them.

"Good morning, Miss Maxine, the Don sent this for Miss Lily." a little boy handed Auntie Maxine a package. Auntie Maxine handed it to Lily.

"Open it."

"Wait, little boy." Lily held on to his shoulder to stall him. "Have a seat right here, did you have tea?"

"No, Miss Lily."

"Let me fix you some breakfast."

"Lily you need to open the package at once."

"It can wait. This child is hungry, look at him; his ribs are showing and his collar bone sunken."

The shirtless boy hung his head and dug his toes in the dirt.

Auntie Maxine grabbed the package from Lily and opened it, then closed it, her eyes bulged.

"OMG! It's not true. No, this cannot be true." Auntie Maxine's hand shook. She fainted.

Lily ran into the house for smelling salts, passed it under Auntie Maxine's nose.

She revived Auntie Maxine. Lily led her into the house and helped her into bed.

"Bring the bag of money to me, Lily."

"It's alright Auntie, you rest. I'll take care of the money."

"What are you going to do with it? It's a lot of money you know; the note in the bag said its two million dollars. Two million dollars, can you believe it?" she started fanning herself, "we need to open a bank account."

"Just relax for now, I can handle it." She held Auntie Maxine's hand, made eye contact and smiled.

"Just be careful with it, it's a lot of money. Write a thank you note to Don Squiggly and apologize for your behavior last night."

"It's okay, Auntie Maxine, I can manage."

Lily fixed the boy something to eat. She stared at the package; picked it up, put it down again. She picked it up once more. She opened the package. The bundles of dollar bills stacked in packets and held together by rubber bands threatened her treacherous heart.

Maybe I should do what Auntie Maxine says, take it and disappear.

Otherwise, she couldn't afford to go to medical school. She didn't get the scholarship. Everything was just a dream. If she took the money, it's a dream come true. Maybe she could repay the Don once she'd completed her course. She could see it as a loan. Yeah. That's what she'd do. It was a loan; she didn't have to feel guilty about a loan. And when she became a doctor, society would benefit. Yeah, that sounded like a good plan.

While the boy ate, she wrote the note to the Don. She walked the package towards the house.

Lily, what the heck are you doing? Are you going to accept blood money? Do you even know where this man got all this money? Do you know how many lives paid for this? Are you mad? Don't be desperate. There are consequences for every choice we make. Could you live with yourself?

Lily's conscience judged her. Her hands shook; she froze in her tracks, blinked, shook her head and turned around.

She wrote another note. "I'm going to ask you to take this to the Don, be careful with it. Please make sure you give him my note. Thanks." She handed him the package.

"Okay, Miss." The boy left. She sat on the bench.

"Lily, bring the package and let's count up our money, love. We're rich. Two million dollars." Auntie Maxine laughed.

Lily didn't respond. Instead, she sat on the bench; her conscience took sides with her innocent heart. She closed her eyes and sighed.

"Lily? Did you hear me? Bring that bag of money now." Auntie Maxine stood in the doorway. "Lily, where's the bag of money?" Her eyes roved around the yard. "Where is it? Did you hide it? Better to bring it inside and hide it under the bed till tomorrow. We can take it to the bank."

Lily kept her arms folded against her chest.

"Lily, answer me, where is it?"

"I sent it back."

"You what? You must be out of your mind. We need that money, and you're insulting the Don. Now you're making enemies with a powerful man. You are a fool, an educated fool!"

"He'll understand. I wrote a very nice note to him."

"Understand? What are you talking about? We need the money. I didn't tell you this before, but I found a lump in my breast and I'm awaiting the result of the biopsy. I need that money, Lily. I need that money to pay for my treatment. What's wrong with you child?" Auntie Maxine covered her face in her hands and sobbed, her body shook.

Lily walked over to her and put her arms around her. "I'm so sorry to hear that, Auntie Maxine; God won't punish us for doing the right thing. He'll help us through this."

Auntie Maxine shrugged her off.

A loud knock on the gate jolted them.

"Come in." Lily walked towards the gate gingerly. The postman gave her a telegram.

Chapter 48

At home in the Ghetto/same day

Lily signed for the telegram, scorned it with her finger-tips like the plague. It bore her name. Recipient: Lily McDermott.

"Open it, Lily." Auntie Maxine urged.

Lily refused. "I can't open it Auntie. Maybe it's bad news."

"Give it to me, silly! What do you expect? Telegram is always bad news, so don't prolong the agony. Open it and face whatever it is. Gimme that." Auntie Maxine took the telegram and read it. A sad smile softened her eyes, her brows pulled together; she made direct eye contact with Lily.

"What is it, Auntie?" Lily grimaced.

"It's Granny." Auntie Maxine walked towards her and hugged her.

"What about Granny?" Lily took the telegram from Auntie Maxine. She scanned the words, her eyes blurred, her knees wobbled, she swayed and her stomach tightened.

"No, no, no! Granny no!" Lily stooped in the middle of the yard and groaned. She ran to the house lay across the bed and hollered. The unthinkable, the unbearable, her worst nightmare materialized. Granny had died. The world as she knew it ended.

The backbone of the family had been broken. Her strong tower had fallen. Granny, had mobilized and stabilized the McDermott family, her indomitable spirit had propelled the family forward, kept them together and nurtured them. When that force leaves, what remains? Lily's throat tightened, she swallowed hard and sobbed.

Gramps? Oh no, poor old gramps. Without Granny he's only half a man. I must go see to Gramps, make sure he stands. Hold his hand and make his tea. Granny always had his tea ready before he woke up. Gramps needs me now.

What about Aunt Liza and her daddy? She didn't know him anymore. He'd abandoned her. The kinship between them had been broken. She couldn't feel him anymore. He remained distant in her mind. She couldn't believe it. Her heart splintered and the tears flowed. A fog gathered in her head.

Auntie Maxine sat beside her on the bed and comforted her. She stroked her hair.

"It's alright, Lily, it's okay to cry. No one is handing out an award for bravery. Cry till you feel better."

"Auntie Maxine, I can't bear it, I think I'm going to die. I always said if Granny died, I'm going to die with her.

Why did she have to die? Why, why, why?" she wept inconsolably.

Auntie Maxine made her some ginger tea. "Come, sit up and drink this. It'll make you feel better."

She sat on the bed and rested her head on Auntie Maxine's shoulder, her tears pooled on Auntie Maxine's dress.

"Come on, drink it." Auntie Maxine patted her back.

Lily sipped through her tears, her grief overwhelming. "I can't swallow, Auntie Maxine."

"Never mind, just try."

"Well, at least I don't have to be a doctor anymore. Granny won't need my services anymore." A renewed flush of tears fell.

Auntie Maxine wiped her tears.

"You'll get over this. You're a strong girl. Granny wouldn't want you to give up on your dream. You go on to be the finest doctor you can ever be."

"It's over, Auntie; it's over."

"Over? What do you mean it's over? You're young and talented and bright. It's not over, it has just begun."

For the first time since Eisteddfod, Lily felt Auntie Maxine's spirit. She savored the moment. She hugged Auntie Maxine and Auntie Maxine didn't push her away.

A car stopped at the gate, then a gentle knock.

"Hello. Anybody home?" a knock again.

"Who is it?" Auntie Maxine pushed her head through the door.

"Liza."

"Liza who?"

"Maxine, it's Liza McDermott, Lily's aunt."

"Liza McDermott?"

"None other than. May I come in?"

"Aunt Liza!" Lily pushed past Auntie Maxine. "Aunt Liza, please come in." Lily opened the gate. Aunt Liza paid the taxi driver and collected her luggage.

Aunt Liza entered the yard past the tin scrapped fencing. Lily led her into the house.

"Oh my God! What kind of place is this you have the child living in, Maxine? I had a hard time finding this place; it doesn't even exist on a map."

"Liza, don't bother to come here with your hoity toity self, you're nothing but a little country bumpkin. Fancy you coming here and looking down on me. The nerve of you." Auntie Maxine stood her ground.

"I've never lived like this, in a ghetto at that. Lily isn't used to this kind of life—my, my, my." Her head swiveled around the yard, the corners of her mouth turned downward. "With your level of intelligence and potential, it should never have come to this, Maxine."

Auntie Maxine stepped towards Auntie Liza, her fist doubled.

Lily stepped between them.

Auntie Maxine gave Aunt Liza an icy stare.

"It's okay, you two, there's no need to greet each other with hostility. Aunt Liza, I am so glad to see you." She embraced Aunt Liza.

Aunt Liza kissed her. "Aw child, I missed you so much, you have no idea. Seems like you've grown taller and you've filled out even more than when you visited us in Canada." She spun Lily around. They laughed.

"How's daddy? Is he coming to see Gr—?" Lily faltered, she choked up, her chin trembled.

Aunt Liza let out a deep sigh and her eyes filled with water. "He sends his love, but he's not sure if he'll make it to the funeral."

"But he must, she's his mother." Lily's brow furrowed.

"He's going through a rough patch in his life."

"That's no excuse and no excuse for neglecting me. You all spoil that man, you and Granny."

"That's the one thing I have to agree with you on, Lily. Spoilt rotten." Auntie Maxine interjected, her arms folded.

Aunt Liza ignored Auntie Maxine.

"Lily, I'm going up to Bellevue to check on Gramps and make funeral arrangements, would you like to come with me?"

"I need to come with you, Auntie." She turned to Auntie Maxine. "Is it alright if I leave with Aunt Liza?"

"Sure, it's important that you go for closure."

"Thanks, Auntie Maxine." She smiled and hugged Auntie Maxine.

Chapter 49

Kingston ghetto/October 1973

The executor of to the will read Granny's wishes. Granny had left a million dollars for her. The will had specified that, the money should be used to help Lily fulfill her dream of being a medical doctor.

So Granny had remembered; she had a big heart.

Lily reeled from the loss. Everything reminded her of Granny, triggering more tears, the cool mornings, the warm evenings, the smell of hot chocolate spiced up with cinnamon, nutmeg, and vanilla. Granny made the best hot chocolate from her cocoa beans. The same cocoa beans she'd sold to amass her wealth. The smell of eucalyptus oil brought back memories. Granny used to put the oil on Lily's pillow when she had a cold, or when she couldn't sleep, the smell of tiger balm, granny used to rub her arthritic joints'

After the funeral, Auntie Liza drove her back and not all the Eucalyptus in the world could relieve the pain in her heart.

Aunt Liza says that time will heal the wound. She says we must never forget our dead loved ones, when we talk about them we keep them alive in our hearts and the pain dulls with happy memories of them.

Lily lay across her bed and allowed the tears to flow. She didn't look at granny in the coffin, she wanted to remember her alive. She gathered her strength and sat up, walked to the mirror and saw red puffy eyes and heard Granny whisper in her heart, '*Lily, move on. Dry up your tears and go work on your goal. Make me proud.*' Lily washed her face and renewed her focus.

Someone pushed the gate open. Lily moved the material aside and saw it was Margaret and her father. Lily bounced off the bed and greeted him, then sprang to embrace Margaret. "Margaret, Is that you?"

"Lily!"

"Margaret!"

"Look at you, you're all grown up, Lily of the Valley!" they squealed with delight to see each other.

"You too, I would've passed you on the street without recognizing you. How are you?" Lily pushed her out and scrutinized her from head to toe. "Foreign life agrees with you, my girl. You look like a diva."

"Thank you. You're beautiful as usual.

Lily tilted her head. "Did Auntie Maxine expect you?"

"No it's a surprise. Actually, we're here to tell you something very important."

"We? We who?"

"Daddy and me. Is Auntie Maxine in? Where are the others?"

"They're at school; Auntie Maxine went to the doctor."

"What's wrong with her?"

"I think she might be having cancer in her breast."

"What? Oh my God! That's terrible, what stage is it at?"

"Dunno."

"You seem sad though, what's wrong?"

"Granny d...d..." Lily couldn't bear to say the word. She fought back tears.

"Your Granny died? Oh Lily, I'm so sorry to hear." She hugged Lily.

"My respects, Lily." Margaret's father offered condolences. "But, on a happy note I have something wonderful to tell you, which I hope will cheer you up."

Lily cocked her head and raised her eyebrows. "And what may that be, pray tell?" a quizzical smile tempted her lips.

"Can we sit here?" Margaret's father motioned to the bamboo bench.

"Okay, I'm all ears, it had better be good." She chuckled.

Cover my eyes and open my mouth. What could he possibly have to tell me that's so important?

He held Lily's hands and made eye contact. "Lily, I am your father." Lily pulled her hands away, quiet tears rolled down her cheeks.

She held her head down and placed one palm over her forehead. "Why should I believe you and why am I just knowing this? This is preposterous!" she stood from the bench and walked away, "You need to tell me how that works. After nearly nineteen years, when you have pleased yourself, you're now going to come into my yard and tell me you are my father, and turn my world topsy-turvy because for some reason, it's now convenient for you."

"Lily, let me explain." Margaret's father moved towards her.

She stepped back. "You've got a whole lot of explaining to do," she exaggerated the word, "Daddy! So start telling me" Lily folded her arms.

"It's like this," He hung his head. "Your mother decided to give you to another man because she was upset with me."

"Why was she upset with you?" Lily narrowed her eyes and sat back on the bench.

"You see, I'd just got a scholarship to study in the U.S. I couldn't give up that offer."

"So you gave me up, instead?" Lily had had enough.

"No, Lily, it's not like that." Rupert waved his hand.

"Look, I don't want to hear anymore of your bull. Please leave." Lily stood and walked to the gate.

"No, Lily, please listen." This man who claimed to be her father pleaded.

"So you can purge your conscience? Just leave before I do something I regret, or worse, that Auntie Maxine comes and finds you here. You know my mother will stone you. Get out!"

"Lily, at least let him tell you what really happened. You need to know your true roots for posterity." Margaret stood between them.

Lily sighed. "Alright, continue."

"So, she told me she was pregnant, and since we had already had Margaret, she wanted us to get married right away, because her mother had threatened her that if she got pregnant again, she would kill her."

"She should have. So why didn't you marry her?"

"I was planning to marry her, but she cursed me and threatened to give you to another man."

"But the question is did you let her know of your plans to marry her?" Lily cocked her head.

"Well, I couldn't get around to telling her. She stormed out of the house, and I didn't see her again before I left for the U.S."

Lily clapped her hands in slow motion. "Bravo, bravo. Nice story. Are you done? 'Because I'm done, I don't know what you expect me to do with this information now, am I to warm to you, cuddle up with you and call you Daddy, heh? Is that what you expect?"

"Nothing like that, I expect that you're going to be upset."

"Upset? Is that what you call it? Right now I can't even find words to find to tell you how I feel. You're telling me this now and it disrupts my whole sense of being. Who the hell am I then? Tell me, who am I? Lily McDermott or Lily Edwards, or just Lily of the Valley? Tell me, tell me!" Lily moved towards him and wagged a finger at him. "You made a complete stranger accept me as his child. Not that he did anything about it. But his family, my family would have sold their soul for me. They nurtured me, cared for me, loved me, and owned me. And now you're asking me to give up all of that love. Do you have any idea how you're hurting me right now?"

Footsteps approached the gate. Auntie Maxine entered the yard. She made eye contact with Lily, then Margaret, then Mr. Edwards.

Chapter 50

Ghetto/A few moments later

Didn't she feel her heart burning, and didn't she feel kinship with this man the time she ran away to his house. That longing that stirred inside her when around him flooded back. She didn't understand it then, but maybe it all made sense. Could it really be true? Was he really her father? What reason did he have to lie, but why now? Auntie Maxine needs to fess up.

Lily glared at Auntie Maxine. "Is this true, Auntie Maxine?"

"If what is true? What is Rupert packing up your head with?" Auntie Maxine stiffened.

"He says he…"Lily faltered.

"He says what? What did you say to her Rupert?"

"Maxine, we're all adults here and she needs to know who she really is. You know I am her real father."

"Rupert Edwards, you're a complete idiot."

"What do you mean?"

"Rupert, you're not her father, Winston McDermott is her father."

"What are you trying to say, you cheated on me?

"I only told you I was pregnant, because I wanted you to marry me. You're a bigger fool than I thought. With all your big university degrees, you're still an idiot."

"No, Winston McDermott is the idiot. Lily was not a premature baby as you fooled him and his family into believing. When you left me you were two months pregnant. I know when a woman is pregnant. Rumor had it that you banned down the belly. I can't believe the McDermott boy bought into that."

Auntie Maxine glanced around and picked up a broken chair and aimed it at Rupert. "You know what is good? Get out of my yard before I use this chair to clobber you. Get out!"

Margaret ran between them.

"Noooo, please don't! You'll get into trouble."

"Trouble, what trouble, he's the one to get into trouble, coming into my yard to slander me, to ruin my reputation, to make me look bad. It's self defense. You better move yourself, because I don't know why you bring this man here to aggravate my spirit. You all trying to make me out to be a deceiver. Both of you get out of my yard now!"

"Nobody is going anywhere. Auntie Maxine, you need to tell me right now, who is my father? I need to know right now." Lily snapped, raised a finger and pointed her blame on her mother, her lips drawn together.

"You are…" Auntie Maxine glanced from one person to the next.

"Who am I?"Lily demanded.

"You know what? I don't have to put up with this shit!" Auntie Maxine walked off, entered the house and slammed the door.

Lily walked to the house and pried the door handle; Auntie Maxine had locked it. Lily banged the door.

"Open the door. Why are you hiding, are you running away from the truth?"

"Lily McDermott, don't let me come out there and sort you out. You know I don't joke. If you bang on the door one more time, I will take away the life I gave you!"

"So you're going to be a murderer now too?" Lily shouted through the keyhole. "Maybe, you're not even my mother, all this time I've been forbidden to call you mother, Mommy. Maybe you should have buried me alive. You all strip me of my birthright."

"Lily, if you know what's good for you, you wouldn't provoke me. Don't take sides with that evil man. Since he says he's your father, where was he all this time? Why didn't he take ownership when I had to struggle with you by myself? Think about that. He's only coming forward now because you passed the worst and he doesn't need to take care of you anymore. Let Rupert Edwards go to hell. If he's not gone soon, I'll know what to do with him." Auntie Maxine shouted back through the keyhole.

Lily moved away from the door and shook her head.

"This is futile. Thank you, Mr. Edwards for coming today to turn my life upside down, thank you for taking away my identity, because now I don't know who I am. Please leave, while I still have my sanity intact."

"Lily, you could do a paternity test to prove who's telling the truth." Margaret hugged her.

Lily sighed and looked away. "What good would that do? Right now I feel like bovine excrement."

"You will know the truth, so you can get closure and move forward."

"Hmm." Lily blinked and sighed again. "You know what, you all better leave before that mad woman comes out and kills somebody."

They left.

Lily paced the yard with tears streaming down her face. Auntie Maxine opened the door and sat on the bench, her face wet.

Lily couldn't believe her eyes. Auntie Maxine showed emotion. She walked over to the bench and sat beside her.

Maybe she wanted to confess. Maybe she wanted to tell her the truth about her paternity.

"What's wrong?" Lily made eye contact.

"I'm dying."

"Dying, what do you mean you're dying?"

"I got back the biopsy result today."

"And?"

"It's positive, I have cancer."

"How bad is it?"

"Stage two."

"What does that mean?"

"It means if I don't get chemotherapy and radiation, I'm going to die."

"Oh my God! I'm so sorry" She hugged Auntie Maxine.

Auntie Maxine didn't push her off, but she didn't reciprocate.

"But the treatment is expensive. I don't have that kind of money. So I am going to die." She cried audibly.

"How much will it cost?" Lily rubbed her shoulder and comforted her. She rested her head on Lily's shoulder.

"Lots of money." Auntie Maxine sniffled.

"How much?"

"I'm not sure, but it's a lot." She blew her nose.

"And you don't have any health insurance." Lily pursed her lips.

"How would I have health insurance, I don't have any big government job." Auntie Maxine shrugged.

"So what are you going to do?"

"Well, I was wondering if I could use the money you inherited from Granny." A coy smile wafted across her face through her tears.

"What the hell? Granny earmarked that money for me to do medicine. First of all I couldn't betray Granny like that and…" Lily stopped and turned her head away, her eyes moistened.

"Lily, you have two fathers, let them pay for your medical degree. I have sacrificed everything to this point for you. Are you going to let your mother die?"

Lily got up from beside her, opened the gate and walked down the alley. Her senses dulled to the usual noises and the smells and the sights. She walked out to the main road and sat by the roadside watching the traffic go to and fro. She got the roaming spirit back. With Granny gone, where would she go? She didn't belong there anyway. She had no identity, she belonged nowhere; she resided in no-man's land. She fought back the tears.

Chapter 51

Ghetto/November 1973

The void in her soul widened. It threatened to consume her. The pain she felt, as sharp as her cry of anguish, burnt holes in her besieged heart. How could people be so cruel? Lily overheard Granny telling Aunt Liza once, that she had no one. Maybe this is what she meant. Did her parents really care about her? She winced and wrung her hands.

Her mother had an appointment at the hospital.

"What time is your appointment, Auntie Maxine?" Lily pulled on a pair of jeans and neatened her hair.

"It's at 9:30 this morning. Are you ready? You will have to pay for the therapy."

"I know."

"Well hurry then, you're dragging your feet as if you're going to my funeral, I'm not dead yet." Auntie Maxine smirked.

The countless times the wishbone broke in Lily's favor left her engulfed in guilt. As a little girl, she had wished many times that Auntie Maxine would die so she wouldn't have to go to live with her in Plum Valley. Her mother's terminal illness changed her feelings. She wanted to be there for her, to hold her hands and, be her shoulder to cry on. Her tangled emotions left her torn. A lone tear fell.

"Come, let's go." Auntie Maxine urged. "I'm really not looking forward to this, because I hear it makes you lose your hair and all."

"Don't worry about it; you need to nip this thing in the bud. I think that's what the doctors are trying to do. For now, it might be unpleasant, but the end result will be good. Your hair will grow back." She patted Auntie Maxine's hair.

"I hope so." Auntie Maxine sighed.

They journeyed to the hospital in silence. The doctor examined Auntie Maxine.

"Your treatment will leave you feeling weak, so you'll need a lot of rest."

"My daughter here will take care of me. Doctor, she's the best daughter I could ever have. You know she wants to be a doctor, but she sacrificed her money instead to get treatments for me."

"That's very noble of you, young lady. Did you apply to the University of the West Indies?" Dr. Burrell's ruddy face warmed into a smile of admiration.

"Yes, I was accepted, but I will only have enough for undergraduate school."

"Hmm. Well, if you actually finish there, and have done the work you need, you might be able to apply to medical school in Cuba, tuition is free there. I could give you the contacts if you make it through undergrad school."

"I'd be so grateful." Lily beamed. "Thank you so very much."

"Well, you don't need to thank me yet until you get through, young lady." He smiled. Lily's heart did a hop, skip, and jump. She could talk about nothing else on the way home. Lily balanced the good with the bad.

Half way down the alley the sound of gunshots followed them.

"Oh shit, what's that?" Auntie Maxine took Lily's hand.

"Gunshots." Lily whispered.

"It seems the garrison is under attack." Auntie Maxine eyes bulged. They quickened their steps and broke into a run, but the gunshots also came from the direction they headed. They froze.

"Take cover, ladies, take cover, come inside, we're under attack from a rival gang. They're attacking us from both ends of the garrison." A man pushed his head through his gate and shouted. He pulled them into his yard. Lily pulled away from him.

"Alright, you know what, you're on your own." the man let go of her and was about to shut his gate.

"No, wait, we'll come with you. What are they fighting over?" Lily asked.

"They're fighting over turf." The man's darting glances scanned the area.

"Turf?" Lily's eyes widened.

"Yes, they claim that the Don stole this piece of land from them and killed some of their men, so it's revenge and reclamation of turf."

"Oh no, that means our lives are nothing but pawns. I didn't know we were living on stolen property. We need to get out of here, Auntie Maxine." Lily closed her eyes and dreamt of the time when she could move out of this God forbidden place. Granny had always said where there's a will there's a way. But how, how would she achieve her goal in the belly of a ghetto, in the middle of a gang war?

Another barrage of gunshots exploded.

"Shush! Don't be silly, child; the Don won't let anything happen to us. He takes care of his people." Auntie Maxine shrugged.

"Auntie Maxine, you speak of this man as if he were God. He's only a man and not a very upright one at that. That's why I couldn't take a penny from him."

Everyone took cover as gunshots ricocheted on the zinc fences; the only shield around them. They hid under the bed. Lily trembled, sweat ran down her back. She pledged that if she came out of this alive, nothing would stop her from fulfilling her dream.

"Ladies, you need to come out from under the bed and listen to what I have to say. They're getting closer; it's each man for himself. I have a few guns. You will have to help yourselves." The man loaded the guns. Her stomach churned at the thought of having to use the gun to take a life. She hoped it never came to that. He gave each member of his family a gun. He left one lying on the table.

"It's okay, I don't need a gun. We won't need that. You can take it."

"You will need it for self-defense. Take it." he chucked the gun into Lily's hand. A dreadful foreboding came over her. She wrapped her finger around the trigger and hid behind the door with the others. Auntie Maxine hid under the bed with the children.

As terrifying sounds drew closer, Lily moved to a backroom. A gun battle ensued between their host and some gunmen. An explosion, the man screamed.

A gunman shot off the lock on the door and burst in.

"Get down on your knees and beg for mercy! All of you!"

Lily hid behind another door. One of the men ordered everyone hiding under the bed to get out.

The man and his two sons had been corralled in and everyone but Lily kneeled before the gunmen. Lily's knees wobbled and beads of sweat gathered on her forehead. Her hands tightened around the trigger. .

"All of you, little rats living off handouts from the Don. Where is he now? We got him by his balls." The man pistol whipped the father.

Her hands tightened around the trigger. She recalled her experience in Barbican.

It could happen anywhere. Evil follows me.

She had to make a decision,

Should I stay in the room and be a coward or go out and play brave?

Auntie Maxine's and innocent children's lives stood in the balance.

Lily said a silent prayer and stepped out.

"Don't move; drop your gun, hands in the air." Lily amazed herself. One of the men made a move and Lily fired a shot, hitting him in his arm. Lily didn't know what her next move would be. The man's sons stood and grabbed a gun. He stepped into Lily's path and started to take over.

"We're not killing anybody here today, that's an order." She pushed the man's son aside. "I will not have blood on my hands."

"What are you talking about, woman? We need to kill them before they kill us."

"That's an order. Tie something around your father's arm to stop the bleeding." Lily pointed the gun at him.

A police siren screamed in the distance. It grew louder as it entered the garrison. A gun battle between police and gunmen broke out.

A policeman entered the house.

"Nobody moves! Drop your guns." The policeman cocked his gun. Lily dropped hers.

Chapter 52

Palisadoes airport/Kingston/October 1974

"Hello, Dr. Burrell, this is Lily McDermott."

"Hello, Lily, so today is the big day, huh?"

"Yes, Dr. Burrell. I'm actually calling from the airport.

"I can just imagine how excited you are!"

"That's an understatement, Dr. Burrell. I have two requests."

"They are?"

"Take care of Maxine, and if I can penpal you while I'm here. I don't want to lose sight of my end goal."

Dr. Burrell laughed on the other end of the line. "Fair enough of the writing, and of course I will take care of Maxine. You just get through these years so you are prepared for the rigors of med school. Okay?"

"Okay." Lily felt at peace with his words. His voice soothed and felt so sure. "As you said, 'just start, you'll finish' so, I'm good. I just need to start; I'll get to the finish line."

"I'm sure I'll see you on the holidays."

"Dr. Burrell, when I grow up I want to be like you." They both laughed.

"One day you'll be Dr. McDermott, ah; it felt so good saying that. I know that you will set a good example for the youth in your community. You can be their role model."

"I hope so."

"Anyway, bon voyage; Keep me abreast of your progress."

"I certainly will, Dr Burrell. Thanks again."

Lily checked in and walked towards the waiting area.

"Lily?" a tall handsome man dressed in a pilot's uniform walked towards her.

"Huh? How do you know my name?" A sudden recollection left her stunned. "Andrew?"

"Same one." His eyes twinkled. "I thought I'd lost you forever. How have you been? You've grown into a more beautiful woman, more beautiful than I remembered, so mature yet so delicate, so delicate, yet so strong." The space between them narrowed.

Lily's knees wobbled. Her head giddy and her heart skipped.

"Andrew! Oh my God! Andrew. I can't believe my eyes. What are you doing here?"

He looked down on his uniform and gestured. "I...I work here, well I mean I stop here, inter-flights."

"Dumb of me, that's right, you're a pilot." Lily giggled.

"Why don't we have a bite? What time is your flight?" His deep baritone voice boomed.

Butterflies took off in Lily's stomach.

"W…well, I have two hours before takeoff." Lily's lips quivered, she flushed, her eyes flashing.

"I also have some time on my hand. So shall we?" his pupils dilated.

"I'd love to." Lily's broad grin gave away her enthusiasm.

They found a table close to the departure lounge.

Andrew took Lily's hand in his. Lily blushed, but didn't try to pull her hand away.

"So how have you been? Married?" he gazed into her eyes.

"Me? Married? Please, I've been busy fighting for my life. You? Are you married?" She smirked.

"Nope. I'm waiting for you." A gentle smile creased the corners of his eyes.

"Yeah right, and you didn't even remember me." She elbowed him.

"I haven't stopped thinking about you since that night. You have been the reason for every breath I take. You may think this is silly, but I decided to become a pilot, so I could find you, wherever in the world you were."

"All you had to do was to search Jamaica for me."

"I didn't believe that any place on earth could hold down a person like you. I knew you would be going places, which brings me to the question. Where are you heading?"

"I'm going to University of West Indies."

"Nice!"

"I'm eventually going to medical school."

"Really?"

"Well, after I get done in Trinidad and Tobago, I'm going to go to Cuba."

"Why Cuba? You could stay there. I hear they have a great medical school, or you could go anywhere else in the world; you'll be top of your class. You're bright, gifted, and talented, not to mention beautiful. You can study in the U.S., the U.K., or Canada. Yeah, why not Canada, your dad lives there?"

"It sounds simple, but it's really not that simple. It's complicated."

"How reputable is the Cuban University. Is it accredited?"

"I believe so, the person who recommended the University is a doctor. He studied there. But, let me get through undergraduate school first." She hesitated, "My mother was diagnosed with cancer."

"I'm sorry to hear that. How's she?"

"The cancer has gone into remission."

"That's great. Back to you though, what's the complication? You said it was complicated. You could just stay at the University of the West Indies. Why not?"

"It's a long story."

"I see. I can understand you don't want to tell me too much, after all, you don't really know me. But I'm going to make sure you get to know me, enough to trust me." He made eye contact and squeezed her hand.

"Oh no, it's not like that. It's, it's just that I wouldn't want to burden you with the humdrum of my life."

"Nothing about you is humdrum, my Lily, my beautiful Lily. You wear your name well."

"Thank you, but maybe if you knew my nickname you wouldn't think it's that beautiful."

"What's that, my sweet?"

"Lily of the Valley."

"That's beautiful, it fits you perfectly. Lily, I think that on that first night we met, you bewitched me. There was something magical about that night, the moonlight and your soft lips, your eyes, sparkled competing with the stars in the sky. Lily what have you done to my heart?" He held his chest, his gaze pierced into her soul. "Lily, you're the prettiest flower in the garden. How did you get that name?"

"It was my nickname at school. It actually means, sweet and poisonous at the same time."

"The sweet I can attest to, but the poison, I can't agree with."

"That's because you don't know how much evil follows me around."

"Then I want to be the good that conquers the evil that follows you. From now on you will never have to face evil alone. My love will follow you around."

They got lost in each other's eyes, distance and space became meaningless. They had found each other again.

"Ladies and gentlemen, flight C363 is boarding. Please take out your boarding passes and start boarding. Thank you."

"Andrew, I must go now before I miss my flight." her lips moved, but her feet froze.

"My love, why don't you change your plans and study in Canada instead?"

"I can't."

"Why not?"

"I couldn't afford the flights I need to take back home. I need to see Maxine as much as possible."

"I will help you."

"I couldn't let you do that."

"Please, Lily, I don't want to lose you again."

"You won't lose me. I promise I'll write. You may also visit me."

"Ladies and gentlemen, this is the final call for boarding of flight C363 to Trinidad and Tobago."

"I must go now."

Andrew bent over and kissed her. Lily felt the earth shift under her feet and her head swam, everything else melted into nothingness. They embraced and kissed again as if their lives depended on it. As they separated, Lily swayed; Andrew braced her up and walked to the airline with her. They kissed again and parted with moist eyes.

Chapter 53

The Drive home/1986

"Are you going to go through the college years too?" Alex stared straight ahead, kept his eyes on the road.

"Would you prefer I skip to the end?"

"Well, it's sort of gotten kind of duppy!"

Lily turned shocked eyes at Alex. "It is not. Oh, that's just not right to say."

He patted her knee. "I'm sorry, please carry on, but skip the undergrad part, I wasn't in much of that."

"Yeah, nobody really was." She turned to Alex, "Most of my correspondence with Andrew was by mail, and I didn't really understand relationships until I went to Cuba for medical school."

"Which, by the way, I suggested."

"Yeah, well that had some odd comings and goings, didn't it?"

"Yes it did, tell me about Maria, and the dean, and Andrew and me, and all of it!"

"But there was so much good stuff at the University of West Indies? You don't want to hear about that?"

"Don't forget I've kind of already heard it. Remember, you were pen palling me, and love letter writing Andrew. When you got to Cuba, you had to buckle down and I didn't hear that much from you."

"Things sure changed when I went there." Lily thought about the four years in med school, the good, the bad, the rigors of studying for her dream, a dream that lifted on the wings of taking care of Granny, something she never got the chance to do.

"So?"

"What?"

"Are you going to pick up at Cuba?"

"Okay, but one day we are going to back to the West Indies stories." She slapped his knee.

"Fair enough."

Chapter 54

Cuba/medical school/October 1978

Bunk beds lined up like sentinels. The deserted dormitory, antiseptic and sterile, greeted her with stark coldness. Lily shivered. She froze at the entrance, memories of her first time at Auntie Maxine's flashed before her. Her struggle to get away from Auntie Maxine ended, but the apprehension she felt as she entered the campus made her think she may have jumped into the fire.

She pivoted to retreat but remembered her reason for being there. She placed one foot in front of the other and marched like a soldier down the aisle, a name tag identified her bed, the lower bunk at the rear of the hall. It was nothing like the University of West Indies.

She packed away her things in the locker assigned to her and sat on the bed. A voice startled her. She turned and a beautiful young woman faced her.

"Soy Maria." The woman greeted her with a warm smile.

"Soy Lillian, but you may call me Lily." Lily answered in meager Spanish.

"Bienvenido." Maria stretched out her hand.

"Gracias." Lily shook her hand.

"Como estas."

"Bien, gracias y usted?" Lily nodded.

"Bien, gracias. Hablas Espanol?"

"Poco, poco."

"Then you're going to have a hard time here," Maria spoke with a strong Cuban accent. "You must learn to master the language in order to do well here."

"You're right; I'm pretty worried about that."

"Being fully immersed in the culture will help you. Don't worry, you'll learn. Are you a fast learner?"

"I think so"

"Well, you're good then."

"I hope so."

Maria seemed friendly enough.

"Come with me, let me take you to the mess hall, you're right on time for dinner."

"Thank you."

"I take it this is your first time here."

"Yes it is."

"Classes begin first thing in the morning."

"I know, I have my schedule, I'm looking forward to it."

"Let me warn you, it's no push-over."

"I didn't expect it to be."

Dr. Burrell had laid out the rigors of medical school to her. The school once functioned as a military base and still wore its stiff atmosphere and rigid regulations: no alcohol, no partying or reveling. She had nowhere to go, and she didn't drink or smoke. She had one intention. She planned to forgo frivolities.

Although male and female dorms separated the sexes, integration occurred, and the catcalling and harassment made Lily uncomfortable. Just the walk to the dining room proved challenging.

"Sexy, can you come to my room tonight?" A man walked up beside her and pinched her ass. A group of men looked on and laughed.

Lily flashed off his hand and glared. "I'm going to report you for sexual harassment!"

"Pay them no mind, they're scumbags." Maria consoled her and gave them her middle finger.

"I want a piece of that ass tonight, heh." Another howled and guffawed. The others joined in.

They stood in a group, intimidating and embarrassing them to pass. Lily held her head up and ignored them.

"Hey you, Jamaican girl, you think you nice? We gonna bring you down to earth here." They laughed.

Maria turned and said something in Spanish.

"What did you say to them?" Lily cocked her head.

"I reminded them that ragging is not allowed and if they continued, I'll report them and get their asses kicked out of the university."

"Thanks."

They answered her in Spanish. That too went over Lily's head. "What did they say?"

"You're really going to have to learn the language fast." Maria made eye contact.

"I know, right, already I feel like I'm drowning. What did they say though?" Lily lowered her head.

"They're calling me a lesbian." Maria shrugged.

"They're calling out sour grapes. Are you a lesbian?" Lily raised her eyebrows.

"Yeah." Maria pursed her lips.

"Oh."

"Do you have a problem with that?"

"Me? What you do in your private life is no concern of mine."

"They can't help themselves; we have a very machismo culture here." Maria continued.

"Isn't that just how men are everywhere?"

"More so here; I believe it trickled down from the head of the stream. Rumor has it that our premiere Fidel has a track record of sleeping with thirty five thousand women."

"Thirty-five thousand women! Really? I'm sure, that story is embellished. No man can sleep with that many women." Lily laughed.

"Even so, it seems to have had an influence on the mentality of the male population. Do you know what we call him?"

"No, what?" Lily wrinkled her nose.

"Mujeriego."

"Mujeriego? What's that?"

"Womanizer."

"Oh." Lily snickered.

"That's not even funny. Some men treat women like ephemeral objects."

"I know. That angers me. We need to be treated with respect." Lily had always stood up for herself around boys.

"Absolutely."

Lily and Maria made it to the mess hall and entered to the clink of silverware and trays, plates and glasses.

Lily gagged at the bland food. She saw nothing appetizing on the menu. She had to gather courage to eat the food or die of hunger. She chose the former.

Maria had warned her of the minimalistic lifestyle in Cuba, and by extension, the difficulties of living on campus.

The U.S embargo made it difficult for Cubans and they'd had to endure it all their lives. No stranger to dire circumstances herself; Lily didn't see hardships as a deterrent. Granny would have said it'll put hair on your chest. Her life experience made her resilient, nothing here would faze her. Being accustomed to minimalism prepared her for any lack she may have to deal with. Rationing due to scarcity in Cuba made her remember Auntie Maxine's phrase, 'You have to learn to suck salt through a wooden spoon.'

In spite of it all, Lily had a bright outlook. She held her head high and walked back to the dorm, oozing with confidence, a wide grin on her face, her heart full of pride. She'd made it to medical school.

Chapter 55

Medical school/Cuba/November 1980

Lily had settled in. Year one and two had come and gone. She made fewer trips home and fewer letters back and forth with Doctor Burrell. However, she'd intensified her letters to Andrew, she wanted him to wait. It would all be worth it if he could wait.

Maria and Lily did everything together. Maria's orientation never spilled over to Lily, and as long as Maria knew her boundaries, they'd stay friends forever.

"I think I'll skip breakfast." Lily slid on a pair of jeans and took her bag to leave the dorm.

"Lily, you can't keep doing that, you'll soon disappear." Maria leaned against Lily's bunk.

"I hate porridge, I'm tired of porridge, and I'm sick of this place! I want to go home, and I haven't heard from Andrew."

"Lily, what's gotten into you?"

"Why can't we have eggs and fruits?" Lily pouted.

"By now you should know that those things are luxury items here. Right now you're wafer thin, so you better go suck up that porridge or die."

"Then I'll die!"

"I'll go and raid the kitchen, see what I can find for you." Maria placed her forefinger under Lily's chin, lifted it and grinned.

"One of these days you're going to get caught, you need to stop doing that. I don't want you to get into trouble on my account." Lily wagged her finger at her.

"I can't have you starving. I love you, Lily. You're my best friend. From the first day I saw you, I just knew that we would be good friends. I'll do anything for you." She kissed Lily on the cheek.

"Hmm" Lily wiped off the kiss.

"Come with me, I'm going down to get you eggs." Maria pulled on Lily's arm.

"Where are you going to get eggs?" Lily resisted.

"No questions; just follow me."

"Nope." Lily pulled away and folded her arms.

"I thought we were friends. You're so mean and selfish, and anti-social, all you do is stay on the dorm and swat." Maria brushed her off.

"I'm here for one purpose and one only, so if that's what you think of me, then I guess we better part company." Lily snapped.

"Come on, Lily, don't be a spoil sport, I just want to take you somewhere so we can have some fun." Maria gave a coy smile.

"I thought you said you were going to get eggs." Lily frowned.

"That too."

It's alright, I'm good. I'm heading to my practical class now." Lily took a sheet from her locker, folded it neatly and stashed it in her bag.

"Why are you taking that sheet with you?"

"Never mind, there's a method to my madness."

"Well, you're mad. Anyway, I don't have class until later."

"See you then." Lily waved and left the dorm.

Lily looked forward to working on her first cadaver, to probe, to cut it open. That day had arrived and she hastened her steps to the laboratory. Before entering the lab, Lily put on her lab coat and put on a pair of gloves. She walked into the lab whistling. Lily scrutinized the surgical instruments lying on the table, checking she had all she needed.

Her lab partner, late as usual, came bustling in a flurry.

"Sorry, sorry to be late. Have you started?" Her voice trembled.

"No."

The students' nerves taut.

The lecturer prepped the group.

"Students, each instrument has a specific purpose and must be handled carefully. You must avoid cutting yourself, or your partner, the same way you must avoid cutting your patients. You must pretend that these cadavers are alive but under anesthetics. They're real people, so be careful, their families are waiting to see them well again."

A sniffling sound emanated from the back of the class. One of the cadavers began moving. It struggled to sit up, and then fell back on the table. It trembled under the sheet. It made a moaning sound, then moved one leg and pushed one arm from under the sheet. Students screamed and ran out of the lab.

Lily sat up from the sheet and burst out laughing.

"Lily McDermott, what the hell are you trying to do? You've just caused pandemonium in the lab. This is not a place for pranks, young lady. You will be penalized for this gross childish behavior." The lecturer barked.

"Sorry professor, I just wanted to lighten up the moment, everyone seemed so tense. I…I'm sorry, won't happen again."

The professor tried to hide his amusement.

"You will stay back and help the lab assistants clean up." He covered his mouth as he spoke.

"Yes, sir." Lily saluted and stood at attention.

The tension dissipated and the class settled.

The cadavers remained covered in containers before them.

"Lily McDermott, what do you expect to take away from this exercise today?"

"Ah, er, well, I hope to be leave here today a more competent student doctor, with the ability to deal with death and dead bodies and, to find a way to deal with the emotional aspect of humanity and to learn the structure of the human body."

The class applauded.

"Thank you, thank you." Lily curtsied.

"Okay students, please press the lever on your cadaver container and elevate the cadavers."

The strong smell of formaldehyde permeated the room as it drained from the bodies. Lily's heart flapped around in her chest, as the cadaver levitated. A couple of skittish students fainted. Feeling squeamish Lily's stomach churned and her head spun. She remembered Mrs. Anderson and Granny. She ran out of the lab crying.

She went to her dorm, flopped on her bed, buried her face in the pillow and sobbed.

Maria walked over to her.

"What's wrong?"

"I'm such a failure." Lily blurted out.

"No you're not; you've been on the Dean's list."

"Well, I guess I will be taken off now. I ran away from the first cadaver. At this rate, I'll never make it." she covered her face and her body shook. Maria hugged her.

"Calm down, do you think you're the first person to react? And you won't be the last. It happens to all of us. Soon you'll be eating your sandwich in one hand, while you dissect."

"To make it worse, I've not heard from Andrew in months." She lowered her head and sighed.

"Hmm, write him a final letter and give him an ultimatum. I'll mail it for you."

"You're so good to mail them for me."

"Anything I can do to help! Now write it and give him that ultimatum."

"You're right; I need to know where I stand. I can't put my life on hold for any man."

"Yep, we need to let them know they're not indispensible."

Lily pulled herself together and wrote her final letter to Andrew. Maria placed the letter in her bag and left the dorm.

Lily's throat tightened. She slumped into bed. She'd remembered she needed to serve her penalty of helping the lab assistants and dashed out of the dorm.

Maria walked off in the distance and Lily caught her dropping what looked like her letter in the trash. She ducked behind a corner and waited for Maria to walk away.

When she made it to the trash, she saw her letter on top. Livid, Lily rushed back to the dorm. She searched through Maria's locker. She found nothing extraordinary. She looked under the bed. She noticed an uneven board in the floor. Lily dug the board out, and underneath rested a box.

Lily lifted the box out and opened it. Inside were letters addressed to her from Andrew. She dropped the box when she heard the door open.

"What are you doing in my things, Lily McDermott?" Maria ran to Lily and fought her for the box, scrambling to gather its contents when they spilled across the floor. Lily bent down and struggled with her to get the letters.

"They're mine, Maria, give them to me."

The dorm mistress entered the dormitory.

"You two, stop the squabbling, you're behaving like animals. Maria Gonzalez, come over here to me at once."

Maria huffed but did as she was told.

"You were seen in the pantry stealing. What do you have to say for yourself?"

"I...I..."

Chapter 56

End of November 1980

Lily approached the Dean's office, the seat of judgment. He had the power to advance her career or not with one stroke of his pen. She knocked.

"Enter." A powerful voice penetrated the walls.

Lily entered and stood before head of the school. "Good day, Dean, my name is Lillian McDermott, a second year medical student."

His reputation and his voice belied his presence. A small wiry old man with a thin moustache and a goatee greeted her. "Ah yes, Miss McDermott, I have heard a lot about you." He stroked his goatee.

"Good things, I hope." Lily dreaded being in his presence.

"Oh yes, except you're sometimes involved in pranks." He cocked his head to one side.

"I try to keep them amusing and safe, sir." Lily flushed.

"I hope so; you could get into my bad books if you take it too far." He formed his hand in a steeple and looked over his glasses.

"Noted, sir." Lily bowed.

"So to what do I owe this auspicious visit, madam? Do have a seat." He pointed to the chair.

"Thank you. It's about Maria Gonzales." Lily sat.

"What about her?" He sat forward, his fingers in a steeple.

"I heard that she has been suspended." Lily shifted in the chair and played with her hands.

"Yes, Miss Gonzalez will be out for a while." He nodded.

"Sir." Lily made eye contact.

"Uh, uh?"

"I'd like to speak on her behalf."

"Speak."

"I know Maria tends to speak out of turn and she's a little mischievous, but she's a kind soul. She means well. She looks for the disenfranchised and gives to those in need. I have benefited from her kindness, sir."

"But stealing is wrong, Miss McDermott." He leaned back in his chair.

"I agree wholeheartedly, but..." Lily sat forward.

"No buts, the common saying goes, 'if you do the crime, you must serve the time.' I'm sure that is also true in Jamaica."

"Most definitely, sir." Lily nodded.

"We really are honored to have Jamaican students here in Cuba. You know that we established diplomatic relations with your country in 1972 agreeing to take some Jamaican students. So far, Jamaican students have been excelling. Look at you. You're at the top of my list."

"Thank you, sir."

"Don't thank me, thank your hard work. Now what were you here for again?"

"About giving Miss Gonzalez some slack."

"Sorry, Miss McDermott, that case is closed. Is there anything else you'd like to talk about?"

"No sir, thanks for your time. Have a nice day, sir."

"Yeah mon, no problem." He used a Jamaican accent and phrase and his beady eyes twinkled. Lily smiled, closed the door behind her, and walked towards the lab.

"I don't know why I even bother." Lily muttered to herself. "She's messed up my life. Now I've lost Andrew. He's never going to want me again. Maria! I hate you, wherever you are!" Water welled up in her eyes and tumbled over its lids. In her haze a figure approached.

"Andrew?" She stood mouth agape. "What are you doing in Cuba?"

"Lily! Baby! I've missed you so much. I can't understand why I haven't been hearing from you. Why don't you write?"

"Again, what are you doing in Cuba? And for the record, I did write."

"So why haven't I received any letters from you? What, did you write them then throw them away?"

"I can explain."

"Well, you better start, because you've got a whole lot of explaining to do, baby." He pulled her in to him, pulled her chin up, and stared into her eyes. "Lily, you're my breath, my life, my reason for existing. How am I supposed to live, if you're not in my life? When I don't hear from you, my whole world shuts down. Right now I'm on borrowed breath." He held both her hands in his.

Lily glanced at her wristwatch.

"Oh no, this is a bad time, Andrew, I'm late for my labs."

"But, baby, I'm here, we need to work this thing out. This long distance relationship is killing me and to make it worse, you don't answer my letters." Andrew pouted.

"I promise I'll explain everything when I get back from class. I've got to go, my professor doesn't like when we're late." She pulled her hands away.

"Lily, your professor can wait."

"No Andrew, you don't understand, I really must go now. I'll speak to you afterwards. You could wait for me in the visitor's lounge. I'm surprised they allowed you through this far." She was happy to see him, but coming to Cuba was a choir.

I don't think this is going to work." He kept her from leaving.

"Are you breaking up with me?" She stared at him, frowning.

"Look, Lily, I came all this way to see you after not hearing from you and you're going to brush me off. I'm trying to talk to you about our future." His eyes moistened.

"Andrew, going to my class on time is about securing my future. This has always been my dream and I don't want to do anything to blow it. I'm six years into school, two more and I'm a doctor. Right now I'm walking on thin ice in my anatomy class."

"Okay, Lily, run along; go and secure your future. I guess I just won't be there." Andrew walked off in a huff. Lily made quick steps behind him.

"Andrew, Andrew, don't walk away from me." He didn't look back. Lily stopped, watched him walking away, and looked in the lab's direction. She had no time for that.

She got to class late. She got into her lab coat and made her way to the lab. She knocked on the door. Anyone late had to get permission to enter. The lecturer peered through the peephole.

"Lillian McDermott, where do you think you're going at this time? You're pushing your luck. One more strike and you're out!"

"I'm so sorry, sir, won't happen again." She sighed and glanced away.

"Find your station and get to work."

Lily's hands shook as she dissected the cadaver. Tears rolled down her cheeks falling onto the lifeless body.

"Lily McDermott, you will have to toughen up if you're going to make it as a doctor. Your timidity is going to blight your future in the field."

"Yes sir." Lily swallowed hard, raised her arm and wiped her tears on her sleeves and sniffled.

Andrew is a stupid, stupid man; I'm not going to run after him. That's what he wants me to do. He thinks I'm going to die if he leaves, heck no!

Lily slammed the surgical instrument down on the table.

"Miss McDermott, your behavior is becoming unbearable and unacceptable. See me after class."

"Sorry, sir."

"You will be sorry."

Lily pouted and immersed herself in the anatomy of the cadaver and soon stopped thinking about her quarrel with Andrew.

Chapter 57

Cuba/same night

Lily felt broken and dejected, her shoulders drooped, with her chin to her chest, she headed for the dorm. She'd done badly in anatomy class and Andrew had acted dastardly, not listening to reason, he'd left. Maybe she should write to him and explain everything, but that seemed pointless, when he'd acted so insensitive. Her head said let him go, but her tenacious heart clung to him. She walked to the visitor's lounge, in case he still waited there for her. Lily saw a silhouette of a man leaning against the window. Her heart skipped. He didn't leave after all. She pushed the door open and entered the room. With his back turned to her, she crept up behind him, placed her arms around his waist.

"Andr…Dr. Burrell."

"Hello, Lily." Dr. Burrell's eyes sparkled.

"I'm sorry; I thought it was someone else." Lily flushed

"Sorry to disappoint you. It's only little me."

"No, it's not like that. It's good to see you. What brought you here though?" Lily stuttered.

"I'm doing some research here and thought I'd just stop by to see how you're doing. I hear you're doing great." He grinned.

"Thanks, but not so good with anatomy. I've been making some silly mistakes." Lily hung her head.

"Tell me about it."

"You don't want to know, don't worry, I've learnt my lesson. I just need to settle down." She waved dismissing any further probe.

"Well do that, it doesn't make any sense to come all this way and waste your scholarship. Remember your goal." He made eye contact.

"Yes, Dr. Burrell." Lily nodded

"Please, call me Alex." A soft smile warmed his eyes.

"Al...Alex." Lily blushed.

"Why don't you and I go for a meal? Would that be okay, it's Friday evening. I believe you're allowed to go out on weekends. If not I could pull a few strings."

"Hmm, I dunno, I mean..." Lily faltered.

"You're afraid of me."

"No, I'm not I..." she trailed off.

"I'll take good care of you. I'm sure your mother wouldn't mind." He stared into her eyes.

"I'm an adult now, Dr. Burrell; she doesn't make decisions for me anymore."

"True. So what is it then, are you coming for a meal with me?" A coy smile gave him a boyish look.

"Hmmm, er, ah, let me freshen up and change into something more comfortable."

"That's fine; maybe we can even go dancing afterward. Have you been to any of the dances here?"

"Oh yeah, I've been with my friend Maria and a couple of other people." Lily beamed.

"Sounds like you're having a great time here."

"Well, you could say that."

"That's good, because it does get stressful at times and you need to release some of the tension."

"Anyway, I'll be right back." She waved. She needed something to take her mind off Andrew, so going out would be a good distraction; otherwise she'd go to her dorm and mope.

The angels must have sent Dr. Burrell…no, Alex.

She felt awkward being on first name basis, but he requested it.

She'd changed into something casual and returned to the lounge.

"My you're looking lovely, Lily." His eyes lit up.

"Thank you." Lily blushed.

They walked in silence.

"How's…" Lily faltered.

"How are…" Dr. Burrell trailed off.

"You go first." Lily bowed.

"No, you go first."

"How's Auntie Maxine doing? Has she been for a check-up lately?"

"Yes, six years without any sign of the cancer. I'm quite pleased with her progress."

"Great."

"How are you coping?"

"Not too bad. I mean the rationing is tough to deal with. You can only get meat or fish once per month and eggs are a rarity. Most times, I don't bother to eat what is served."

"So how do you manage?"

"To be honest, I've never been a big eater, plus I've never had luxury back home, except when I lived with my grandparents and my aunt. Living in the ghetto has prepared me well. It's peaceful here though and everyone is seen as equals. I like that. You know back home there's class distinction, the upper class, the middle class, and the lower class. Don't know exactly where I fit in then. I'd say lower class." She laughed. "Here, there's no class distinction."

"I like your humility. I must remind you though, don't take anything at face value, everything is not always the way it seems, and you haven't been everywhere in

Cuba yet." He held on to her as a horse pulled carriage and a car competed for space on the narrow roadway. "Careful."

"I find this blend of modern with ancient really intriguing. It feels like twilight zone. In one instance you're living in the nineteen hundreds and then you're catapulted to the sixties, with sixties cars."

"Kind of like time travel."

"Exactly."

They found a café.

Alex pulled her chair out and seated her.

"What will you have?"

"What's on the menu?" she took up the menu card.

They perused the menu and placed their orders. Light pleasantries took Andrew off her mind, at least in the moment. The laughter proved therapeutic. She didn't know Dr. Burrell...Alex could be so much fun. They went dancing then headed back to the dorm before her midnight curfew.

They entered the visitor's lounge. She saw a man with his legs stretched out and fast asleep on the sofa. They tip-toed past the man, Lily wondered who allowed him to be there at that hour. She did a double take.

"Andrew! What are you doing here?"

Andrew, bleary-eyed, jumped from the sofa and swayed. He rubbed his eyes and regained his composure.

"What do you mean what am I doing here and what is the meaning of this? Who is this man?"

"Andrew, please meet Dr. Burrell, my mentor."

"Dr. Burrell, your mentor? How comes I'm just hearing about you having a mentor?"

"Well, the truth is, Andrew, our communication line broke down as you know."

"And whose fault is that? Look at the time you're coming in and with a man. Do you really expect me to believe you? Mentor indeed. Some mentor, he's an indecent man, preying on you, because you're vulnerable."

"I'm not vulnerable, Andrew. I'm a grown woman who can take care of myself. Who do you think you are? You're not my father! Don't you ever speak to me like that ever again!"

"No decent young woman who already has a boyfriend would behave like you. I'm so disappointed in you Lily; you are just like every other woman."

"And how so?"

"Fickle and air-brained!" he barked in her face.

"How dare you!" Lily glared at Andrew.

"I thought you had more class, but obviously not, you chose this dog over me!"

Alex let go of Lily's arm and punched Andrew in his face. Andrew staggered. The two men exchanged punches.

The security guard intervened, warned them and escorted them out. Lily mortified, covered her face and wished the earth would swallow her.

Chapter 58
Cuba/December 1980

"Frankly, Maria, I don't know what you could possibly say to fix back my love life. You've thrown a torpedo into my heart and totally obliterated any chance of love with Andrew. What were you thinking?" Lily shook her head.

"I'm so sorry, Lily, I didn't mean to." Maria dipped her chin.

"What do you mean? You threw away my letters and took the ones he sent me for yourself, and now you glibly say you didn't know what you were doing? Why, Why, Maria?" Lily wanted answers.

"I'm sorry."

"If you say you're sorry one more time, I'm going to scream." Lily doubled her fists and held them against her side.

"Let me tell you why."

"Please tell me why!" Lily's voice screeched.

"Isn't it obvious, Lily?"

"What's obvious?" Lily shrugged.

"Lily, I'm in love with you."

"What?" Lily hesitated, trying to process what she meant.

"Yes, I was jealous. I wanted you for myself." Maria's face reddened.

Lily studied Maria's face. She was serious. "Don't be ridiculous, you and I could never be a couple. We were just friends, Maria. I don't have that kind of inclination, no disrespect, but that's not for me. You're only thinking of yourself."

"You're right, I was being selfish, and I'm truly sorry for what I've done." Maria put a hand on Lily's shoulder.

"I'm sorry, Maria, but I'll never be able to forgive you, let alone trust you." Lily peeled Maria's hands from her shoulder.

"I can understand that. I mean I really understand."

"You have no idea how devastated I am. Anyway, I have things to do." She waved away Maria and walked away.

"Uh, Lily" Maria caught up to Lily.

"What is it?" Lily stopped.

"I am very grateful to you for speaking on my behalf. I was allowed to come back this term because of your effort. I was actually meant to sit out for a year. My respects and gratitude are to you, Lily. I'm forever grateful to you."

"You're welcome. But I don't want to be friends with you anymore, and it's not about what you are, but what you've done. You've really hurt me and shaken my confidence in you. If I can't trust someone, I can't be friends with them."

"Is there anything I can do to bring back Andrew?"

"Nope." Lily shook her head and folded her arms.

"Maybe, I could write him a letter and explain everything."

"Don't be silly. It's too late anyway, we're done." Lily sighed and left Maria standing.

On her way to lunch, she stopped to check for mail. She collected her stipend slips and two foreign letters: one from Aunt Liza and the other from Andrew. Her hand trembled. She wanted to rip Andrews's letter to pieces, but at the same time, she wanted to rip it open. She found a secluded area, her knees wobbled, she leaned her back against a wall for support, her fingers shook; she tore at the envelope. She closed her eyes to calm herself and took a deep breath. Her heart palpitated. She gritted her teeth opened her eyes and opened the letter.

'My darling Lily,

I have been a real oaf. My behavior is inexcusable. I made a complete fool of myself and embarrassed you. I apologize for talking to you the way I did, and I apologize for my vulgar behavior. I hope by the time you get this letter, you will have forgiven me.

When you walked away, it felt like a knife was thrust in my heart. I barely made it through that night. I am deeply depressed and lost without you.

Lily, my feelings for you haven't changed, in fact my love has grown and I can't bear to be away from you. I wish you could come to Canada and finish your degree.

My love, my life, everything reminds me of you and every breath I take belongs to you. My world is empty without you. These past few days have been torturous, not knowing where I stand. Please don't give up on us, no matter what. Love, like life, is a journey, I have chosen to sojourn both with you. You're the most beautiful soul I have known. You're beautiful inside and out. I need you.

Please forgive me, my love.

Love always.

Andrew.

Tears blurred her vision. Her heart raced and her hands shook. She felt relieved, she smiled through her tears, like the sun that shone through the raindrops, her rainbow had returned.

She sang all the way to the canteen. Lily had to contain her legs to prevent them from skipping like a goat. She wanted to kiss everybody she met.

At the canteen, she ate the insipid lunch with gusto.

Head in the cloud and pep in her step, Lily walked back to the dorm.

"Hey, Lily, wait up." A male voice behind her called out.

She turned.

"Oh, hi, Dr. Burrell, I mean, Alex. I thought you'd left."

"Oh no, I'll be here for a couple of months working on the research project. Care to grab a bite with me."

"Uh, oh, sorry, I just had lunch."

"I was trying to catch you before you had lunch, considering you don't really like the food."

"Oh, that's so sweet of you, but I'm okay."

"Well, maybe we could have a drink?"

"At this hour?' Lily glanced at her watch. "And on a Thursday?"

"I could pull some strings."

"I think I'll pass on your offer this time." Lily grimaced.

"I need to talk to you, can you spare a moment?"

"Sure, do you mean now?"

"Yeah, do you mind?"

"No, not at all."

They sat by a fountain. Alex made eye contact with Lily. "I don't know how to say this…"

"Is Auntie Maxine alright?"

"She's fine. That's not what I want to talk to you about, Lily. I want to tell you how I feel about you."

Lily glanced away.

"I know this may come as a shock to you, but ever since I laid my eyes on you, I've been swept off my feet. In the capacity as your mother's doctor, I tried to conceal my feelings, but now the setting is neutral, it's more appropriate to share my feelings with you."

Lily hung her head.

"I hope I'm not embarrassing you."

Lily blushed.

"I love you, Lily.

Chapter 59
Canada/July 1982

Aunt Liza's letter indicated that she'd prepared to jump the broom. Her wedding imminent, Lily flew to Canada.

Andrew met her at the airport. They bonded again. He'd held her close. He held her hand while driving all the way to Aunt Liza's. Lily had just taken a few days off to attend the wedding, so the time they had together would prove to be short. They'd kissed long and deep, burning all the missiles between them.

"Come, Lily, freshen up and get dressed, we have to move fast." Aunt Liza's friend greeted her downstairs.

Lily finally stepped into the bridal room to greet Aunt Liza. Her close friends filled the room and buzzed around her like worker bees. Lily counted five of them.

"Aunt Liza, just look at you, you're a bride today. I'm so happy for you." Lily effervesced. They exchanged hugs and kisses.

"Who would have thought that at my great age of forty-nine I'd be walking down the aisle?" Aunt Liza giggled like a little girl, her pupils dilated.

Her friend dressing her for the wedding pulled up the zipper of her flowing wedding gown. The high waist dress dazzled with lace and sequins, camouflaging Aunt Liza's middle aged figure. She looked regal.

"With your age long dropped off the calendar, yeah, who would have thought?" one of Aunt Liza's friend poked her. "You're looking great."

"Thank you." Aunt Liza preened herself in the mirror and flashed the skirt of her gown.

"Well, look at that, belated rain is still good for parched earth." Another one said.

"This downpour had better be real heavy, because this earth is super cracked and parched." Aunt Liza made fun of herself. The chatter and the laughter filled the atmosphere with jollity.

"Aunt Liza, I'm so very happy for you." Lily cupped Aunt Liza's face in her hand, smiled and kissed her forehead.

"Thank you, Lily, I recall, when you were just little, you would kneel at your bedside and pray that I get married so that I wouldn't get old, because Granny, bless her soul, used to say, I'm going to be an old maid."

"Oh, yes, I remember. I thought it meant if you got married you would not get old. That was rather dumb of me." Lily grinned.

"Well, you were only little. Here I am old but not an old maid." Aunt Liza laughed and everyone with her.

"You're not old, Aunt Liza." Lily rubbed Aunt Liza's back.

"Well, if you don't hurry, you may still be an old maid; Jack may leave you standing at the altar if you're late." Her friend shooed her. Their laughter sounded like the cackling of old hens that had lost their egg-laying days.

Lily listened to them, her eyes moving from one woman to the next. They behaved like teenagers, giggling and poking fun at each other, reminiscing about their younger days.

"My Benji had to make numerous trips to Daddy before he could get my hand. I felt sorry for him. Daddy would always send him the extra mile on what he needed to qualify to get me."

"Lord have mercy girl, my Mickey thought he was the cat's pajama, until I gave him competition. Before you know it, he was on his knees proposing. Sometimes you have to do that to wake them up."

Lily's wandered to Andrew and Alex. She stopped hearing the women; their chatter became a blur of noises in the background until Aunt Liza brought her back.

"I invited Andrew to the wedding. I believe he's going to pop the question tonight." Aunt Liza informed Lily.

"Do you really think so?" Andrew's letters had been coming frequently and she'd responded timely, but the physical connection suffered from long distance.

"How much do you wanna bet?" Aunt Liza challenged her.

"I don't know; recently our relationship has been a little strained. I dunno." Lily frowned.

"That's why he's going to do it, to secure your hand. You're a nice catch, girl, beautiful and intelligent and, you're going to be a medical doctor." Aunt Liza's friend said.

"He'd be a fool to let you slip out of his hands." Another added.

"Well I hope so." Lily said.

"You hope he'll be a fool." Aunt Liza said and they laughed again.

"You all know what I mean." Lily laughed.

"You all know the saying, 'love and deep waters don't agree.'" Aunt Liza warned. "You two need to be in the same place for this thing to work."

"But there's also the saying, 'absence, or is it distance? Something like that 'makes the love stronger.'" A friend offered consolation.

"Something like that." another friend. They chuckled.

"I bet you have many suitors, waiting in line." Yet another asked.

Lily didn't respond, but closed her eyes. She thought of Alex. He'd been so attentive and he'd been finding every opportunity to be in Cuba. He filled those lonely moments with meaning and purpose, encouraging her when she felt like giving up, but he couldn't replace Andrew in her heart. She'd made it clear to him that they could only be friends. He'd been the best friend she could ask for. She lacked nothing. He showed her respect and care.

"Uh, Lily, is that true?" Aunt Liza pressed.

"Oh, please, I don't pay them any mind. I have only one person in my heart and one thing on my mind." She shrugged.

"Liza, girl, we need to leave for the church, the limo is here." One of her friends ran into the room.

The bride looked like a dream, her train trailing behind her, she entered the limo. The bridal party, including Lily, a bridesmaid, poured into the limousine, their long gowns flowing.

The packed church flowed with with carnations. The décor matched the bridal party's dresses, burgundy.

Lily spotted Andrew in the audience. He beamed at her. Her anticipation of his proposal intensified, her heart played drums in her chest. She felt giddy with the thought of her wedding day. She imagined Andrew standing next to her. She imagined him going down on his knees, taking out a ring from his pocket and placing it on her finger. She smiled and winked at him.

"I love you." He mouthed the words. Butterflies stirred in her chest, and a tingling ran down her spine.

Chapter 60
Canada/July 1982

The bridal party gathered around the head table for the reception. Andrew had come over and kissed her.

"You look amazing. You're outshining the bride.'" Andrew whispered in her ear.

Lily flushed. "Thank you."

"I love you." Andrew leaned over and kissed her.

The Master of Ceremonies gushed pleasantries while the guest luxuriated in the ambiance. Members from the audience toasted to the newlyweds' happiness. Aunt Liza and Uncle Jack, now man and wife, looked into each other's eyes, fed each other, and kissed to the oohs and aahs of the audience. Each time someone tinkled the crystals, the bride and groom had to kiss each other. If they never kissed again for the rest of their lives, they would have kissed enough that day. Lily blushed and giggled like a teenager. If only Granny and Gramps could've seen it. Gramps couldn't make the trip.

Lily believed that any minute, Andrew would announce he wanted to say something special. She hardly ate; she had a nervous stomach, anticipating the moment. Her gut feeling told her he'd been waiting on the right moment. She looked across at him and gave her sweetest smile. She waited breath abated, listening to her gut feeling.

It seemed everyone in the room but Andrew made a toast to the new couple. Andrew finally stood.

"Ladies and gentlemen, tonight is a very special night, a night long in the making. Destiny has brought these two people from diverse backgrounds and forged their hearts together. We're here tonight to celebrate with Mr. and Mrs. Bloomfield as they commit to matrimony. Marriage is a very serious institution and a huge step." Andrew spoke with a booming voice through the microphone, the epitome of confidence. Andrew continued his toast.

"On this account, I'd like to say how impressed I am with you both. I just want to wish that you'll both have a very happy and successful life together, because statistics have shown that many marriages end before they reach their second anniversary mark. I don't want to sound cynical, but I have my doubts about the institution, but kudos to all who wish to take the plunge. A very happy one to you both. On that note, I'd like us all to raise our glasses to Mr. and Mrs. Bloomfield."

Lily cringed and sunk in her chair. Her heart sank on his last lines, 'but I have my doubts about the institution.' What could he mean by that? What intentions did he have towards her? 'But kudos to all who wish to take the plunge,' what kind of man is he? Why pledge his undying love when he had no intention of taking their relationship to the next level. He didn't make any announcement pertaining to them and their future.

A lone tear fell from her eyes, but she forced her lips to smile, and she lifted her glass.

The bride and groom opened the dance floor. Others joined in and soon the floor filled with couples gyrating to Jamaican reggae. Lily noticed that Andrew had slipped out and left.

"Aunt Liza, it seems you've lost your bet."

"What are you talking about?"

"You said Andrew would have proposed tonight."

"The night is young yet. Be patient."

"It seems he's left. And he didn't even say bye. I've looked everywhere for him. Did you hear what he said about marriage? He doesn't seem like the marrying type after all." Lily's eyes watered.

"I must say I was surprised at what he said, but maybe it's just hard talk. You know men, they have to play tough." Aunt Liza soothed her and rubbed her shoulder.

"Whatever it was, I found it very disappointing. I'm done with him. I'm booking a flight back to Cuba first thing in the morning." She folded her arms.

"Don't be rash. So Andrew is the only reason you're here?"

"No Auntie, I'm here for you too, but the wedding is over and you won't have time for me. You'll be going off on your honeymoon." She managed a smile.

"I can't say I'm not looking forward to it."

"Have a happy one, Auntie. I'm just glad you've found love at last." Lily made eye contact.

"You will too, my dear, don't do anything rash. If it's yours, it will come back." Aunt Liza looked long and hard into her eyes.

"I hope so. I'm going to search for him outside." Lily stepped off.

"Okay, my love."

Lily walked out into the courtyard. Two figures stood close kissing. The dim lighting made it difficult to make out the persons. Lily drew closer.

"Andrew?"

The man turned around.

"So sorry, I thought it was someone else." She covered her mouth and walked away. She stood in the courtyard, her arms folded. She felt despondent.

"Lily, what are you doing out here all by yourself."

She turned and Andrew stood in the dark. "I've been looking everywhere for you. Why did you just disappear like that?"

"You're the one who disappeared."

Andrew led Lily inside and to the dance floor. A slow song, they embraced and he whispered. "Your mood has turned sour. What's wrong?"

"What's wrong? Really?" she stopped and pulled back.

"I can't understand why you seem so angry, did I do something wrong?"

"Do you want to hear the truth, Andrew? Your toast sucked. How could you say those negative things at my Aunt's wedding? She should have never invited you." Lily stepped back and walked out of the hall, and to the courtyard.

Andrew followed her.

"I can't understand why you're getting so worked up. Look, I was nervous and I just said something." He held her hand.

"Clearly, you spoke what was in your heart. Thank you for letting me know in public what your intentions are." She pulled away her hand.

"Come on, Lily, don't be childish."

"Childish?" Lily glared, "Frankly, Andrew, I don't think we're working out." Her eyes moistened. She turned to walk away.

"Lily." Andrew held on to her and pulled her back. He pulled something from his pocket. He knelt down, looked into her eyes.

"Will you marry me?"

Chapter 61
Cuba/October 1984

Lily went to the visitor's lounge, whistling. Andrew must have come to give her a surprise. He'd told her in his last letter that he'd be visiting her. She pushed the double door and anticipated the romantic greeting.

"Oh, it's you, Alex."

"What do you mean; 'oh it's you, Alex'? Don't I count?" Alex made a face and teased her.

"Of course you count. You know how much you mean to me, but I thought it was Andrew." Lily flushed.

"Oh well, lucky him. Does he even know what he's got?" he tickled her.

"What's he got?" Lily giggled.

"He's got the most beautiful woman in the world." He held her hand and spun her.

"Go away; you're a mess, Alexander Burrell. Stop, you're making me dizzy."

"I want you to be dizzy for me, like you're dizzy for Alex." He continued to spin her.

"Andrew, stop, seriously, you're making me quite dizzy."

"Dizzy, dizzy, Miss Daisy. You just called me Andrew." He continued spinning her and laughing.

"Andrew, I mean Alex! Stop! Leave me alone!" She shrieked.

"Okay, I'll leave you alone." He stopped.

"Don't be silly, Alex." Lily swayed and almost fell. Alex caught her. She staggered and then regained her composure. "Can't you ever be serious? I don't know how you even became a doctor."

"I would never let you fall." He gave a coy smile.

"Anyway, what's up with you?" she blinked.

"Lily, come over here and sit. What I have to tell you is unpleasant." He sat on the lounge and patted the space beside him.

"So, why are you so jolly then?" Her eyebrows raised.

"I'm trying to put you in a good mood, I guess."

"Okay, enough of that now, what is it?" She sat beside him.

"I hate to be the harbinger of bad news, but..." he faltered—

"Alex, what is it? I'm stronger than I look."

"It's your mother." He held her hands and made eye contact.

"What about her? Is she..." Lily tailed off.

"It's the cancer; it's back." He squeezed her hand.

"Oh no, how bad is it?" Lily's eyes froze open.

"Pretty bad, it's come back more aggressively."

"What do you mean?" Her eyes narrowed.

"It's spreading to other parts of her body, like her lymph nodes."

"Oh my God, what's the prognosis?" she hung to his every word.

"You may only have her around for a short while."

"What do you mean a short while?"

"The longest…a year."

"Oh no, I have to go home and take care of her." Lily's eyes moistened. She turned her back to Alex.

"Lily, I don't think your mother would want you to drop out of medical school to do that." He turned her to face him.

"It's not what she wants; it's what's best for her." Quiet tears rolled down her cheeks.

"She'd be fine with a nursemaid to take care of her; you could visit to make sure everything is okay. In fact, in your absence, I'll check on her." He put his arms around her shoulder.

"No Alex, I can't expect you to do that. In any case, I don't have any money left to continue the course, let alone to pay for a nursemaid." She shrugged and pushed his hand off.

"Lily, you can't give up now, you've reached too far. You're almost at the goal post, you only have a year left to finish. You must let me help you."

"I couldn't let you do that." She stood up and paced the floor.

"Why not?"

"I'm not a charity case." She stopped pacing and confronted him.

"So you'd rather drop out of medical school than accept help. Lily, I'm your friend, I feel offended that you see my help as charity. Isn't that what friends are for, helping out each other?"

"That's true."

"So, what's the problem then?"

"Andrew wants me to stop, we've been engaged now for over a year and he's been complaining that we don't get to spend enough time together."

"What? How could he? That's quite a big sacrifice to make."

"I'm confused, Alex. I really don't know what to do?"

"What do you mean; you don't know what to do? Being a doctor has always been your dream, am I right? Come and sit here with me."

"Yes, you're right. But life is unpredictable and sometimes dreams are just that, 'dreams' that's all they are, they're not reality. We have to face the harsh reality of life sometimes. Who would have known that my mother's cancer would return? Who is to know if Andrew will wait?"

"But that's just how life is, you said it yourself. So we have to take chances. Take a chance and let him wait. If he loves you, he'll wait; he'll respect what you're trying to do. Lily, take my advice."

"Oh, Alex, I'm torn, I don't know what to do." She sat beside Alex.

"I understand, but I'm here, if there's any way I can help, just let me know." He embraced her. She rested her head on his shoulders. Tears rolled down her cheeks, wetting his shirt. Lily sniffled and sobbed. Alex's arms felt like home, she clung to him and felt all her stress dissipate.

"Hello?" a male voice from behind greeted them.

Lily and Alex pulled apart and turned.

"What is this? What is going on here? Lily, are you out of your mind? Could someone please tell me what's going on here?" Andrew walked up to them his chest heaving.

"Andrew, it's not what it seems. I can explain. We were just talking about you." Lily got up and walked towards Andrew. Alex stood up.

"What could you be talking about me to this man?" Andrew doubled his fist and approached Alex. Lily jumped between them.

"Please, Andrew, don't create a scene. Let's talk."

"There's nothing to talk about, Lily, you've made your choice." Andrew gave Alex an icy stare.

"Let me explain." Alex motioned with his hands open.

"Don't come any closer; I won't be responsible for anything I do to you. I want no explanation from you; you and I are not into anything." Andrew pointed with a stiffened finger.

Alex stepped back.

"If you know what's good for you, just leave before I do something I regret." Andrew closed in on Alex.

"Make me. Make my day." Alex held his ground.

Andrew moved closer, height over weight. Alex's bulk made Andrew look like a string bean. Lily stood between them.

"Alex, Andrew! Stop it!" Lily stretched her hands out between them to keep them apart. She had neither the height nor the weight, but she hung in the balance of cooler heads.

"Lily, you know what? Just forget it. This engagement is off. It's not worth it." Andrew threw his hands up and walked away.

"Andrew, don't be silly! Come back here!"

"Lily, don't. Let him go." Alex held onto her.

"No, b...but..." she stuttered—her gaze unfocused and her limbs limp. Lily flopped onto the lounge chair, curled up in a ball, and wept. Alex sat beside her and tried to comfort her.

Chapter 62
Plum valley/May 1985

Lily and Margaret walked up the steep incline to join the others. The sultry afternoon sapped her energy and being back in Plum Valley brought back a wealth of unpleasant memories and a well of tears.

"It's a pity it takes a morbid occasion to bring us together like this." Lily sighed, her eyes red and swollen, from weeping. She swallowed hard, but the lump in her throat remained.

"Yes, it's a pity indeed. We should really try to keep in touch in the future." Margaret wiped her incessant tears.

"We can make amends as of today. After you left us, my world turned upside down. I would have done anything to come and live with you and your daddy." Lily managed a smile.

"And you should have, because he's your father."

"Please, Margaret, don't say that again, you have no proof."

"Do you think people mistaking us for twins had no bearings? Look at us, we sound alike, we have the same mannerisms, we look like twins. We are full sisters."

"That is because we have the same mother." Lily countered.

"So why is it that we look so different from our siblings?" Margaret pointed out.

"As I said, Margaret, I'd rather not talk about it." Lily shrugged.

"You're denying yourself of knowing about your true heritage. I don't think that's fair to you. I think you should do a paternity test since you're in doubt."

"To be honest with you Margaret, this whole thing has affected me more deeply than you can imagine. Since that revelation by your father, I have lost my sense of identity. But, the truth is I don't want to ever find out that Granny, Gramps, and Aunt Liza are not my family members. I would be devastated, and not to mention how it would make me feel like an imposter. It would mean that all this time, I've not been my true self. I don't want to know."

"But, it wouldn't be your fault."

"Did you know that Granny gave me all her life savings to study medicine?"

"Oh my goodness, that's incredible. You're really indebted to these people." Margaret nodded.

"I'll never be able to repay them, especially Granny. So can you understand how I would feel if it proves to be true that they're not my family. I'd feel like a complete user." Lily shook her head and bit her lip.

"The indictment would not be yours. Auntie Maxine would be the irreprehensible one, presuming on the kindness of other innocent people, robbing them of resources, you know what I mean."

They approached the top of the hill, Auntie Maxine's family burial ground. Lily spotted Mr. Tremble. She walked over to him.

"Hello, Mr. Tremble." Lily smiled through tears.

"Lily, Lily of the Valley, my dear Lily, you've grown into a fine young woman. My heart is bursting with joy to see you. Only you're capable of bringing joy on a day like this. Give poor old Tremble a hug." He reached out and hugged her.

"It's so good to see you. You look as fit as a fiddle yourself." Lily looked him over.

"Looks are deceiving, my dear, the arthritis is killing me. I hear you're a doctor now. I'm so very proud of you. You followed your dreams." He hugged her again.

"Thank you, Mr. Tremble. I'm so happy to see you."

The small gathering consisting of close relatives and a few friends converged at the graveside. The pastor gave a tear jerking ceremony, warning those alive of their impending demise.

Lily felt remorse over the many broken wishbones and the secret and evil wishes she had made each time the bone snapped, but she couldn't blame herself. Her mother had fought a good fight and lost to the enemy. As she watched the men lower the white coffin into the hole, she convinced herself that Auntie Maxine would have been proud of her accomplishment; she had stuck it out and had become a medical doctor. The time Auntie Maxine invested in her; the sacrifices she made had paid off; the beatings, the insults, the neglect, the abuse? It all balanced on a precarious pendulum. In spite of it all, Auntie Maxine meant well. She just didn't know any better. Lily tried to rationalize the years of abuse, to pardon the dead.

The mourners sang choruses promising another life somewhere across the river. A sound of applause emanated from the sky. A flock of blackbirds in a nearby apple tree, disturbed by the crowd, flapped their wings and chattered as they flew off. Lily walked closer to her mother's grave. The men covered the hole in the ground and her hatred for her mother with mortar. She knelt awkwardly at the gravesite and placed a bouquet of white lilies and scribbled the words, *'I love you mother'* in the wet cement.

Alex held her gently by her shoulders and helped her to stand. He held her close. Andrew hovered around, both men's rivalry evident. They glared at each other, daggers drawn. Lily eased away from Alex.

"Alex, no hard feelings, but right now I just want to be alone."

Lily walked away from the crowd and made her way down into the valley to the house built by Auntie Maxine's father. Rickety with floorboards creaking, it gave her a glimpse of her roots from her mother's side. She'd only visited her grandparents there once or twice, so it held no special magic for her, however, she'd had a paint job done to it, to create a little cheer. She sat in the living room all alone and allowed herself to cry. Childhood memories came flooding back; a kaleidoscope of mixed feelings engulfed her. Her body shook as she let the fountain flow from her soul.

Lily pulled herself together as the crowd moved down the hill. She helped serve refreshments; it took her mind off her tangled emotions. She greeted the guests.

Well wishers thanked her for the hospitality and shared condolences and left.

The dreary evening turned into twilight and the pall over her gave her a chill. She and Margaret and the other siblings huddled together and mixed their tears.

Alex entered the room, clearing his throat.

"Ah, er, I don't wish to disturb you all at this time, but there's a very important matter your mom asked me to oversee."

They pulled away from each other and turned to face Alex. Andrew stood in the doorway.

"Oh hi, Dr. Burrell," they chorused.

"Hi. Ah, your mother wrote a will on her dying bed and made me the executor."

"Auntie Maxine wrote a will, what does she have…" Margaret trailed off.

"Margaret!" Lily cautioned Margaret. "Go ahead, Alex, please read it."

Alex read.

"I, Maxine Jeanette Molly Francis hereby bequeath all my earthly possessions to all my children, to be shared equally among them." Alex listed the few items.

He continued.

"I, Maxine Jeanette Molly Francis hereby request that my three daughters take full custody of Peter, my youngest son, and ensure that he receives a good education and that his well being is seen to by them. I am also enclosing a letter especially for Lily." Alex gave the letter to Lily.

Lily read it.

"My dearest Lily;

> I must start by saying how very proud
> I am of you. You have weathered the storm
> and turned out well. You may not know
> this, but you grew to be my backbone and

my right hand, and I'm forever indebted to you.

I know I may not have been the best mother, but I'm sure you learnt a lot from me, including not being like me."

Lily broke down in tears. She couldn't read anymore. Margaret took the letter and continued reading. Andrew walked over to Lily and put his arms around her shoulder.

"What I'm about to say next may come as a surprise to you, but I think I owe it you. I must give you what belongs to you. I'm giving you back your legacy. I hope you will be able to forgive me, because what I've done is not fair to you. While I was busy trying to cover my shame and protect my ego, I destroyed your self-worth and your identity. So today, I'm going to tell you the truth and hope that you can move forward knowing your true roots.

Rupert Edwards is your real father.

Please forgive me, my beloved daughter. I go to my grave with a free conscience and love in my heart for you.

Yours truly,

Mommy.

Lily fainted.

Chapter 63
Jamaica/1986

"Lily, this is your day, my love, but you look so down, what's the matter?" Aunt Liza had flown down to Jamaica for Lily's wedding.

"I'm okay, Aunt Liza. Just apprehensive that's all." Lily forced a smile. She sat facing the vanity mirror.

"So true, Aunt Liza, she should be bubbling." Margaret added, studying Lily's face.

Margaret and the other bridesmaid had already dressed and came to help Lily with the finishing touches. "You know something, Lily; you have me puzzled..." Margaret tapered off.

"Puzzled, why are you puzzled?" Lily pressed her.

"Why did you invite Alex to the wedding?" Margaret folded her arms and cocked her head.

"I need him here." Lily said without emotion.

"Why would you need him here, Lily?

"What, do you have a problem with it?" Lily turned to Margaret.

"Not really, just wondered." Margaret recoiled.

"Alex has been my backbone and my dear friend. I just feel safe when he's around, that's all. He's the only person who truly understands me." Lily turned back to view her reflection in the mirror.

"Then marry him." Margaret chuckled.

"Don't be silly, Margaret. You know Andrew is my first love." Lily took up the brush from the vanity and played with the bristles. "Throughout this year, as I have stepped up and accepted who I am, the only person who understands what that means, and how it could affect me has been Alex. Andrew acts as though it's not important." She turned back to the mirror and studied her own face. "And maybe he's right. Maybe it isn't important, but what if it is?"

Margaret dismissed her. "That's a bit more than I want to think about."

Aunt Liza stayed out of it. "Anyway, Lily, I'm going downstairs to make sure all the last minute details are in place. Margaret, girls," she waved her hand at the crowd, "Why don't you ladies join me." She kissed Lily on cheek and left the room.

Lily continued to peer into the mirror.

"I am Lillian Elaine Edwards." Lily studied her reflection and mouthed her identity. "I am Lillian Elaine Edwards, Lillian…Elaine…Edwards." She turned sideways, she stared at her profile, and she stared into her eyes, touched the contour of her lips, and wondered, did she look like her father? Did she look like an Edwards? She peered at herself as if she'd been a newborn; she felt a rebirth into a different psyche. The veil had been lifted from her heart. The void in her soul filled with a new sense of being. Her life had taken on new meaning.

She felt remorse and sadness for burying her old self, she felt guilty for embracing her new self.

Lily placed her tiara upon her head, "I guess it doesn't really matter, I won't be McDermott or Edwards after today." She stood and gathered in her train, and made her way to the street. Lily looked the perfect fairy-tale princess. She'd arranged to be driven in a horse-drawn carriage around the resort town of Ocho Rios then back to the hotel for the ceremony and then the reception hall at the hotel.

The carriage awaited her.

The bridal party wore baby pink and the men wore white tuxes. Lily's bouquet of pink and white carnations tied together with pink silk ribbons had dew drops, still fresh from the floral shop.

With the help of the carriage driver, she stepped up into the carriage. Lily looked regal and felt like royalty. Butterflies danced in her stomach and her heart palpitated.

The carriage pulled up alongside the outdoor wedding site.

Lily alighted from the carriage; her bridesmaids met her there. The gaily decorated grounds created a paradisiacal atmosphere.

Chairs dressed up in dusky pink coverings stood neatly in rows, their occupants glanced around as Lily, circled by her entourage, made her way to her place of entrance. They cheered.

Lily walked over the small arched bridge, her heart thumping in her chest. Her head buzzed and her ears rang. Her lips trembled into a smile. Everything moved in slow motion.

The bridesmaids walked down the aisle and took their places. A flower girl walked ahead of her sprinkling white Lily petals. Mr. Tremble smiled with her, folded his elbow in hers and led her up the aisle. Lily's knees wobbled and her stomach churned. Excitement's heat spread to Lily's face, her lips curled into a smile all the way to the altar.

Andrew looked immaculate in his white tuxedo and dusky pink shirt and burgundy tie. He thanked Mr. Tremble and stared into her eyes, a broad grin plastered his face.

"You look radiant, baby. You're the most beautiful woman in the whole world." He whispered as she stood beside him.

"Thank you; you're looking awesome, my handsome prince." She smiled.

Alex sat in the front row, his lips pursed and his arms folded.

"Ladies and gentlemen…" the marriage officer commenced the ceremony.

Lily's mind wandered during the procedure except when the man asked Andrew if he would take her as his wife.

"I do." Andrew gazed into her eyes, his gaze fixed.

"Do you, Lillian Elaine Edwards, take Andrew Gregory Richards as your lawfully wedded husband?"

Lily's head spun, her heart rate raced. Lillian Elaine Edwards? Who is that? Her world sharpened then fazed, sharpened then fazed. With clarity she captured the audience, tilted her head towards Alex.

Alex stiffened; he tilted his head back at her.

Lily raised her posture, turned to Andrew, his gaze still as fixed as before. The world stopped spinning, silence.

"Lily, Lily." Andrew whispered.

"Uh, er, Yes." Jolted back to the present, she pulled on her ear.

"Do you Lillian Elaine Edwards, take Andrew, Gregory. Richards as your lawfully wedded husband?"

"I…I…Andrew, I…I can't."

"What?" the fire in Andrew's eyes faded, "Lily, what are you saying?"

He held her hands in his. She pulled away her hands. "Sorry, Andrew, I can't do this." Shock and realization fought over her emotions. A tear fell from her eyes but she felt okay.

Andrew sighed, his eyes moistened, his gaze fell. He held his head down and walked away.

Lily closed her eyes and let out a deep sigh and sank to the floor.

"Lily, what the hell do you think you're doing, this is so embarrassing?" Margaret nudged her foot.

Lily looked up. "I'm sorry, Margaret, sorry for the trouble." Her thoughts about who she was rolled over and over in her thoughts.

"What are we going to do with all the food and the gifts?"

"Feed the guests, and…I—" Lily spluttered.

"You've put Andrew in a very embarrassing situation." Margaret shook her head and stormed off.

The audience murmured in disappointment and left the venue one by one.

Aunt Liza didn't say a word; she just rubbed Lily's shoulders. Alex stepped up, and sat on the step beside her. He patted her knee. "I didn't see that coming."

Their eyes met.

"I love you, Alex."

"I love you too, baby."

The End

Hazel Andrea Smith

I am grateful to my grandparents, Mama, (Mother Mack) and Papa, (Cappie, easily my hero), and my auntie Dot Dot, for my happy childhood. Their gentle nurturing inspired my confidence. They doted on me and filled my youthful world with love, warmth, and happiness.

My husband, Dr. Vidal R. Smith Jr., my children, Hans-Christian and Cristal Morning and my darling grandsons, Joel and Brandon; thank you for your patience while I stole time away from you all to finish this book. I appreciate my husband's support and patience as he shared our bed with my laptop at wee hours in the morning when inspiration woke me.

Hans-Christian, thank you for being my sounding board as you listened to my ramblings. Thank you for the critiques and suggestions. You will be a writer one day.

Thank you Randall Andrews and R.L. Andrew for your coaching. You are marvelous critics and instructors. Also, to Kay Kelman, another islander for your wonderful cover art.

And last but not least, in fact, mostly, thanks to Jehovah for blessing me with creativity.

The author Hazel Andrea Smith is a mother of two grown children. She is also the grandmother of two boys.

She is a trained teacher, a business management major and also a human development consultant.

She is an author of at least a dozen children stories, short stories, self-help books, and poetry. She has kept these close to her and enjoys reading them over and over again. She reads the children stories to her grandsons, but now she wants to share them all with the children of the world and the world at large.

She is starting with this publication, "Lily of the Valley." Why is she starting with the novel? Because it was her first literary piece and it is inspired by real events.

She is now a retired dean of discipline. She loves working with young people and impacts their lives positively by the values and attitudes she reflects. She teaches by example. She continues to shape the lives of young adults through the capacity of being a human development consultant.

She enjoys listening to music, and plays the guitar. She is also fond of reading and writing. Her favorite genre is historical novels and she loves watching period dramas. When she is not writing she is busy baking, making jams and jellies, and gardening. She also loves interior decorating and painting. She is very spiritual and spends a large part of her life teaching people about God.

Family time is important. She spends a lot of time with her family and believes it is very important for families to keep communication lines open at all times. She believes that Quality family time is very important in order to build strong individuals who are centered and positive.

Her favorite phrase is "To begin is half the work." No matter how impossible a task is "just begin." Another phrase she is inspired by is "always expect the unexpected." And "do to others as you would have them do to you."

She has a keen eye for finding the opportunities in disappointments. She strongly believes that when things don't work out as planned it means that there is a better plan in the out working. She believes that if you look at the bigger picture you will find it. So she doesn't have time to stay down.

You can find all of JaCol's authors at
www.jacolpublishing.com